ALSO BY J. B. VELASQUEZ

Every Last One: The Rise of Sylvia Boone

Tourist Trapped

SLEEPERS

J. B. VELASQUEZ

WILD RUMPUS PRESS

ISBN: 979-8-9875541-4-2 (ebook)

ISBN: 979-8-9875541-5-9 (paperback)

For Sofie

CHAPTER 1
EVERYTHING IS FINE

SOMEONE IS SOFTLY HUMMING "HAPPY BIRTHDAY." Am I dreaming? No. I'm not asleep. I blink my eyes open. I'm lying on a green velvet couch and cuddling a stuffed pig. Where am I? A tall middle-aged man with curly reddish hair sits in an armchair just a few feet away. He's holding a red balloon and . . . smiling.

"Happy birthday," the man says in a half-whisper, leaning forward. He's wearing a light grey suit and his pants are two inches too short, revealing a whimsical kitten pattern on his socks. He's still smiling. It's giving me the creeps.

"Where am I?" I ask as I slowly push myself into a sitting position. The tiny room we're in is empty except for the couch, the chair the man is sitting in, and a side table holding a framed photo of a woman. An acoustic guitar rests on a floor stand in the corner. There are no windows. Just a door.

He reaches toward me with the balloon.

"I know you must have lots of questions—"

"Who are you?" I ask, taking the balloon. What am I supposed to do with this?

"My name is Rafael. I'm here to help you." Still smiling.

"What am I doing here?"

"All in good time, friend. All in good time. If you don't mind, I need to ask you a few questions first."

I look to the exit, back to Rafael, and back to the exit. I rush to the door and turn the knob back and forth—locked. "Why are we locked in here?"

"It's for your safety. Please. Sit. I'll tell you everything you need to know, I promise." Rafael gestures toward the couch. "Please."

I'm skeptical but I sit down again, still holding the balloon. I let it go and it gently rises to the ceiling. The stuffed pig—it's Piglet from *Winnie the Pooh*— stares up at me. I add that to the queue of questions rapidly accumulating in my mind. I don't know where I am or how I got here. But more importantly, I don't know who *I* am. What's my name? Why can't I remember my name? I can't remember *anything*.

My breath starts to pick up and I press my temples with both hands, some uninformed attempt to squeeze memories back into place, and when they don't come, I make this groaning, whining sound and start slapping my head with both hands.

"Calm down," Rafael says. "Breathe."

I take a deep breath and exhale forcefully through my mouth.

"Good," he says.

I nod and take another deep breath.

"You're okay, Hugo. Everything is fine."

"Hugo? Is that my name?"

"Yes."

"Why don't I know that? Why don't I know my own name?"

"Do you know where you live?"

I concentrate with all my might, but can't remember anything at all.

"No."

"Do you know where you were just before you woke up here in this room?"

I search the floor for the answer. "No," I say, shaking my head. "Do I have amnesia? Did I hit my head or something?"

"No, no, of course not. Let's calm down. You're okay. Everything is okay," Rafael says like a paramedic trying to sooth an accident victim who hasn't yet noticed his limbs are missing.

"I don't think so." I shake my head. "Something's wrong. You're not telling me something. Why were you singing 'Happy Birthday?'"

"Because it's your birthday, silly!" He's smiling again. Does he think this is funny?

"How old am I?"

Rafael looks at his watch. "About seventeen minutes."

"What?" He's messing with me. "What are you talking about?"

"You were just born," he says, still smiling.

"Stop smiling! Stop treating me like I'm an idiot!" I bark.

His smile immediately drops from his face and is replaced with a look of concern. "You're upset. That's totally normal. Can I get you some tea?"

"No, I don't want any fucking tea! Why can't I remember anything?"

"Because today is your birthday. You just got here," Rafael says as if it should be obvious by now.

I stand and suddenly feel lightheaded so I sit back down again. "This doesn't make any sense," I say mostly to myself. I point to the door. "What's behind that door?"

"You'll have a chance to meet everyone soon."

"Who's everyone? Do they have amnesia, too?"

"You don't have amnesia."

"Where am I? What *is* this place?"

"I'd like to show you—what's beyond that door. As soon as you're ready."

"I'm ready. Show me," I say without hesitation.

"Oooh," he chuckles softly. "Let's not get ahead of ourselves. You were just born."

"Stop saying that. People aren't born as grown men."

"What do you mean?" Rafael seems genuinely confused.

"What do you mean what do I mean? People are born as babies."

Rafael shakes his head. "What's a baby?"

I groan and bury my face in my hands. This guy is either completely off his rocker or he's deliberately trying to confuse and infuriate me. I try mightily to remember anything—my mother, a friend, a single moment from my life. Every thought dissolves before it forms.

"I want you to take a look at this picture." Rafael takes the framed photo from the side table and hands it to me. "Do you recognize this woman?"

I take the picture from him and study it. She's gorgeous. "No," I say, shaking my head. "Who is this?"

"Are you sure you don't recognize her?"

I look again. "No. Should I?"

A satisfied smile spreads across Rafael's face. "No. No, that's perfectly fine." He takes the picture from me and lays it face down on the table.

"Who is that?" I ask.

"It's nobody. Where did you get that little pig?"

Piglet stares at me as if waiting for me to provide some kind of explanation. "This? It's not mine. I just woke up and I was holding it."

"Who does it belong to?"

"I don't know. I don't . . . I don't know *anybody*!" I'm struck with an intense feeling of loneliness. What is happening? "Why are you doing this?" I ask weakly.

"I'm not doing anything," he says. "I'm here to help you."

"Help me what?"

"Discover your purpose."

"How are you helping me do that exactly?"

"Do you like music?" This question seems to come from nowhere.

"How is that relevant?"

"You'll see. Do you?"

"Yes. I like music." Who doesn't like music?

"Good. Do you know how to play?"

"Music?"

"Yes." Rafael nods vigorously with wild eyes and that stupid fucking smile.

My brow furrows and I search the floor for an answer. Oh, shit—I *do* know how to play music. A wave of relief hits me like fireworks—something about myself that I know to be true. I look up at him. "Yes!"

Rafael makes a celebratory clapping gesture like a child waiting to open a Christmas present. He stands and reaches for the guitar. He's holding it in the most awkward manner, like he's never held a guitar before—like it might explode. "Do you think you can play this?"

I take the guitar from him. It feels natural in my hands and I place it on my knee.

"Go ahead. Anything you like." He's smiling again.

"Just play anything?" I ask.

"Yes, anything at all." Rafael sits down again and rests his chin on his balled fists, elbows on his knees. He's like the host of some children's television show.

I cradle the neck of the guitar in my left hand and position my fingers into a G-chord. I'm thrilled to know what a G-chord is. I strum the strings once to make sure it's in tune. Sounds good.

"Go on," Rafael says eagerly.

I close my eyes. "Blackbird" comes to mind. I feel like I know it. I don't know how I know it or where I learned it, but my fingers know exactly what to do. I don't sing, but I hear every word in my mind. This is deeply satisfying. When I finish, I open my eyes.

Rafael claps enthusiastically. "That was wonderful! Just wonderful! Did you write that?"

"What?" Is he kidding?

"That song. Did you write it?"

"No. It's The Beatles."

"Oh, sure. I knew that. You gotta love The Beatles—big fan. So, let me ask you this. Do you know how to *write* songs?"

"Do I know how to write songs?" I repeat. "I don't know." I search my memory for any songs I may have written but every song I think of is someone else's.

"I think so." I feel some degree of certainty about this, but I'm not sure why.

"Excellent! That's excellent."

"Why?"

"You're struggling to find yourself, right? The one thing you know about yourself is that you like music and you can play the guitar. And you can play it very well, if you ask me. I bet you can even sing. Try another one and sing this time."

A dozen songs run through my head—songs by The Stokes, Talking Heads, Nirvana, Radiohead, Bowie, Dylan. My brain's a damn jukebox.

"Hard to pick just one," I say.

"Anything." His knee is bouncing wildly in anticipation.

"Okay, here's one." I pick up the guitar and place it back on my knee. I strum a couple of chords and clear my throat. My fingers begin to pick a soothing, haunting melody. After the first few measures of the intro, I bump the side of the guitar twice with my fist and sing the opening verse to "Hotel California."

I feel a sense of ease as I sing, as if connecting with something uniquely authentic within me. I don't just play the song. I feel it course through me. It feels more *me* than my own name. When I finish the song, Rafael gives me a standing ovation.

"Bravo! Superb! You're a natural! Hugo, this is what you were born to do. Don't you agree?"

"I don't know. How am I supposed to know something like that?"

"What did it feel like singing that song just now?"

"I mean, good. It felt good." What I mean by that is that it felt *familiar*. "I don't understand. How do I know that song but I don't know anything about my life?"

"This *is* your life, Hugo. You were born knowing everything you need to know to fulfill your purpose in this life. You're a musician, Hugo. And your life has just begun."

He's not telling me everything. He's calling me Hugo, but how am I supposed to know if that's really my name? What did he do to my memory? Whatever it is, I'm not going to find out in this little room. I have to get out of here and the only way he's going to let me leave is if he thinks I'm ready—whatever that means. He seems committed to this nonsense, so I'll have to go along with it until I can get more information. I have to get out of this room.

"So let me get this straight," I say. "I was just born—right here on this couch, as a fully grown man. And that's why I don't have any memories. My name is Hugo and I'm a musician. And . . . that's my life's purpose."

Rafael nods ecstatically. "Yes! That's it—you got it!"

"So does that mean I'm ready? Can we get out of here now?"

A weirdly satisfied smile spreads across his face, like a proud father gives his son. "I think you're ready. Would you like to meet the others?"

I nod. "Yes. Yes, I would."

CHAPTER 2

DON'T SAY NUGGIES

I CRACKED OPENED another beer before emptying the last of a bag of frozen chicken nuggets onto a warped baking sheet. There were only five full nuggets along with some smaller batter-only bits—barely enough for Ava. She'd be home any minute. I shook out some frostbitten broccoli onto the same pan and pre-heated the oven. There was a package of instant ramen hiding in the back of the cupboard. I didn't mind eating that. I used to live on the stuff.

I'd have to split the remaining eleven dollars and thirty-eight cents in my checking account between groceries and gas for the next two days. Luckily, I already had a jar of pasta sauce in the cupboard so I could pick up some spaghetti for tomorrow. It was just the two of us after all, and thankfully, Ava wasn't too picky.

I never really learned to cook, so most of our meals came from the frozen food section or take out. After Celeste died, Ava and I received a steady stream of meal deliveries from family and friends. Some weeks we had so much food we couldn't eat it all and had to throw some of it out. That generosity only lasted a couple months. Even the most well-intentioned are incapable of abiding the endurance of grief when it's not their own. Life goes on.

I never knew what to expect from Ava when she got home from school. It was Tuesday, which meant theater rehearsal, and that usually put her in a good mood. Car tires crunched gravel out on the driveway. Muffled music emitted from a car stereo, accompanied by giggling and nonsensical shouting. She got a ride home with another kid who lived nearby. If she was in a good mood, she'd say hi. If not, she'd go straight to her room and I'd know to give her space.

"Hey dad!" Ava called when she came through the door—good mood.

"Hi sweetheart! How was theater?"

Ava had been cast as an understudy for one of the Plastics in her high school's stage adaptation of *Mean Girls*. I'd hear her rehearsing in front of her dresser mirror every night. It reminded me of how I used to be with guitar at her age—completely absorbed. That was good. She'd been through so much since her mom's passing. Theater came at the right time.

"Fine," she said. "I have a Math test tomorrow. I need to study."

"Okay. Dinner should be ready in about twenty minutes."

She was a good kid—got good grades, didn't get into trouble. I didn't have to remind her to clean her room or do her homework. I was pretty lucky, I guess.

Celeste had always been more clued into Ava's life. I was always there, don't get me wrong, but when it came to parenting decisions and keeping our lives organized, Celeste was in charge. Ava and I had a decent relationship, but she never came to me with the big stuff unless it involved fixing a bike or helping with a science project. When it came to anything serious, Celeste was the one to step up and I was happy to leave it to her. She was just better at it.

I never imagined I would have to carry the responsibility of both parents. I knew I wasn't adequately filling her mother's shoes. How could I?

The oven beeped. I plated the chicken along with the overdone broccoli, sprinkling it with salt. I placed the plate on the table with a fork and a plastic bottle of ketchup turned on its top to allow the remaining condiment to drip slowly toward its opening. I tore off a paper towel and tucked it under her fork.

"Ava! Dinner!" I called from the kitchen. I poured ramen from the pan into a cereal bowl for myself and sprinkled it generously with red pepper flakes from a stash of packets we'd saved from two years of pizza deliveries. I sipped the broth as I carried the bowl to the table, set it across from Ava's seat. "Ava!"

"Coming!" Ava shouted back with a tinge of irritation. She was a lot like her mother—prickly, opinionated, and beautiful.

Ava plopped down and squirted two blobs of ketchup onto her plate followed by air and red spittle. "We need more ketchup," she said flatly.

"I know. I get paid Thursday and I'll pick some up." I ignored the subtle raise of her lip in minor disgust at the burnt broccoli. "Any special requests?"

"Hey, why do *you* get ramen?" Ava asked indignantly, ignoring my question.

"Because we ran out of nuggies."

"Don't say nuggies."

"You want ramen instead?"

She nodded with raised eyebrows. In that moment, she was seven again with a butterfly barrette in her hair and a missing front tooth.

"Trade me." I slid my bowl of ramen toward her. She pushed her plate toward me.

"Eww, I don't want your fork!" She wasn't smiling, but there was an air of playfulness I recognized. I'd learned to read the various layers of sarcasm and cankerous hostility that randomly erupted from this child—sometimes genuine, sometimes for her own amusement.

"How's the studying coming along?"

Ava shrugged and stuffed a mouthful of noodles into her face.

I should have known that was a dead end. "Tell me about the play."

Ava nodded as she finished chewing and swallowing. "Zachary Barnes just found out he has to move to Utah next month, so that means Jake Fowler gets to play Aaron."

"Is that good?" I took a bite of rubbery chicken.

"No! Jake Fowler is terrible. But he has a huge crush on Stephanie Gibbons, who plays Cady, and they get to kiss."

"You don't have to kiss anyone, do you? I mean, if you end up having to play . . . what's her name?"

"Gretchen. No, Gretchen doesn't kiss anybody."

"Oh, okay," I said, trying to sound nonchalant. The thought of Ava kissing made me uneasy. She's fourteen. Rationally, I knew she was old enough to handle it. I kissed girls when I was her age. Then again, I never talked to my parents about it. If Ava had been kissing boys, I doubted she would have let me in on it. If Celeste were still here . . . it was useless going down that road. Everything would be better if she were still here.

"Stephanie's having a birthday sleepover this weekend at La Paloma. Everyone's getting *spa treatments,*" she said, wiggling her fingers.

"Spa treatments? What do her parents do?"

"I don't know," she said in that defensive tone when asked questions she couldn't possibly know the answers to, or even care to know.

"Were you invited?"

"Yeah, but I told her I couldn't go."

"Why?"

"Because, dad. You can't show up to a party without a gift. Hayleigh Brighton said she's getting her a Marc Jacobs bag. Last year Stephanie took Vera Clark to see Billie Eilish."

I nodded slowly as her problem became clear. "And you don't want to show up with some cheap present."

Ava stirred the noodles in her bowl. "We don't even have enough for a *cheap* present." She said it without sarcasm, without any hostility at all. It came from someplace fragile within her and my heart sunk like an anvil.

"Do you want to go?" I asked, trying to infuse hope into a bleak reality.

Ava shrugged. "All the theater kids are going—just the girls."

Before I could second guess myself, I blurted, "Tell her you can go."

"What?" She glared at me with incredulity.

"Tell her you're in," I said, doubling down on a decision my mouth had made without consulting my brain.

Ava shook her head as if trying to shake away the nonsense. "What are you talking about?"

"Well, maybe we can't get her a Mike Jacobs bag—"

"*Marc* Jacobs," she corrected me—always correcting me.

"What about music?"

"Dad, kids don't buy music anymore. They have Spotify."

"Oh. Right," I said. "Well, what do you want to get her?"

"Are you being serious right now?" Her eyebrows lifted like clouds.

"Sure! I mean, let's be reasonable."

"She's really into Remi Swan."

"Is that a band?"

She made a sound that might have potentially turned into a full giggle. "No, dad. It's a brand of skincare products."

"What does a fourteen-year-old need with skincare products?"

"Fifteen. I don't know. A lot of kids are into that stuff."

"Okay. That sounds reasonable. How much is it?"

Ava pulled her phone from the pocket of her hoodie. The corners of her mouth pulled downward as she scrolled. She shook her head. "This stuff is really expensive. One thing of hydration serum is forty bucks."

I rocked my head from side to side, weighing the feasibility of this extraneous expense. "We can do that," I said, trying to sound confident.

"Dad, it's this little." She held up her thumb and forefinger denoting a lipstick-size container. "That would be so lame."

"Let me see." I held out my hand. She hesitated before handing me her phone. I scrolled through pink and yellow colored products, expertly targeted to her demographic. "Okay, look, they have these gift sets." I mumbled as I read through the list of products, for which skincare purposes I had no clue. "I don't know what all this is, but it's got five things and it comes with this little bag." I handed the phone back.

"That's seventy-five dollars," she said with a pained expression.

"Still cheaper than the spa treatments she's handing out like sticks of gum. I assume you're getting a meal out of it, too?"

"Dinner. And breakfast the next morning."

"See there? Worth it."

She looked at me with the same dubious glare her mother used to give me whenever I proposed something half-baked, which was fairly often. "Are you sure? I know we're behind on the electric bill."

"Hey, you let me worry about the bills. How did you know about that?"

"You talk to yourself."

"Oh." Do I? "Well, if this is something you really want . . ."

"Okaay?" she said with skepticism. "Thanks."

"You're welcome, sweetheart."

"I'm gonna text Stephanie that I can come." She half-skipped back to her room leaving half a bowl of ramen on the table.

I put on an old Sonic Youth record and cracked open another beer. I spent the next half hour cleaning up after dinner and straightening the house. Ava would be up studying for another hour. I was grateful I didn't have to be on her case about school work. She was a good kid. She deserved to go to birthday parties at the very least.

I needed to find a better job. The music store barely paid the bills and I'd already burned through the accidental death insurance money. This wasn't sustainable. I'd been on the job boards for months and had applied to dozens of jobs. Everyone wanted a bachelor's degree or a certification in this or that.

I didn't think I'd need to go to college once my band started taking off. We were pretty big here in the Southwest and we were touring six months out of the year. When Ava was born, I decided to take a year off and that ended up costing us a record deal. The guys were pretty pissed about it. They don't talk to me anymore.

When Ava started pre-school, Celeste went to nursing school. The plan was that once she finished and started working that it would be my turn to go to school, but it was never the right time. We still needed both incomes to keep our heads above water. We couldn't afford fancy vacations or new cars but we paid the bills, mostly on time, and had enough left over to give Ava a nice Christmas every year.

Things were different now. Ava and I didn't have the same connection we used to. She used to light up when I'd come home. She'd come into my music room and lay on the floor and draw or just listen to me play. She just wanted to be near me. Maybe part of it is her age. I knew teenagers didn't like hanging around their parents, but it was more than that. I thought I reminded her too much of the life before—when she had two parents. I was a glass half-empty.

The tonearm on the turntable repositioned itself to its starting position, but instead of flipping the record, I walked down the hall and saw light coming from Ava's bedroom door. I rested my forehead on the closed door and I could hear her reciting lines from the play. I knocked softly with one knuckle.

"I just wanted to say goodnight." It's not all I wanted to say. I wanted to tell her that things will get better. But I didn't know if that was true, so I didn't say it. I wanted to tell her I loved her, which *was* true. But I didn't say that either.

CHAPTER 3
POD FIFTY-FOUR

RAFAEL STANDS and walks to the door. He places a hand on the doorknob and waits for me to get up and stand next to him. He nods and I nod back. I'm eager to get out of this little room.

"Just remember, everything is okay," he says reassuringly. "You belong here and we're all very happy to see you."

"Okay."

He opens the door and motions for me to walk through. I'm not sure what to expect out there but my curiosity nudges me through the door. A group of people in party hats are gathered around a dining room table. The dining room is open to a spacious living room and a kitchen to one side. It's clean and has new furnishings, like a model home.

There's a small round cake on the table with paper plates, forks, and napkins. One of them makes eye contact with the others and they start to sing "Happy Birthday," off key. Rafael joins them.

Besides Rafael, there are two men, one tall and skinny, the other short and tubby. And there's a woman—attractive. She doesn't look too happy to be here and she might be mouthing the words instead of actually singing.

When they finish singing, they clap and Rafael gently guides me with a hand on my shoulder toward the table.

"Everyone, this is Hugo. He's a musician—a very talented musician," he says.

The tall one approaches me and holds out his hand. "It's nice to meet you, Hugo. I'm Geoff."

Geoff is quite tall with bulging eyes and an extremely pale complexion. I shake his large bony hand.

"I'm Theo," says the fat one with curly hair and thick glasses. He's got crumbs on his short sleeve button-up. I shake his pudgy hand. It's moist.

The woman is looking self-conscious and removes her party hat.

"This is Piper," Rafael says. "Say hi, Piper."

"Hi Piper," she says with distain.

"Hi," I say. I want to know more about this one.

"You guys!" Rafael chides. "Why didn't you light the candle?"

"I thought Geoff was going to bring the lighter," Theo says.

"And I thought Theo was going to bring it," Geoff says.

Piper rolls her eyes. She clearly doesn't want to be here.

"It's fine," I say. "Thank you. It's very . . . thoughtful."

"Can we eat the cake now?" Theo asks Rafael who seems to be in charge here.

"Yes, go ahead. Make sure Hugo here gets the first piece. It's *his* birthday."

"Oh, no. I'm not hungry. You guys go ahead."

"Well, of course you're not hungry," Rafael says with a chuckle. "We don't get hungry here."

"I get hungry," Theo says.

"You only *think* you're hungry," Geoff says.

Theo cuts himself a heroic slice. Geoff cuts modest size slices for everyone else.

"Mmmm," Rafael says with a mouthful of cake. "Are you sure you don't want any? It's got raspberry filling." He has white icing on his upper lip. "So good."

Piper isn't eating her cake, but poking at it with a plastic fork. She looks bored.

"So what does everyone do here?" I ask finally.

"I'm a molecular biologist," Theo says. "I'm working on a new Alzheimer's treatment protocol. Alzheimer's is a progressive neurodegenerative disorder that affects the brain later in life causing memory loss and cognitive decline."

"I know what Alzheimer's is," I say. Do they really think I was just born in that room over there?

"I'm an aerospace engineer," Geoff says.

"They needed a tall guy to work on those rockets!" Rafael quips. "Isn't that right Mr. Rocket Scientist?"

"He's kidding," Geoff tells me. "Rockets are way taller."

"Yeah. I get it. Funny." Wow.

"We like to kid around here," Rafael says. "Isn't that right, Pipe?"

Piper is in a zone. She reminds me of someone, but I can't remember who. Apparently, I don't know anyone besides these four. That can't be right.

"Piper!" Rafael says.

"Huh?" Piper says snapping out of it.

"I said, we like to kid around here, don't we?"

"Uh, yeah. We kid all the time. It's a riot," she says in perfect monotone.

"Piper here is a systems administrator. Computer stuff," Rafael says.

"Oh cool," I say to Piper even though she didn't offer up

that information. She only raises her eyebrows and stabs her cake with a fork. What is her deal?

Rafael snickers nervously and shakes his head. "She's a genius. You all are! You are all such bright stars." He's laying it on pretty thick. Geoff and Theo seem to be buying it. "I was hoping, since today is Hugo's first day, you guys could show him the ropes a bit."

"I'm sure you have lots of questions," Theo says.

I nod. "I do."

"Sit down," Rafael says as he takes a seat at the head of the table.

I sit and notice all eyes are on me. "Um. So where am I? What is this place?"

"Great question," Rafael says. "It's a—"

"It's a prison," Piper says out of nowhere.

"Piper!" Rafael chides playfully. "See? She likes to kid, too."

"This is Pod Fifty-Four," Theo says. "Here in Level Six, pods are like your family."

"Level Six?"

"It's one of the seven levels of spiritual evolution," Theo says.

Geoff nods.

I open my mouth to reply but I have no words. "I . . . what?"

"You've lived other lives before this one," Theo explains. "That's why you know how to play music and why we know how to do what we do. We've advanced to a point in our spiritual development where we've come to understand what we're ultimately meant for. And this is the stage where we get to practice that and only that for the betterment of humankind."

"Well put, Theo," Rafael says.

"And then what?" I ask. "What is Level Seven?"

"Level Seven is when you become legend." Theo turns toward the fireplace in the living room and points to a portrait of a stone-faced man with a thin mustache and a bad haircut. "You get your portrait made and those at lower stages get to look to you for inspiration. Like Steve Gower."

"Where is he now?" I ask.

Geoff looks to the ceiling. "He's everywhere."

Piper rolls her eyes.

"And his wisdom is recorded in the Book of Illumination," Theo says.

"What's that?" I ask.

"It's a guide," Rafael says. "For when you need a little inspiration. We'll get you a copy."

"So what happened in my previous lives?" I ask.

"Level One and Two are mostly for learning to walk and talk," Theo explains. "At that stage you were just crawling around and making unintelligible sounds."

"I was a baby," I say.

"What's a baby?" Theo asks. He looks confused.

"A baby," I say. "You know, like a little baby," I use my arms to demonstrate holding a baby. The others just look at each other with furrowed brows.

"Like a tiny person?" Rafael asks. He's oddly curious.

"Yeah."

"Sometimes we have impressions from past lives," Theo explains. "But they're often misinterpreted. I can see how you might make that interpretation. I'm sure it probably feels like you're really small when you can't even lift your head and you keep pooping your pants."

"I take it there are no babies here," I say.

"Well, Glenna back at the lab is pretty tiny," Geoff says. "But she's just very short."

"There are others?" I ask.

"Oh yes!" Rafael says. "Lots of others. I'll introduce you to your work associates later. This is your core pod. Pods are assigned based on a diverse cross section of the work force. We find it helps stimulate your productivity to interact with others from different fields of study. Having a musician among us is going to really round out the pod."

"I see. So what about the next few levels," I ask.

"Level Three and Four have to do with social development," Theo says. "You learn to navigate your social environment as a separate individual. You develop a personality and an ego."

"You also learn basic Math and language skills," Geoff adds.

"Thank you, Geoff. In Level Five, you continue your academic learning and embark on your first career. You might try different careers to see what you're better suited for. You accumulate material possessions as a way to wield power and influence over others. You get into transactional relationships to gain status or to combat a growing sense of loneliness and isolation. Many people do not advance passed this level and have to repeat it several times before they get it right—before they learn the truth."

"And what truth is that?" I ask.

"The truth that you are meant to do one thing for the betterment of humanity and that material possessions and empty relationships are only distractions from your one true purpose."

"You entered this life," Rafael interjects, "already knowing what you were meant for. That's a wonderful place to be." He's smiling again.

"What are you meant for?" I ask him. "What's your job?"

"I'm a pod facilitator. You can think of me as a counselor or a—"

"Or a hall monitor," Piper says.

"That was one time," Rafael says, laughing nervously. "What were you doing in the hall during working hours anyway?"

"Looking for the bathroom," she says.

Rafael laughs. "She is such a kidder! We don't have to go to the bathroom here," he says shaking his head.

"Why not?" I ask.

"Because you've evolved beyond that," Rafael says. "You don't have to sleep or eat either."

"But you can eat if you want to," Theo says and takes another bite of cake.

I can't help feeling like this has to be a dream. In dreams, things that would be completely illogical in the real world somehow make sense. This gives me a strange sense of acceptance for what I am now being told—that today is my first day in a new level of spiritual development. I'm not hungry or sleepy. I don't have to pee.

Piper doesn't seem to be buying it. What does she know? I wonder if I'll ever get a chance to talk to her alone. I don't think she likes me very much.

There's a clock on the wall. It only goes to eight.

"What's with that clock?" I ask.

"What do you mean?" Rafael asks looking at the clock.

"Why does it only go to eight?"

"Because there are only eight hours in a day," he says like he's talking to a child. Only children don't exist here.

"That's a holdover from a previous life," Theo says. "In previous lives we needed to sleep a third of the day to recharge so our days were a lot longer. We used to be exhausted all the time because we were doing jobs we hated. In this life, we just have to reboot every eight hours."

"Reboot?"

"At about five minutes to eight, you'll come back here and lay your head on the table. Your brain automatically reboots at eight o'clock so we lay down for safety reasons."

"You don't want to fall down if you happen to be standing up when you reboot," Geoff says.

"Especially if you're as tall as Geoff!" Rafael says, smiling and pointing at him with his thumb.

"So we just work all day?" I ask.

"Yes! Isn't that great?" Rafael says. "You get to literally spend your whole life doing exactly what you were meant to do and nothing else! It's fantastic!"

"Do we ever get vacation? What if we have families?"

Rafael shakes his head. "No. That's Level Five stuff. None of that is important here. But you do get breaks. We've found productivity increases when we take short intermittent breaks throughout the day."

"And we get time off for celebrations," Geoff says. "Like what we're doing now."

"Yes!" Rafael says. "Today is a special occasion. We're so happy you're here." He sounds sincere, if not a bit maniacal.

The clock on the wall says it's just past one o'clock. I'm an hour old. As much as I'd like to protest against the idea of being born as a full grown man, I keep forgetting what babies look like. Yes, they're small, and not metaphorically so as Theo suggests. There is something categorically different about them other than their size. I imagine a stroller being pushed by a fully grown adult and when I mentally look inside, it's just a smaller adult with beard stubble and a phone.

"Phones," I blurt out.

"Pardon?" Rafael asks.

"Are phones a thing? Or is that something I'm remembering from my previous life?"

"Yes. That's another way people used to distract themselves from the pain of living in lower stages of spiritual evolution. We have no need for distraction here."

I can almost feel the weight of a phone in my hand and the pull to view it, but I can't make out any of the applications on its screen. When I imagine a phone, it's not distraction or avoidance I feel. It's something more like anticipation, or longing. I'm connected to something or someone on the other end of that phone. But who?

"Will I ever see anyone from my previous lives?" I ask.

"Doubtful," Rafael says.

"But not entirely out of the question," Theo adds. "For example, if you were to expire around the same time and you were both at the same spiritual level, it's conceivable that you might find each other in the next iteration. But, you wouldn't recognize them."

"I died?" I ask. It's the first time I've given it any thought. "How did I die?"

"Probably doing something you hated," Rafael says with a chuckle. "Good riddance!"

"We can't remember anything from our past lives," Geoff says.

"It doesn't matter!" Rafael says enthusiastically. "You've made it to this level! You're one step away from complete and total freedom."

I see Piper inconspicuously shaking her head. I don't know if she doesn't buy into any of this or if she's just fed up with his evangelistic fervor. Rafael does seem to be a bit of a zealot, which is fine. But I'm not one to go all in on something I don't fully understand. If there's an alternative explanation, I'd like to hear it.

A soothing chime resonates throughout the house.

"Party time's over, everyone," Rafael says. "Time to get back to changing the world!"

Theo slices into another piece of cake. "For the road," he says.

"It was a pleasure meeting you, Hugo," Geoff says.

"Nice meeting you," I say.

"Have a great first day," Theo says, licking icing off his thumb.

"Thanks." I look over at Piper who is pushing her chair back under the table. "It was nice meeting you," I say. It seems like the most basic acknowledgment, but given her lack of engagement, it's all I really can say.

"See you around," Piper says. Her eyes linger on me a second longer than I might have expected and she walks out the front door. Something in her look infuses me with curiosity, like she knows something I don't.

"Are you ready to see your studio?" Rafael asks, rubbing his hands together.

I'm eager to see more of this place. "Sure."

"After you," he says opening the front door.

CHAPTER 4
INSOMNIA

THE ALARM WRENCHED me from sleep and into a throbbing headache. I couldn't have gotten more than a couple hours. Some nights, sleep didn't even come at all. It had been like this since Celeste died. I was up watching old sci-fi movies until two and then stared at the ceiling for another couple hours before sleep finally bestowed its mercy upon me. I've tried melatonin, magnesium powder, edibles—nothing works. I tried Ambien once, but I set off the smoke alarm trying to cook a whole pound of bacon in the oven. It was still in the package.

I checked my phone for any job emails—nothing. Not surprised. I wasn't qualified for anything that paid more than what I was currently making, which wasn't much. I showered and pulled on a pair of jeans before shuffling into the kitchen to put the coffee on. Ava was sitting at the table eating a Pop Tart and scrolling through her phone.

"How'd you sleep?" I asked.

She pulled earbuds from her ears. "Fine."

"Are you ready for your test?" Math wasn't her favorite subject but she managed to get all A's anyway.

She shrugged. "Pretty much."

"I'm sure you'll ace it like you always do."

She started to put her earbuds back in.

"Is that all you're eating for breakfast?" I asked and she rolled her eyes. "I can scramble some eggs." I opened the fridge and pulled out the carton, but there was only one egg left. "I can scramble you one egg."

"No, thanks. Mr. Peters is bringing donuts to homeroom."

"Nice. What's the occasion?" I asked, returning the egg carton back to the fridge.

"He lost a bet."

"What was the bet?"

"He bet Su-Jin Jeon he could beat him in a cube-off."

"A cube-off?"

"Yeah. Do you even know what a Rubik's Cube is?"

"Of course. I had one when I was younger than you."

"Well, apparently, Su-Jin won some competition, so Mr. Peters challenged him to a cube-off and if he won, Su-Jin would have to wash his car, and if he lost, he said he'd buy the whole class donuts. Su-Jin solved it in two minutes flat."

"That's impressive. But Pop Tarts and donuts aren't exactly a great breakfast."

She mocked my words silently with her face. "I'm gonna be late for the bus." Ava pulled her backpack over her shoulder and put her earbuds back in.

"Have a good day at school."

"Later, homie," she said over her shoulder, throwing me a peace sign on her way out.

"Good luck on your test!" I shouted just before the door closed behind her. It's funny how quiet the house got when she left—and how loud that quiet could feel. It used to be Celeste running the show—packing the lunches, signing permission slips, making sure Ava clothes were weather appropriate. Now it was just me, clumsily filling in the blanks and hoping Ava didn't notice. But of course she did. How could she not?

I poured a cup of coffee and leaned against the counter, taking slow sips, ensuring every ounce of caffeine got into my bloodstream. My head felt fuzzy, like it had been packed with styrofoam. My eyes still hadn't fully focused. I couldn't tell if it was the alcohol or the lack of sleep—probably both. At first, I drank to escape the intrusive thoughts that kept me up at night. By the time I admitted the alcohol didn't help me sleep, it had already become a nightly routine.

I pulled my sun-beaten *vintage*, I liked to call it, Toyota pickup into the parking lot of the Taggert Crossings shopping center and pinned the Alvernon Music Store name tag onto my shirt. I liked my job. It was laid back and the owner liked me. I just wished they paid me more.

"Hey Hugo!" Lenny called as I walked through the glass door. Lenny had been working here longer than me. He handled instrument rentals for school kids and coordinated lessons with local instructors, among whom I was one. I taught guitar. Besides Guitar Center, we had the largest selection of guitars in town. And I knew my shit. I made a little extra from lessons, but my commissions are what kept me going. Technically, I was a salesman, but it didn't feel like sales. I knew what people were looking for and I knew the gear.

"What's up, Lenny?"

"Fisticuffs tickets go on sale this Friday. Ernie and Raj are going. Want me to deal you in?"

I wasn't crazy about the Fisticuffs. Lenny went every time they were in town. We used to go to shows all the time, but not since Celeste passed. Most people give up after you keep negging on their invites, but Lenny still asked every so often.

"When is it?" I asked.

"Not until April but I'm pretty sure they'll sell out before the weekend is over."

"Sorry, man. I have to pass this time. Ava's going to a birthday party this weekend and we have to get a gift. Money's tight."

"Don't worry about that, man. You don't have to pay me right away. I know where you work," he said with a grin.

"I don't know." I wasn't one for handouts. I didn't like feeling like I owed anybody anything.

"I'm getting you a ticket. If you can't make it, I'll see if Jody's sister wants to go. I heard she might be breaking up with her boyfriend soon."

"Alright. Deal," I said with a chuckle. Jody's sister would never go out with Lenny. But I admired his confidence. "Thanks."

"Don't mention it."

"Hey, do you think I could pick up some extra lessons this month?"

"It's been slow, man. Plus, there's a rotation. You're better off playing for tips out on the sidewalk."

"Don't think I won't."

"Hey, why did you stop playing over at Cactus Annie's?" Regret flashed on his face as soon as he said it. I stopped playing after Celeste died. "Shit. Sorry, man. That was a stupid question."

"Don't worry about it. It's cool." I didn't expect him to remember every detail of my life. But seriously, I didn't think I'd ever sing again.

"I didn't mean to—"

"Seriously, dude. It's fine." I offered up a weak smile.

"You used to do pretty good down there though, didn't you?"

"Not bad. Plus, I got a free meal." On good nights I could make up to four hundred dollars, all in tips. Cactus Annie's was a small neighborhood bar and grill with a cozy outdoor patio. I mostly played covers. Occasionally, I played an original, but the patrons weren't there to hear original music. They just wanted to eat their fish and chips and burgers and drink beer in the acoustic equivalent of a popular sit com rerun. That was fine with me.

"You should start playing again. I'd come see you." He wasn't just saying it either. He didn't know me back when we were big. I took some relief in that fact. It was hard to explain to people who knew me then why I gave it all up. Plenty of famous musicians had kids and it never stopped them from having a successful career. It was just different for me. The thought of being away from my newborn for more than a weekend was unfathomable.

"I'll think about it," I said. But that wasn't true. That part of me was ancient history.

It was slow in the store that day. Couldn't stop yawning. It was almost time for my 3:30 guitar lesson—this twelve-year-old kid named Declan. His mom Darcy was kind of into me. She was sort of attractive, in a botoxed, manicured fingernails, cougar kind of way, but she had a lot of baggage, and no filter. She told me all about her divorce after her son's very first lesson. She wanted to make sure I knew that her therapist thought it was time for her to *get out there.*

"Coming in hot!" Lenny said as Darcy barreled into a store-facing parking space in her Land Rover. If it weren't for the concrete bollards out front, I'd be afraid she might crash right into the store. She pulled down the sun visor to re-apply her lipstick while Declan labored to extract his guitar case from the back seat. "Need me to run interference?" Lenny asked.

I snickered. "No, I can handle it."

"You sure? Last week, I thought I was going to have to turn the hose on her."

"Oh, come on now."

"I think you should just go out with her so she can get it out of her system."

"That's a terrible idea."

"Could be fun. She's like a bubble ready to pop."

Darcy tossed her blonde hair back, repositioning her sunglasses on top of her head as she walked through the front door. She smiled when she saw me.

"Sorry, I'm such a mess. I didn't have time to change after the gym." She was wearing yoga pants and an athletic halter top, but her hair and makeup looked perfect and she was wearing dangly ear rings—not exactly gym appropriate.

"Okay." I wasn't sure what else to say about that so I turned to Declan. "Hey buddy. Did you practice this week?"

He shrugged. "Yeah."

"That's great. You're a little early but we can go ahead and get started. You ready?"

"Yeah."

We started to walk back to the practice rooms when Darcy touched my arm.

"How do you think he's progressing?" Darcy asked with a look of concern.

"He's getting better and better," I said trying to come off upbeat.

"'Cause I was wondering if you thought he should start coming twice a week."

Declan rolled his eyes.

"That's up to you. He's on track with his weekly lessons, but it couldn't hurt."

"I listened to your old band this week. You guys were so good! Declan is lucky to have you as an instructor."

"Oh. Thanks. That was a long time ago."

She playfully swatted my arm. "Don't be modest!" She leaned toward me and in a half whisper said, "I bet you had all the ladies eating out of your hand." Her breath smelled like cinnamon.

"Not exactly."

"Whatever you say, Mr. Rock Star."

"Well, we should probably get started. Let me know if you want to add another day. Mondays are pretty open."

"Okay. Have fun, sweetheart," she said to Declan. "I'll be next door at the boba place."

I followed Declan back to the practice rooms and I didn't look back. "We'll be in here today," I said, opening the door to let him enter before me.

As he opened his guitar case, I could tell his face was beet red.

"You okay?" I asked, shutting the door behind me.

"Yeah." He's always a bit low energy but that day he seemed extra moody.

"You know, if you need to talk, I'm a pretty good listener."

He sighed. "It's my mom. She's so embarrassing."

"Oh hey, don't even worry about that."

"She doesn't think I need extra lessons. She just wants another excuse to come in here." He looked at the floor. "She's trying to get you to ask her out if you can't tell."

I blinked, caught off guard by his bluntness. "And that would be weird, right?"

"I mean, yeah."

"You have nothing to worry about. I have a strict no dating policy with students and their moms, alright?"

"She can be kinda pushy."

"Trust me. She's a very nice lady, but between you and me, she's not exactly my type."

"That's what I told her!" He seemed a little relieved.

"So are we cool?"

"Yeah."

"Cool. So let me hear how far you got on 'Hey Jude'."

He stumbled through the first few measures and then stopped.

"You're doing great. Why'd you stop?"

"I suck," he said kicking his foot at nothing.

"What are you talking about? No, you don't."

"I'm never going to be able to play like you."

"Don't say that. Listen here. You're twelve years old! I started playing when I was fifteen and I sucked for a long time before I was good enough to play in front of anyone. You can't expect to play like Slash right off the bat. You have to work at it—for a long time."

"What's Slash?"

"Really? Lead guitar for Gun's 'N Roses?"

Declan just stared at me blankly. Of course he didn't know who Guns 'N Roses were.

"So how long do I have to suck for?"

"You just need to put in the practice."

"How long?"

"It depends. When I started playing, I practiced for hours every day. I couldn't wait to get home from school so I could play. I had this beat up second-hand Squire and a little ten-watt Fender amp. My mom had to force me to stop and come eat dinner and then I'd finish as fast as I could so I could go right back to my bedroom to keep playing."

"I guess they didn't have video games back then."

"No, they did! I played a little, but my main focus was guitar. I couldn't get enough. But the main thing is, at that stage, I wasn't any good, see? I sucked, too, for a long time. If you can't embrace the suckiness of being new at something, you'll never move beyond it. Great players, they all sucked in the beginning."

"Did they suck as bad as me?"

"Yep. Now let's try it again, from the top."

When we finished the lesson, Declan seemed to be in better spirits. We walked out into the main store lobby and his mother was waiting there with two cups of boba tea.

"How'd he do?" Darcy asked. She handed Declan his tea. "I got this one for you," she said holding the second one out to me. "Just a little thank you for being such a great instructor. It's passionfruit."

"Thanks," I said, taking the pink beverage. "He did really well today. I don't think he needs extra lessons. He probably needs to spend more time practicing and we talked about that."

"Okay, well, whatever you think." She turned to her son. "Guess what?"

"What?"

"I signed up for guitar lessons!"

"What?!" Declan said with trepidation.

I looked over at Lenny behind the counter, shrugging apologetically.

"I figured, you know, why not? You'll be at your dad's this weekend and I've been meaning to take up a new hobby." She turned to me. "God knows he has his new hobby—Miss Barely Legal."

"Mom!"

"Sorry. I just thought it would be nice if we both had something else in common. We could even start our own band someday!"

"Mo-om!" Declan pleaded.

"We could be like that mother-son duo on American Idol!"

Declan moaned. Poor kid.

"See you Friday, Hugo!" Darcy ushered her son by the shoulder out of the store.

"What just happened?" I asked Lenny.

"You said you needed more lessons," he said with a shrug.

"Dude!"

"Hey, I tried to put her with Marty, but she insisted you be her instructor. You got to admire a woman who knows what she wants," he said trying to hide a salacious grin. He was enjoying this.

"I guess I do need the money. Ava has this birthday sleepover at La Paloma and I have to get her a gift. Apparently her friends go all out for birthdays."

"She has some bougie-ass friends."

"I don't want her to feel left out. She finally found a group of friends she relates to. You know how it is at that age."

"Yeah. I was a total outcast."

"Weren't you in band?"

"Yeah. I played the clarinet and had a revolting acne problem. Wasn't exactly a chick magnet."

"And look at you now!" I said with a mocking grin.

"Oh yeah, I'm a regular Don Juan," he said sarcastically. "That's why I'm playing poker with Ernie and Raj this Saturday. You want in?"

My first impulse was to decline. But I couldn't think of a good enough excuse. "Saturday?" Ava had that sleepover. "Yeah. Sure. I'll be there."

CHAPTER 5
STUDIO

EVERY HOUSE in this neighborhood is small, probably because they don't have bedrooms. They all seem to be new construction—well-maintained with perfectly manicured lawns and fully grown trees. I notice, while there is variation in the landscaping, every species of plant is identical to one another. For example, there are three or four cherry blossom trees on this lane and they're all the same height and have the same size canopy. The yellow tulips in our flower bed are like four repetitions of the same cluster in a neat row—each cluster containing the same number of flowers, all the same height.

Each cottage has their pod number attached to the right of each front door. Paved walkways wind from each door toward a center pathway that separates the cottages on each side. We walk down the path, which is lined with benches, shrubberies, small fountains, and flower beds, toward what I can only describe as an outdoor elevator.

"What is this thing?" I ask him.

"A teleporter," he says, like it's the most normal thing in the world.

"A what?"

"A teleporter. It's the fastest way to get around town."

I don't see any cars, or streets for that matter. "What town?"

"Slumbervale."

Rafael approaches the vestibule and bends to a retinal scanner near the door. It beeps and says, "Hello Rafael." When the doors open, we step into the teleporter and he says to me, "I think you're going to like what we've got set up for you."

A computerized voice says, "Where would you like to go, Rafael?"

"Gower Productions," he says, over-pronouncing his words.

"Right away," the computer replies.

"What exactly is my job going to be?" I ask

"You're a musician. You're going to write music."

"What kind of music?"

"Whatever you feel inspired to write."

"That's pretty open-ended."

"Yes," he says, eyebrows reaching into his receding hairline.

I feel no movement inside the teleporter, but in a few seconds the doors open with a ding. We walk out onto a court-yard surrounded by taller buildings on each side. It reminds me of a small town center, but without streets or cars. People are milling about, congregating in small groups, entering and exiting buildings.

"The studio is right downtown!" Rafael says gleefully. "You're lucky to work down here."

"It's nice," I say. I've never seen any place this clean in my life, which, I suppose, hasn't been that long.

We walk into one of the buildings, which has a colorful mural of several rock legends on its side: Hendrix, Joplin, Jagger, Prince, Madonna, Cobain, Dylan, Jerry Garcia, and others. We walk through the glass entry doors, which say *Gower Productions* in gold lettering, into a lobby, which has leather couches and framed gold and platinum records on every wall. Vintage concert posters line the walls of the hallway that leads back to the main studio.

Rafael opens the door and I am transfixed by what I see. Rows of guitars, keyboards, microphones, drums and other instruments line the walls. A black baby grand sits in the center of the room. On one end is a window to an engineering booth where a guy with long dreadlocks and a greying beard sits. He sees us as we walk in, removes his headphones, and greets us through a side door.

"Here he is," he says holding out his hand. "I'm Vincent, your producer."

I shake his hand. "Hugo."

"I know. I can't wait to make music with you, man!"

"Vincent works with all our musicians," Rafael explains. "You'll get to meet some of the others later. You'll write the music and Vincent here will do all the mixing and recording stuff." He makes some hand gestures that reveal his utter lack of knowledge of how music is recorded—like it's some kind of sorcery.

"You just concentrate on writing songs," Vincent says. "When you think you've got something, you call me and we'll lay down some tracks. I'm here to support you in any way I can. If you need some other instrument or you want to collaborate with other musicians, just let me know and I'll make it happen. We have everything you could possibly need here."

"This is unbelievable," I say picking up a 1950's Rickenbacker—convertible fireglo finish, mint. How did they get this? It's got to be upwards of ten grand. How do I know that?

"Believe it," Rafael says. "You can finally spend your time

doing what you love—doing exactly what you were put on this Earth for."

"It's like a dream come true," I say.

"That it is," Rafael says. "That it is. Well, I'll leave you to it. I'll be here before eight to walk you back to the pod to reboot. Have a great first day!" He grabs both my shoulders and gives them a squeeze. "We're so happy you're here!" He shakes Vincent's hand and leaves.

"So," Vincent says. "What kind of music do you like?"

"I don't know." I really *don't* know. I know lots of different kinds of music but I can't seem to identify any personal preferences.

"That makes sense. It's your birthday! How could you know?"

"Right. But if I was just born, how do I already know so much music? Where did I learn it all?"

"That's a trip, ain't it?" He scratches his neck. "There are so many things about the universe we can't possibly understand. Everything you know is carried over from previous lives. They've prepared you for this moment."

"But what about everything I don't know? Why don't I know anything about myself?"

"You know everything you need to know to make a difference in this life. That's all that matters."

"Okay. So what now?" I look around the studio. "I mean, how do I start?"

"You're going to have to develop your own process. Everyone approaches it different. Some start with writing lyrics. Others start with a riff and go from there. You're going to have to find your own style. Tell you what. You've been eyeing that Rickenbacker there. Why don't you take it for a spin?"

"Yeah?" I say. I pick up the guitar and slip the strap over

my neck. There's a bowl of guitar picks on the table and I fish one out. Vincent hands me the cable, which is plugged into a Marshall amp, and I plug it into the output jack of the guitar. The hairs on my arm stand up when I hear the static of the connection. My fingers find the G-chord and I strum slowly to hear each string in succession. Vincent turns the volume up on the amp a notch or two.

"Just play anything that comes to mind," he says.

I nod and close my eyes, reaching into the darkness of my memory, hoping the right song appears. My fingers find D major 7 and I strum. Then I move to G/D. My head nods to a rhythm that pulses through the darkness and I alternate between these chords. I don't even know the song until the words come at the right moment—"Everybody Wants to Rule the World."

Vincent is sitting on a black leather couch when I finish the song. He doesn't clap the way Rafael did when I played "Hotel California." He doesn't say anything for a long time—just sits there barely nodding his head.

"Was that okay?" I ask. I'm not fishing for compliments. I really can't tell what he's thinking.

"Brother, that wasn't just okay. That was next level. I know you didn't write it, but you sang it like you did—like it came from somewhere deep inside you. See, you were born with a deep well of truth and you instinctively know how to tap into it. Do you think you can write something like that?"

"I don't know."

"If you could write a song a fraction as good as what you just played, I think you could be a huge star."

"Really?" Okay, now maybe I am fishing for a compliment.

"I don't lie, Hugo. I just wish we had been recording. Can we try another one?"

"Sure."

"How about something a little more uptempo. Something with an edge to it. You got something like that?"

"Yeah, I think so. Let me see."

Vincent brings over a microphone stand and plugs the cable into a PA. He jogs back to the recording booth and puts on his headphones. Through the intercom, he says, "Alright, what do you got?"

"I got one" I say into the mic. But the Rickenbacker doesn't feel right for this song. I unplug it and return it to the rack. I select a gorgeous sunburst Les Paul and I plug the cable into the output jack. The size and weight of this guitar feels oddly familiar. The hum from the amplifier is electrifying and I send a crashing power chord into the quiet room. The opening riff comes at me like a schoolyard bully. I retaliate with the next power chord and find my way into the rhythm.

I don't even know the name of this song until the end of the first verse—"Everlong." Vincent is nodding fervently in the booth. The guitar is an extension of me. By the time I get to the chorus, my voice is a drift car finding its grip into a straightaway.

At the end, I let the final chord linger until the amp gifts me with just the right amount of feedback. Vincent is jumping in the booth. He's lit up. So am I. My heart is racing and my skin is electric. I push my hair back with both hands and take a deep breath.

Vincent approaches me with a big smile. He places a hand on my shoulder and says, "If you ever doubted that this is what you were meant for, I hope that clears things up."

I don't know what to say. He's right. But just because I can play these songs, doesn't mean I know how to write them. What am I supposed to write about? I'm less than two hours old. I have almost zero life experience.

"I don't know if I could ever write anything that good," I say.

"I mean, it's a good song, no doubt about it, but what makes it incredible is the way you made it your own. It's your energy. You put yourself into it, see? Anything you write is going to be that much more powerful. It's you, man."

"You really think so?"

"I do. Now, I know what you're thinking. 'What am I supposed to write about? I was just born!' I know. But like Steve Gower says in the Book of Illumination, 'Your wisdom is the composite of many lives.' Everything that ever meant anything to you is already in there, even if you don't know it by name. You've loved and lost. You've faced many challenges and heartbreaks. All that emotion, all that pain, you have it right there inside you, even if you don't have access to those particular memories. And the only reason you had to go through all of that is so that you could turn it into music in this life.

"I don't even know where to start."

"What are you feeling right now?"

"What am I feeling?"

"Yeah, I know it's been kind of a head trip these last couple hours. You must be feeling some kind of way."

"Confused. Frustrated. Skeptical. To name a few."

"I'd say that's a pretty good place to start. Take that feeling and make it real. Let it lead you. What do you need from me?"

"I'm not sure."

"Why don't you just play around? If something sounds good, write it down." He points to a stack of notebooks on a coffee table. "There's no pressure to come up with a hit on your first try. Just have fun with it."

"Okay."

"Oh, and if you need any inspiration, this laptop has every song ever recorded." He hands me an open laptop.

"Woah," I say as I scroll through the extensive music library. I recognize a lot of these songs and artists, but I'm not sure it's going to help me write anything original.

"I got some errands to run. Make yourself at home. I'll be back to check in on you later."

"Okay."

I sit back on the couch and take it all in. This place is amazing. I could spend the rest of my days in here. Still, there's this persistent doubt I can't shake—like it's too good to be true, like it could all be taken away at any moment.

CHAPTER 6
COUGAR

I ARRIVED at the music store for Darcy's first guitar lesson at 9:00 a.m. I tried my best not to assume ulterior motives on her part. *Just act normal—don't make it weird,* I told myself. Part of me wanted to ask Ava what she thought about me dating again. Not because I wanted to date Darcy, because I didn't—just in general. I was perfectly content not dating until after her graduation. I really wasn't interested in all that, but I still wished I knew how she felt about it.

Darcy was waiting in her Land Rover when I arrived. I offered a two-finger salute as I walked past her car and into the store. What was that? I'd never done that before in my life. I was already making it weird.

"How long has she been here?" I asked Lenny who was putting up a promotional display in the middle of the store.

"At least ten minutes."

There were cameras in each of the practice rooms. I just knew he'd be watching us the whole time.

Darcy walked through the doors wearing a short skirt, open-toe sandals, and a low cut top revealing ample tanned cleavage. I noticed she had long acrylic nails that had been painted in pink and orange swirls. That was going to be a problem. She was carrying her son's guitar case, which was plastered with stickers. He should have taken it to his dad's to practice over the weekend, but I decided I wasn't going to say anything.

"Are you ready for me?" Darcy asked.

Lenny gave me a sideways look.

"Ready." I led her to the practice rooms and glanced back at Lenny, gyrating his hips against the cardboard display and making a sex face I never wanted to see again for as long as I lived.

In the practice room, Darcy sat in a folding chair and bent forward to unlatch her son's guitar case, nearly spilling out of her top. She crossed spider-veined legs and placed the guitar on her lap.

"Like this?"

"Perfect. Have you had lessons before?"

"I'm a virgin." She giggled.

"Okay, well, first things first," I said, ignoring the innuendo. "Your nails look very nice, but—"

"Thank you." She held them out to admire them.

"But they're going to get in the way when you're trying to press the strings with your fretting hand."

"Oh, boo! I just had these done, too," she said with a pout and then brightened. "But you're in charge. I'll do whatever you want me to do."

I could feel her eyes on me when she said this, but I managed to avoid making eye contact. "Let's start with the open strings." I wrote the notes vertically on the dry erase board behind me: E, A, D, G, B, E. I picked each string from top to bottom, naming each. She watched me intently. "Okay now you try."

She picked each string, saying each note out loud. "Like that?"

"Good! But I think your guitar is a little out of tune. Let me see it real quick."

She handed me the guitar, then sat back, folding her hands in her lap. She flipped her hair and readjusted her posture. She forced a smile but her gaze drifted toward the wall."

"You okay?" I asked as I continued tuning her B string.

She nodded a bit too eagerly. "Yes. I mean . . . it's a little strange being in here. Like I'm sitting in my son's classroom at school."

"Well, I teach adults, too—"

"No, I know." Her eyes looked glassy. Her lip trembled and she turned her reddening face to the wall and shook her head. "Sorry."

"What's wrong?"

"God, what am I doing?" Her voice cracked. "This was a bad idea." She dabbed a tear before it reached her cheek.

"What are you talking about?"

"I'm sorry. I have to go." Darcy reached for her purse.

"Why?" What just happened?

"I'm wasting your time. I don't really want guitar lessons."

"You don't?" I was confused.

"Look at me! I got my nails and hair done for this. I'm so pathetic." A thin line of mascara started to drip down her cheek.

"No, you're not." I put down the guitar and handed her a box of tissue.

"My therapist said I needed to get out there and I told her about you and how I thought you'd never ask me out in front of Declan, so she said I should *be creative*. So I figured I'll just schedule my own lessons. But you're obviously not interested in me." Her throat clenched around her words. "Oh, what am I doing? I'm going to be forty-five this year and you're what, thirty?"

"I'm thirty-seven," I said, which I thought would help, but it didn't.

She scoffed. "I don't know what I was thinking. I guess I thought since my ex found a younger woman, maybe I'd feel better if I found a younger man. That sounds so stupid when I say it out loud." She sobbed into a wad of tissues.

I felt bad for her. "Look, I know it's hard. You've been through a lot and maybe it seems like finding someone else will solve everything, but I think you have to let it happen naturally. You don't have to do all this. Just be yourself and when the right person comes along, it'll be effortless."

"You really think so?" Darcy asked while wiping tears and mascara from under her eyes.

"Sure. You have a lot to offer."

"Really?" She twirled a lock of hair around her finger.

"Of course. You're a very attractive woman."

When she bit her lip, I realized I'd said too much. Darcy lunged toward me like a cougar and planted her mouth onto mine. A moan escaped as she pressed into the kiss. She squeezed my thighs with both hands and I jumped from my chair.

Aware of the camera, which was installed for my own protection in cases like this, I put my hands up like someone was pointing a gun at me and blurted, "No! I don't want this."

Startled, as if coming out of a trance, the sobering realization of her actions began to sink in.

"I'm sorry." Darcy quickly put the guitar back into its case and latched it shut. When she reached for her purse on the chair, it toppled over, spilling its contents onto the carpet. She frantically tried to put everything back—keys, lip balm, a hair clip, two prescription bottles, cough drops, a pen, and other sundry items. She sniffled and wiped her nose while attempting to scoop up as many items as possible, dropping some in the process. One of her fake eyelashes came loose and she tried to reattach it. This was hard to watch.

Eventually, she gave up trying to recover every little thing and rose to her feet. She pulled her purse over her shoulder and reached down to pick up the guitar case with as much dignity as she could muster. Her hair looked like she's been in a wind storm. Her fake eyelash clung to her cheek. She lifted her chin as she crossed the room. I opened the door and before walking through it, she said in a formal tone, "See you next Wednesday for Declan's lesson."

I cleared my throat. "See you Wednesday," I mumbled looking down at the floor.

I walked back over to the area where random purse contents remained on the carpet. Some of it was just trash—a protein bar wrapper, a rubber band, used tissue, pencil shavings. I placed as much of that as I could into the waste basket. Then there were a few items she might have wanted to keep had she not been in such a rush—a single ear ring, a punch card for the boba place next door, and a folded brochure for something called Lunatech. I placed these items into a plastic bag so I could return it to her next week.

When I left the practice room, Lenny began to clap, slowly at first and then increasingly vigorous and celebratory.

"Alright, alright, calm down," I said. "I take it you were watching on the monitor?"

"That's must see TV," he said and showed me his phone screen. Apparently, he'd recorded it.

"Oh, come on, man. Don't fucking post that."

"I won't." Lenny shook his head in disapproval. "That could have ended a lot better."

"You think?"

"No, I mean, you could have definitely hit that."

"Yeah, and I'm sure you'd be happy to sit here and watch, perv."

"Duh."

"You're incorrigible."

"Why do you have to be such a Boy Scout?"

"I'm not a Boy Scout just because I don't want to take advantage of a vulnerable woman."

"She didn't look very vulnerable to me."

"Trust me. She's not in a great place. I feel bad for her."

"What's this stuff?" Lenny asked, nodding toward the bag of random effects.

"Oh, it's just stuff she left behind when she was rushing out. She might want it back next time she comes in."

"You think she's coming back?" Lenny asked, suppressing a laugh.

"She said she'd be back on Wednesday for Declan's lesson."

"Gutsy."

I pulled out the brochure for Lunatech. The tagline caught my eye earlier: *Earn money while you sleep!*

I read on: *Lunatech's patented neuro-interfacing technology—*

"What's that?" Lenny asks.

"Something called Lunatech."

"Let me see." Lenny snatched the brochure from my hand and studied it. "Neuro-interfacing technology? This seems pretty sketch. What are they paying you for?"

I shrugged.

"It says to inquire about their income earning sleeper program." He mumbled as he continued reading.

I took the brochure from him and flipped to the back. "There's a number here. Says to call for more information. Couldn't hurt, right?"

"Wait. You're actually thinking about it?"

"Why not? It's free money."

"There's no such thing as free money, dude. They're paying for access to your brain, your dreams, your darkest secrets. This is how it all starts, man. This is how the machines take over the world. Are your seriously thinking about selling your mind to the machine uprising?"

"It's better than being broke."

He paused, letting that reality settle, then grinned. "You could let Darcy be your sugar mama."

"You're sick."

"I'm just being practical. You could move in with her in that big house in the Foothills, spend all day floating in her pool, drinking her *aged* wine—if you know what I mean."

"Not interested."

"Alright, alright. Just trying to help you think outside the box, that's all. But seriously, this Lunatech thing sounds fucking dystopian. Don't do it."

He wasn't wrong. But he didn't have kids. If the robots did end up taking over, at least I'd have someone to protect. I slipped the brochure into my back pocket.

CHAPTER 7
EMERGENCY

IT'S BEEN NEARLY four hours since Vincent left me alone to start writing music. I've spent most of my time listening to songs I recognize and some that I don't. I'm impressed with this digital music library. You can search music not just based on artist or song title, but you can search different genres and moods, too.

You can even enter a prompt into the AI search. For example, I typed: What's a timeless song for a first date? It generated hundreds of titles, including "This Magic Moment" by the Drifters and "Unchained Melody" by The Righteous Brothers and "Never Tear Us Apart" by INXS.

Vincent was clear no one expects me to write a song in one day and to take my time getting acquainted with the studio. I'm sitting at the baby grand and I have the laptop open on the piano lid. I've managed to play along with some of the tracks. Finding the right keys seems to be more of a struggle on piano than on guitar, but I can usually find the main chord progressions. I look down at the empty notebook in my lap. I feel like I should have written something down by now. I'm interrupted by a knock at the door.

"Come in," I say, grateful for the distraction. It's Rafael.

"Am I interrupting?" Rafael asks leaning halfway into the room.

"No, unfortunately, you're not. I got nothing."

"Well, that's okay," he says shutting the door behind him. "Nobody expects you to write a song on your very first day. But what do you think about this studio? It's great isn't it?"

"It's amazing. I can't think of anything it doesn't have. Vincent seems pretty cool, too."

"Oh, yeah. He's worked with some of the greatest musicians we've ever seen. He's a real professional."

Rafael sits next to me on the piano bench and I scoot to the right to give him room. "Let's see." He cracks his knuckles and places his hands on the keys. "Do you know this one?" He plays the opening to "The Entertainer," a popular piano song among non-pianists.

"Yeah, I think I know that one," I say and when it gets to my part, I finger the melody.

"That's it!" Rafael says and continues, laughing. "We sound so good!" It's not a hard song, but he seems to be having the time of his life. I used to think he was overreacting to things, but he's genuinely enthusiastic about everything. He's a strange man. I like him. When we finish, he says, "That was fun! I wish I knew more songs. That's the only one I know. I can see why you love playing music."

"Yeah, I just wish I knew how to write it."

"You'll get there. Take your time. You're not even a day old."

"Right. It's weird though."

"What?"

"I know I was just born, but I feel like I've been alive for a long time. I mean, granted there's a lot I don't know, but it feels more like I can't remember rather than the fact that I haven't learned it yet."

"That is weird. Obviously, you can't remember what you haven't learned," he says stroking his chin. "You've lived other lives to be sure. But we can't always remember everything from those lives, only what's relevant to this one."

"Yeah. It feels like there are important, meaningful things I should know about myself."

"All you need to know to fulfill your spiritual journey is that you love music and you have a deep desire to share it with the world. Nothing else matters."

"I do love music," I say. That's undeniable. Although I still have the sense something is missing, I don't know what it is. I shouldn't focus on what I can't possibly know. I have to focus on what I do know—music. "Who's in charge here?" I ask.

"I report directly to a division officer within Human Resources. You and Vincent and other creatives are technically in the Arts and Entertainment Division, but while there is a hierarchy in place, you report to me, even though technically, I'm not above you. It's my job to liaison between you and your division heads. Does that make sense?"

"Not really. So I don't have a boss?"

"You do. You just don't interface with them. Any communication that comes from your division heads will come through me and vice versa."

"So you meet with my boss?"

"Not exactly. We correspond."

"You've never met them?"

"In person? No."

"Huh."

"Say, maybe you should go outside. I understand nature can be a vital source of inspiration."

"That makes sense."

"There's a really nice park just around the block. I can show you."

Rafael leads the way through the quaint downtown courtyard, pointing out different places worth visiting along the way. He waves at several people he knows and they wave back. He's probably the most outgoing person I've ever met.

Rafael puts a finger to his ear and says, "Say again." I didn't notice he was wearing a tiny earpiece before. "Uh huh .. . Okay . . . I'm on it." He turns to me and says, "I have to deal with something."

"Is everything okay?"

"Oh yeah," he assures me with a wide smile. "Everything's fine. It's all good in the neighborhood! I'll meet you back at the house. It's fine," he says, showing me his palms, which effectively communicates the exact opposite.

"You sure?"

"Yep. See you soon!" He's walking backwards, then turns and runs away.

What kind of emergencies should I be worried about? Rafael seems so relaxed and cheerful. It's unsettling to see him in an emergency situation.

It's a beautiful park. A pathway winds toward a footbridge, which crosses a small stream. I can't help but notice a lack of variation in the color of the grass. Two birds fly out of a towering Eucalyptus tree. A hummingbird flies toward my head and I instinctively duck. It hovers in front of my face for a few seconds and then darts away.

Am I able to come here whenever I want? It might be a good place to write music. Nature does inspire creativity. I'm not sure how I know that but it seems true enough.

There's a couple of people standing on the footbridge having a conversation. A woman is sitting on a bench with a pile of notebooks on her lap. She looks deeply engrossed in whatever she's working on.

I stroll toward a pond with ducks and lily pads floating on its still, clear surface. Dragonflies buzz near the reedy banks. I stroll by the woman whose brow is furrowed in deep concentration. One of the notebooks slips from her lap onto the grass and I reach down to retrieve it for her.

"Thanks," she says.

"What are you working on?" I ask.

"Oh, I'm trying to get familiar with these files. It's my first day."

"Me too!"

"Happy birthday," she says. Her smile fades and she looks away absently.

"What is it?"

She shakes her head. "It's funny. When I said that just now, I had the impulse to ask you how old you were, but you told me you were just born. *We* were just born. I don't know why that question popped into my head all the sudden. Sorry, I'm really out of sorts today."

"I guess that's understandable. I suppose we still have a lot to learn. I keep thinking I'm supposed to know more than I do. Like I'm trying to remember something, but I don't know what it is. Does that make any sense?"

"Yes! I feel exactly the same way. It's like I have dementia or something."

"I hope it's temporary."

"I think it is."

"Or . . . "

"What?"

"Nothing. It's stupid."

"What were you going to say?"

"It's nothing. I'm just being paranoid."

"Well, now you have to tell me." Her smile puts me at ease.

"What if . . . what if there *is* something we're not remembering? What if . . . I know this is going to sound crazy but, what if they're deliberately keeping something from us? Like what if they erased our memories somehow?"

"I had the same thought. It certainly feels that way. But why would they do that? I asked Lorena—she's my pod facilitator. She said they're just shadows from our past lives and newborns are susceptible to sensing them at first, but they eventually fade with time."

"Oh. Yeah, I guess that makes sense." I don't know if it makes *more* sense, but it is an explanation. "So what pod are you in?"

"Sixty-two. You?"

"Fifty-four. What's your job here?"

"I'm in training for the sentinel program."

"What is that?"

"Sentinels make sure people are where they're supposed to be and that they're following the rules."

"Like a cop?"

"Sort of. They didn't explain it like that. They talk a lot about safety and keeping order. I guess when I say it out loud, that does sound like what a cop does. We don't have guns or anything. But I have to learn all these protocols and safety codes."

"And this is your life purpose?" I don't mean to be condescending but I'm afraid that's how it came out.

"Apparently so."

"That looks like a lot of work."

"Yeah. It's a lot of information. I feel like . . ." Her brow furrows again.

"Like what?"

"I was going to say . . . I feel like I'm in school again. But I've never been to school."

"Must be a Level Five thing?"

"Yeah. Must be." Her face does not reflect satisfaction with that logic. She shakes her head and brightens, like she's shaking away any pesky doubts. "So, what do you do?"

"I'm a musician."

"Oh, cool! I love music."

"They want me to write songs, but I don't know if I even know how."

"I'm sure you'll figure it out. They wouldn't have given you that assignment if they didn't think you were cut out for it."

"I guess you're right."

A female voice comes through speakers I cannot locate, "Rebooting commences in twenty minutes. Please return to your pods. Rebooting commences in twenty minutes."

"Well, I guess we ought to get back," the woman says, stuffing her files into a soft-sided briefcase.

"I'm not even sure how to get back."

She points. "There's a teleporter over there."

Luckily, Rafael is trotting down the path towards us. "Hugo! Sorry. I didn't forget about you. I had to deal with something." He's a little out of breath.

"No worries."

"I see you made a friend," he says, smiling at the woman.

"I did. Rafael this is . . ." I turn to the woman. "I'm sorry. I didn't catch your name."

"Darcy."

"Nice to meet you, Darcy. I'm Hugo." I shake her hand and turn to Rafael. "It's her birthday, too."

"Well, happy birthday!" Rafael announces with glee. "Welcome to Slumbervale."

"Thank you," Darcy says.

"What pod are you in?" Rafael asks as we walk toward the teleporter.

"Sixty-two."

"Funny you two meeting on your first day. What are the chances?" Rafael quips. He carries the conversation and Darcy keeps giving me this knowing look as he prattles on. I nod with wide eyes to let her know we're on the same page—he's a bit weird. She stifles a giggle. When we get to the teleporter, Rafael insists she go first.

She scans her retina.

"Hello Darcy," the computer says and the door opens.

"See you around," she says to me as she steps inside.

I wave.

"Nice to meet you!" Rafael shouts for no reason. "She seems nice," he says to me as the door closes. "Very nice."

When we get back to the pod, Geoff and Theo are already there.

"Hey, Hugo!" Theo says. "How was your first day?"

"Good, I think."

"Did you write any songs?" Geoff asks.

"Give him a break," Rafael says. "It's just his first day."

"Sorry," Geoff says.

"That's okay," I say and turn to Rafael. "So what was the emergency?" I ask.

"Emergency? Oh, right." He sighs heavily. "It's Piper. She had another one of her episodes."

"Episodes?" I ask.

"Not again," Theo says, shaking his head. "Was she raving about how we're all being imprisoned against our will?"

"Something like that. I don't know where she gets this stuff," Rafael says, shaking his head. He turns to me. "When she's under a lot of stress, Piper can get kind of . . . well, paranoid. She starts talking crazy and we find her in strange places. Don't worry. She's safe now up in restoration."

"Restoration?"

"She'll be back to her grumpy self again in no time."

"Does that mean we get to have a taco party?" Theo asks Rafael. "Last time she came back from restoration, we had a taco party," he informs me.

"Yes, we can have a taco party," Rafael concedes.

"What's restoration?" I ask.

"Oh, it's kind of like a . . . mental tune-up," he says with a raised index finger, like he just made that up. "Ooh, look at the time! We better get settled in."

I look up at the clock. Two minutes to eight. Everyone takes a seat at the dining room table and lays their heads down like they're in a pre-school classroom. It feels silly, but I do the same. I watch the second hand tick around. One minute to eight. I look back at the others and they all have their eyes closed. My curiosity compels me to keep mine open just to see what happens. The second hand ticks closer to the eight. Five seconds . . . three seconds . . . and when it gets to one, my consciousness is blown out like a candle flame.

CHAPTER 8
SCRATCH-OFF

I LEFT work at 3:00 to pick Ava up from school and take her shopping for that ridiculously priced birthday gift. She was sitting on a bench outside the fine arts building when I pulled into the parking lot. When she saw me, she pulled her backpack over her shoulder and walked to the truck with her typical scowl.

"How was school?" I asked when she got in and closed the door.

"Fine."

"Are you excited about your sleepover?"

"Yeah," she said without any excitement in her voice whatsoever. "Oh, dad. I have a permission slip for you." She reached into her backpack and ripped out a bent up packet of information that came loose from its staples as she tugged it free from her overstuffed bag.

"What's it for?" I asked.

"The New York trip, remember?"

"New York? When is it?"

"Spring Break," she said with a quick shake of her head, as if I should've already known this.

"Let me see." Now I remembered receiving an email about it. Keeping up with all the school's emails was a full-time job. This trip was specifically for theater. They'd be going to two Broadway plays and touring The New York Conservatory for Dramatic Arts, as well as visiting other iconic New York sites. She would absolutely love this. "Ay-ya-yay! Three thousand dollars? Are they going to be feeding you caviar everyday?"

"Whatever. I already knew I couldn't go," Ava said, swiping the forms from my hand.

"Hey! You're going to give me a paper cut. I didn't say you couldn't go."

"It's too expensive," she said. "We can't afford it." She might as well have punched me in the gut.

"Let me see." I held out my hand and she shoved the papers back toward me with an eye roll.

"I mean, yeah it's a lot, but if it's not until March—"

"The deposit's due in December."

I looked closer. They wanted a thousand dollar deposit by December 16th. "That's a month away!" What a time to expect large sums of money—right before Christmas.

"Told you. Whatever. It's fine. Can we just go?"

"It's not fine!" I didn't mean to shout. "Dammit!" I flung the packet onto the dashboard and gripped the steering wheel tight to restrain myself from doing any further damage. I exhaled and looked over at Ava, who was leaning away from me against the passenger door. Fuck, I scared her.

"I'm sorry, sweetheart."

"Jesus. Are you okay?"

"Yeah. I'm sorry. I . . ." Get a hold of yourself, man! I took a deep breath. I retrieved the colorful packet and gathered the pages that had come loose. I handed it back to her, my hand shaking. "We're going to figure this out, okay? I'm going to find a way to get the money."

"Dad, it's really not that big a deal. It's not like I was actually expecting to go."

"This is important to you and I'm going to find a way," I said definitively. My eyes burned with moisture that I quickly blinked away.

Ava sat there, looking straight ahead. "Can we go?"

"Yeah. Let's go," I said, putting the truck in gear.

I'd think of something. I had a 1976 Les Paul that's worth well over six thousand dollars. It was the exact same guitar Mike Ness, the lead singer for Social Distortion, played when I saw them in Anaheim in '06. It's the same guitar I toured with the two years before Ava was born. I bought it after we took second place at a Southwest Regional Battle of the Bands contest in El Paso. First place got a record deal. We got a ten thousand dollar check to split four ways, which was the most money I'd ever made as a musician at one time. That guitar was worth more than my truck.

But that would have to be an absolute last resort. One of us would have to be dying before I could sell it. I had a couple other guitars—an Epiphone, a Stratocaster, but neither of those are worth much. I also have a Taylor acoustic that I could probably get a grand for, but I can't go without an acoustic guitar. That's what I write all my songs on, not that I've written anything in a while.

I turned on the radio and we didn't speak the entire way to the mall. That's where the makeup store was. Luckily, it's right near the entrance so we didn't have to pass a bunch of stores I knew I couldn't afford to buy her clothes in. I was embarrassed about my behavior earlier, but I was hoping this would cheer her up a little and we could turn a page. At the front of the store was a sandwich board that read: *Sale! 20-40% off select items.*

"Look at that!" I said, nudging Ava's shoulder.

She managed a charitable grin. Her mother did the same thing when I'd be excited about something she didn't really care that much about.

There was a young lady standing at the entrance, welcoming customers with a smile that looked pasted onto her youthful face. I told her what we were looking for and she directed us toward the Remi Swan collection. We wound our way back to an entire section branded in pink and yellow.

"Here it is," I said. "This is the one, right?"

She picked up the gift bag and examined its contents.

"And it's on sale!" I said. "Twenty percent off!"

We made our way to the check out counter. The line snaked through a labyrinth of impulse buy items. Ava was rifling through bins of lip gloss and sniffed a couple.

"You want that?" I asked her.

"No, it's okay."

"Go ahead. Get one. Do you need anything else?"

"No, dad. I'm good."

When we got up to the counter I grabbed a tin of lip gloss from the bin and placed it next to the gift bag to be rung up. I paid and Ava bumped me with her shoulder as a gesture of gratitude. It wasn't much of a gesture, but I'd take it.

The air felt less tense on the way home. "You want burgers or tacos tonight?" I asked. Friday nights we usually got take out.

"Either. I don't care." She was staring out the passenger window.

"Listen. I'm sorry about how I reacted earlier."

She turned to me but didn't say anything.

"I shouldn't have freaked out like that."

"It's okay. I know you're stressed about money."

"I don't want you to worry about it, okay? A kid shouldn't have to worry about money. That's for me to worry about."

"I'm not worried about money, dad. I'm worried about *you*."

"Me? I'm fine. Don't worry about me."

"Are you still not sleeping?" Ava asked. "You were up super late last night."

Granted, my money troubles were far worse now than they ever were when we were a dual income family. But the insomnia didn't originate with anxiety over money.

The week before Celeste died, I was supposed to take her car in to get the brakes fixed. It was long overdue. She set up the appointment, but she picked up an extra shift that day so I agreed to take it in. But that was the day I got a call to perform at Cactus Annie's because the duo they booked cancelled last minute. I had been working on a few new songs to work into my set list and time got away from me. So I missed the appointment completely and by the time I remembered, it was too late to bring it in and I had to reschedule for the following Saturday. But Celeste didn't make it to the following Saturday.

She was pissed that I'd forgotten, but halfway through my set that night, I looked up and there she was, still in scrubs from her shift that day. Ava stood beside her and waved to me. That was the last time either of them heard me sing.

"You don't need to worry about me," I said.

She held my gaze for a moment and then turned toward the window. "Dad?" she said, still looking out the window.

"Yeah?" I braced myself for a question I was afraid I wasn't prepared to answer.

"Never mind."

The fuel gauge lit up on my dashboard so we pulled into a gas station to fill up. After I replaced the gas nozzle, I ran inside to buy a scratch-off. Even though I knew the chances of winning were extremely slim, I'd found that when I was in possession of a brand new lottery ticket, my financial anxieties tended to dissipate. Sometimes I'd hang onto a ticket for more than a day or so without scratching it, just to prolong that sense of hope and possibility. I knew it was stupid.

I bought a Cherry Doubler scratch-off. I could win up to fifty-thousand dollars. Of course, I wouldn't. But the possibility now existed.

We pulled into the drive through and I ordered burgers, fries, and shakes—chocolate for her, vanilla for me. It was the same order every time.

At home, Ava tore into her burger like she hadn't eaten all day.

"Slow down," I said. "You're going to get heartburn."

She opened her mouth to reveal half-masticated cheeseburger. I did the same right back. She was laughing now—genuinely. I wanted that moment to freeze, just for a little while. In that moment, she was looking at me the way Celeste did that time I put pureed sweet potatoes on my nose to get baby Ava to eat. It didn't work, but she applauded my creativity nonetheless.

"Oh, dad."

"Yeah?"

"Do we have any plans for Thanksgiving?"

"No. I thought we could get one of those fully-cooked turkey dinners. Comes with everything."

"Oh," she said, deflated.

"Why do you ask?"

"Gammie texted me today. She said we could go to their house." Gammie is what she called her grandmother—Celeste's mother. I got along with her okay. It's my father-in-law who I couldn't stand, or rather, he couldn't stand me. He never liked me—almost didn't come to our wedding. Initially, he refused to give her away, but after Celeste pleaded with him and threatened to move far away, he gave in. He thought she could do a lot better and he was probably right. At the funeral, he wouldn't even make eye contact with me. I got the feeling he knew about the car situation and silently blamed me.

"Do you want to go?" I asked her.

She shrugged and slurped the last of her milkshake down.

"If you want to go, that's fine. I can drop you off. I'll probably just hang back here though." I took another sip of my shake.

"Why do you hate Pop Pop?" Pop Pop is what she called her grandfather. Even though he probably wished I was dead, he loved his granddaughter. I guess he was a decent grandpa.

"I don't. I don't hate him," I said. "It's complicated. You should see your grandparents. It's been a few months, hasn't it?"

"Fourth of July," she said.

"Well, see? I bet they miss you."

"So you're just going to sit around here?" Her lip curled with mild disgust.

"Yeah, I can just order a pizza. I'm just going to be watching the game anyway. Don't worry about me. Seriously, you should go."

"I want you to come, too."

I sighed heavily. "I think everyone will have a better time if I'm not there."

"I won't," she said meekly.

I scratched behind my ear. "I'll think about it. Okay?"

Ava nodded but remained crestfallen as if she knew I was only placating her. She gathered her grease-stained burger wrapper and napkins and shoved it into the paper bag. She sat there for a moment, like she was about to say something, but then got up and went to her room.

I grabbed a beer from the fridge and took a long drink. The

scratch-off ticket I bought was sitting there on the counter. Here's the dilemma. If I scratched it now and lost, I also lost the anticipation of winning. But if I won, I got to send Ava to New York and could turn this whole night around. As I stared at its glossy finish, that feeling of possibility returned.

Using a penny, I scratched off the first row: lemon, horseshoe, clover—nothing. That's fine. Three more rows to go. The second row revealed banana, horseshoe, diamond. The third row revealed heart, gold bar, rainbow. One row left. I took a deep breath before scratching. Banana, heart, *cherry*! The cherry meant double the prize amount. I scratched off the prize amount—one hundred dollars! That was two hundred dollars with the cherry!

I hollered and ran back to Ava's room. I flung the door open with the ticket in hand.

"What the fuck, Dad!"

"I won two hundred dollars!"

"Seriously!?"

"Look!" I held out the ticket for her to take.

"You never win these," she said, examining the ticket.

"I know, right? This can be like a deposit on the deposit."

She nodded with raised eyebrows—dubious and unconvinced. She handed the ticket back and I looked it over again before noticing a familiar smell—skunky, herbal. I don't see any smoke anywhere. She watched me as I scanned her room. I knew I should say something. It was my responsibility to say something.

"Do you smell something?"

She shook her head. "No."

I tried. If I accused her of smoking weed, I'd then have to prove it. I didn't have the energy to search her room right now. Technically, we hadn't even really talked about drugs so it's not like she was breaking any house rules. I didn't even know how I felt about it. I mean, I still smoked occasionally. I smoked a lot more before she was born, constantly when we were touring. I didn't want to be a hypocrite.

Was it even that big of a deal? It wasn't like her grades were suffering. She was the most responsible kid I'd ever known. She was a little young though. I smoked my first joint when I was thirteen. Maybe I'd just keep an eye on it. As long as she was doing well in school, maybe it wasn't worth getting all worked up about it. It wasn't a problem until it was a problem, right?

The truth is, if I was being totally honest, I didn't want to rock the boat. That was the honest to God truth. I'd already ruined the day with my outburst. No need to pile on.

"Okay, well . . . night."

"Night."

CHAPTER 9
ARTISTIC INTERPRETATION

THE NEXT THING I KNOW, I'm opening my eyes. I don't remember closing them, but when I open them again it's two minutes past eight. It doesn't feel like I've been asleep. I don't feel the least bit groggy. I lift my head. Rafael is already awake. He's drawing something on a piece of paper but I can't tell what it is. Theo and Geoff still have their heads on the table.

"Good morning!" Rafael says.

"Good morning," I say. "What happened?"

"We rebooted," he says without looking up from his paper.

"What does that mean exactly?"

"It's a natural mechanism for the brain to restore itself to full capacity."

"Why are they still rebooting?" I ask, gesturing toward the other two.

"We don't always reboot at the same speed. They'll be up soon. Look!" He holds up the piece of paper he's been drawing on. "It's us." He's drawn the five of us, including Piper, in pencil. It's not great.

"Oh," is all I say. I mean, it's really not great. We're all standing in a line facing forward the way a first grader might draw his family. I'm holding a misshapen four-string guitar. Geoff is comically tall compared to the rest of us. Piper is scowling. At least he got that right.

Geoff lifts his head.

"Hey, Geoff, look," Rafael says. "I drew us."

Geoff takes the picture in his big hands and studies it. "That's amazing," he says in a languid monotone. "Look at me. I'm so tall."

Rafael is nodding with the biggest grin I've ever seen. "Yes, you are."

"Would anyone like a coffee," Geoff asks, sliding the picture back toward Rafael.

"None for me, thanks," Rafael says.

"I'll have a coffee," I say. Although I don't feel tired or groggy, coffee does sound like a good way to start the day.

"Do you take cream or sugar?" Geoff asks.

"I'm not sure." I guess I've never actually had coffee before. "Surprise me."

"Okay," he says and walks into the kitchen.

Theo begins to stir. He sits up and adjusts his square framed glasses. "What's this?" Theo picks up Rafael's picture.

"It's us," Rafael says gleefully.

"Guitars have six strings," he says matter of factly. "Isn't that right, Hugo?"

"Well, yes," I say. I glance at Rafael who's taken back the picture and is studying his work with a furrowed brow. "But you have to allow for artistic interpretation."

"Yeah, Theo. This is my artistic interpretation," Rafael says, nodding at me.

"Oh, sure," Theo says. "Of course."

"That's why it's nice to have a creative in our midst. You scientists can be too literal sometimes."

Geoff returns to the room with two coffees and a bear claw. He hands me a coffee and gives Theo the bear claw.

"Thanks," I say and take a sip. "Mmm . . . that's good."

Geoff looks pleased he got it right. "Not too sweet?"

"No, it's perfect." I don't know what to compare it to, but it is good.

"Alright," Rafael says, placing his hands flat on the table. "Let's start rounds. Would you like to start us off, Geoff?"

"Sure. Today I'll continue to work on a new small core combustor design. It's the first axially-staged single sector combustor expected to reduce take-off emissions by more than eighty percent."

"Fascinating," Rafael says and turns to Theo. "Theo?"

Theo holds up a finger while he finishes chewing and swallowing the bear claw in his mouth. He licks his fingers and says, "I'm working on synthetic monoclonal antibodies to help prevent beta-amyloid proteins from forming plaques in the brain." He looks at me. "It's basically an immunity approach to Alzheimer's treatment."

"Wonderful stuff," Rafael says. "Hugo, I know it's only your second day but if you could just let us know what you plan on working on today."

"Oh, well, I hope I get a little further than I did yesterday. I'm not sure. Maybe I can put together a chord progression and work from that."

"That sounds amazing," Rafael says. "You have to start somewhere. Am I right?"

"I guess so."

"Okay. Well, fellas, let's get out there and change the world!" Rafael claps his hands and stands, but before he can fully rise, the front door opens and Piper walks in. She is escorted by two people in grey uniforms. One of them gives Rafael a thumbs up before shutting the door and leaving.

"Piper," Rafael says. "How do you feel?"

"Fine," she says. She's standing just inside the doorway with a glazed look in her eyes.

"Well, get in here," Rafael says and walks over to her. He puts an arm around her shoulder and guides her toward the group. "We're so happy you're back."

"Hey, Piper," Theo says and takes another bite of his bear claw.

Geoff waves.

She seems different—subdued, rather than defiant. She doesn't acknowledge me. Does she even remember me from yesterday?

"We were just doing rounds," Rafael says. "Would you like to report?"

Piper shakes her head slightly.

"That's okay. That's totally fine. We're just glad to have you back."

She smiles demurely.

"Raf said we could have a taco party," Theo announces.

"Yes, but not right now," Rafael says.

"No, not now. Later today though, right?"

"Fine. Let's all meet back here at 6:00 for Piper's taco party. Okay?"

Theo pumps his fist in victory. "Can we get the fresh jalapeños this time?"

"I like the pickled kind," Geoff says. "The fresh ones are too spicy."

"I'll make sure we have both," Rafael says, peeved.

Piper still hasn't even glanced at me. Something's not right with her.

"Alright, pod, we have important work to do today!" Rafael says. He turns to me and lowers his voice. "Hugo, would you mind escorting Piper to work? I'll meet you over there in a few minutes. I need to check in with restoration."

"I don't know where she works," I say.

"She knows where it is."

"Um, yeah okay."

She turns toward the door and Rafael leans in close to me. "I just don't want to leave her alone right now. Just keep an eye on her."

I nod and follow Piper outside.

"Do you feel okay?" I ask her as we walk toward the teleporter.

"Hugo, right?"

"Yeah. Do you remember me from yesterday?"

She looks at me for the first time today. "Yesterday was your birthday. You're a musician."

"Yeah. That's right. What happened to you?" I ask.

"I was in restoration."

"And before that?"

She stops walking and turns her head down to the left. "I can't remember. Was I at work?"

"I don't know." Rafael said they sometimes find her in strange places. What did he mean by that? Wherever they found her, she doesn't remember. Restoration had something to do with her not remembering.

When we reach the teleporter, Piper looks into the scanner, which greets her warmly. We get in and Piper tells the computer to go take us to "Central Systems."

When we arrive, the doors open to the interior of an immense office building. People in suits are buzzing around making clopping sounds with their shoes on the tile floor.

I follow Piper down a wide hallway with offices on each side. Piper walks a few feet ahead of me before realizing I'm behind her. Theo asked if she was raving about being held prisoner. I wonder if she still thinks that now. She stops and turns back to me. "What are you doing?"

"I have to ask you something."

"Okay."

I'm not sure how to bring this up. "Do you ever feel like you're a prisoner here?"

She laughs. When she stops, she laughs again. "That's so silly! Why? Is that what you think?"

"No. No, I'm just trying to figure all this out. Because I'm new. Are we really here to make the world a better place with our unique skills and talents or whatever?"

"Of course. Why else would we be here?" Her electric eyes penetrate me.

"I don't know." I really *don't* know. But I feel like there is something else. I thought she knew, but whatever happened in restoration seems to have erased it.

"Come on. I'm going to be late." We walk to the next intersection of halls and turn left. When we reach the first door, she stops. "This is me."

"Oh. Okay." I look back trying to remember the turns.

"Thanks for walking me," she says. "I'm not supposed to be alone after restoration."

"Of course."

She lingers for a moment. "So you're writing a song, right?"

"Well, I don't have anything written yet, but that's the plan."

Piper leans casually against the door frame. "What will you write about if you're only a day old?"

"Good question. I'm not sure."

"Well, I'm looking forward to hearing it."

"Me, too."

"Okay, well, I guess I'll see you at the taco party," she says rolling her eyes.

"I like tacos," I say. "I mean, I think I do."

"Everyone likes tacos," she says, leaning into the door as it opens into her office.

When the door closes, I'm standing alone in a nondescript corridor. Rafael said he'd meet me but I feel silly just standing here so I start walking back the way we came. When I turn right at the corner, I almost run into a guy in a gray uniform—the same uniform the people who brought Piper home this morning were wearing.

"What are you doing out here?" he asks authoritatively.

"I was walking someone to her office. She was just in restoration."

"I.D.?"

I.D.? I check my pockets, first my jacket, then my jeans. I don't have any I.D.

Rafael is trotting down the corridor. "He's with me, sir!"

"Oh, hey Raf. How's it going down there in fifty-four?"

"Great!" Rafael is still catching his breath. "I see you've met our newest talent. This is Hugo."

"He doesn't have any I.D."

"I have it right here. The printers must have been delayed. Sorry." Rafael produces a laminated I.D. badge.

The officer removes a handheld device from his utility belt and scans the card. His expression softens and he hands me the badge.

"Nice to meet you, Hugo. Well, you two have a nice day."

"You, too," Rafael says. "Thank you."

The man turns down the hall and Rafael and I walk back the way he came.

"Was that a . . . what do you call them?"

"Sentinels. They're here to keep us safe."

We turn down another hallway.

"Piper seems different today," I say.

"What do you mean?"

"Well, yesterday she seemed to have more of an attitude, like she had a chip on her shoulder."

"Yeah, that's our Piper," he says with a chuckle.

"But today, she seemed . . . I don't know, less prickly."

"It's just temporary. Restoration has a lingering effect. She'll even out here soon enough."

"She didn't remember anything that happened to her or saying anything about being a prisoner."

"Yeah, she won't remember any of that. Restoration scrubs those memories so they don't interfere with her important work here."

"Isn't that, I don't know, wrong?"

Rafael stops in front of the teleporter. "Hugo, we are here to exercise our one true gift. Anything in the service of optimizing our productivity or improving the quality of our work can only be a *good* thing."

"Right."

"It's my job to make sure you and the rest of our little pod are happy and have everything you need to be productive and fulfilled. Piper is very important to me and to Slumbervale. I would never let anything get in the way of her advancement. Same goes for you. You got that?"

I nod.

"Good. Now let's get out there and make a difference in the world! What do you say?"

"Yeah, okay." I can tell Rafael really believes this stuff. I can't say I'm completely sold. And although Piper is buying into it at the moment, will she think any differently when the effects of her restoration wear off? Nobody else seems to have any doubts. Maybe it would be easier if I could just get on board.

CHAPTER 10
FULL HOUSE

THE NEXT MORNING, I woke up on the couch and sat up like a fallen tree in reverse. It was after 10:00 and the sun was forcing my eyelids into slits. The Lunatech brochure that Darcy left behind was laying on the floor next to two empty beer cans. I read it through once again front to back. I reached for my phone, knocking another beer can off the coffee table, and dialed the number.

After navigating a typical automated phone tree, I was forwarded to a live scheduler.

"Hello, this is Andrea at Lunatech. Are you calling to attend one of our informational seminars?"

"I think so. I just have some questions."

"Of course. Our consultants will go over everything and answer any questions you may have about our program. We have an opening tomorrow morning at eleven o'clock if you're available."

I gave her my first and last name, email and phone number, and she gave me the address. She said it's in Suite 204 on the second floor of a red brick office complex, across the street from a mattress store and a Chuck-E-Cheese. I copied down the information on the back of the brochure.

I traipsed back to Ava's room and peeked in. Still asleep. I still needed to go grocery shopping for the week so I pulled on some jeans and a t-shirt and headed out. I grabbed the usual frozen dinners, eggs, milk, bread. I did spring for the good ice cream and a big bag of those super spicy chips Ava likes. I got two cases of beer to bring to the poker game tonight.

As soon as I walked back into the house I could smell the coconut and vanilla of Ava's shampoo. She must have just gotten out of the shower. I walked back to her room where she was packing a bag for her sleepover.

"Don't forget your toothbrush," I reminded her.

She rolled her eyes—hard. Didn't justify my instruction with a verbal response. I guess I deserved that. She's not five.

"Sydney and Dani are already there," she said.

"Danny?"

"Dani's a girl, dad. Chill."

"I'm chill."

"Whatever."

"I just need to put away these groceries and then we can go."

I wondered if she knew that I knew. She was definitely not acting guilty. Maybe it really was nothing. I only thought I smelled something.

We pulled up to the valet in front of La Paloma. This place was nice. I took Celeste here for an anniversary one year. The valet opened Ava's door.

"Text me if you need anything," I said.

"Okay."

"You got the gift?"

"Yep."

"I'll be here tomorrow at 10 to pick you up."

"Okay."

"Have fun!" I said as she got out. The valet closed her door and she walked toward the front steps. She turned around again to give me a hard look, as if to say *go already!* I pulled away slowly and watched as she ascended the front steps. A bellboy opened the front door and she walked on in without looking back. It reminded me of her first day of kindergarten, her giant backpack bobbing up and down with each step. She didn't look back then either. She has always been so independent. I felt proud. But also sad for some reason.

On my way over to Ernie's house, I got a text from Lenny:

> Just a heads up. Seth Fucker is going to be there.

He means Seth Tucker. Lenny accused Seth of stealing away some girl he was dating a while back, but he's had beef with him since before that. They went to high school together. Now he's a local news reporter for channel 4.

> Who invited him?

> Probably invited himself. Entitled prick.

I guess he was kind of a douchebag. He's never done anything to me though. I just texted back a laughing emoji.

When I pulled up to Ernie's house, Seth's Cybertruck, with a license plate that read: NUZMAN, was taking up the whole driveway so I had to park in the street two houses down. I rung the doorbell and heard someone yell for me to come on in. Ernie's house looked like his grandmother decorated it—doilies everywhere. He even had a china hutch, with china in it. They called out my name in unison when I entered the kitchen area. Ernie, Lenny, Raj, and Seth were there.

"Hey, Hugo," Ernie said as I transferred the beers into the refrigerator, "Congratulations on that winning lottery ticket!" Ernie was a heavyset Chicagoan. He was married, but I'd never met his wife. "Let's see it!"

I took the folded ticket out of my wallet and handed it to Ernie who passed it Raj.

"What are you going to do with it?" Raj asked and then handed it back to me.

"He's going to blow it all here tonight," Ernie said, laughing.

"Nah, my daughter has this school trip to New York this Spring. I'm trying to save up for that."

"You're a good father," Ernie says.

It's nice to hear that even though I don't believe it's true. I nod my thanks.

"I heard about your cougar," Raj says making claws with his hands. "Did she leave any scratch marks?" He was nudging Ernie with his elbow. Raj is the youngest of the group and the least experienced with women. He moved here from India to get his engineering degree from the U of A and hadn't been on an official date until his last year of grad school. It was just the one date—he never got a second. Raj got positively giddy when the subject of women came up.

I glanced at Lenny, who shrugged with a guilty grin while

shuffling a deck of cards. I'm sure that's the first thing he told everyone.

"Hugo here was a perfect gentleman," Lenny said in my defense, but then raised his hands the way I did when Darcy assaulted me, and everyone laughed.

"That's so wild, man!" Raj said, boyish excitement bursting forth. "Was she hot? What did she look like?"

"Like a Real Housewife," Lenny said.

"No way!" Raj said. "I would have let her teach me a thing or two."

"I'm surprised you didn't show them the footage," I said to Lenny.

"You have footage?" Raj asked enthusiastically.

"That's just great," I said out loud to myself.

"Only with your blessing, good sir," Lenny said in a terrible British accent.

"Fine, but I'm not watching."

Everyone gathered around Lenny's phone while I went to the kitchen to grab a slice of pizza. Somehow I'd become both the hero and the butt of their jokes all at the same time.

"Are we going to play cards or what?" I asked finally, hoping to change the subject.

"Yeah, yeah," Ernie said in his midwestern accent. "Why don't you call the game, since it's your first time? What do you want to play?"

I shrugged. "I don't know. What do you normally play?"

"We switch it up. Five Card Draw, Seven Card Stud, Texas Hold 'Em, Omaha—"

"Texas Hold 'Em," I said. I thought I remembered how to play that one.

"Okay, boys. It's a twenty dollar buy in," Ernie said passing around a pewter Chicago Bears beer stein. He started counting out and distributing poker chips.

"Can we do a practice round?" Seth asked. He hadn't said much this whole time. "It's been a while since I played this game." I'm glad he said it and not me.

"Sure," Lenny said mockingly. "Can I get you a sippy cup for your beer?" Everyone laughed except Seth, who shook his head dismissively. I could tell Lenny had already put back a couple. His humor got increasingly biting the more he drank.

After a practice round, the game began. I was sitting to the left of Lenny. Then it was Raj to my left, then Ernie, and then Seth. The first few rounds were fairly low stakes and I folded on a couple, but I ended up winning one hand with a flush, which boosted my confidence enough to raise on the flop in the next round. I won the next two hands with two pair and a straight, respectively. An hour in and I was already up sixty bucks. Ernie and Lenny already had to buy more chips.

"I've got an idea," Seth said. "Why don't we play tournament rules where we increase the blinds at regular intervals." The amount of the blinds determine the minimum raise on each round of betting. We started with a two dollar blind. "What do you say we double the blinds every hour to keep the game interesting?"

Lenny rubbed his forehead, but didn't say anything. Nobody opposed the idea, or at least nobody was willing to go soft. Seth acted like he didn't know how to play this game in the beginning, but he'd acquired a nice little pile of chips there. When Lenny commented on it, Seth shrugged and said, "Beginner's luck."

"My ass," Lenny said, cracking open another beer. I could tell he was getting pissed, and probably a little drunk. He really hated this guy and wasn't even trying to hide it.

Another two hours passed and the blind was up to sixteen bucks. I lost a couple of big hands and ended up buying another thirty dollars in chips, but had at least two hundred dollars in chips stacked in front of me now. Seth had about the same, maybe more. Lenny was sweating bullets and bought another forty dollars in chips. I opened another beer.

On the next hand, I got two jacks on the hole and I was under the gun, so I raised twenty bucks right out of the gates. Raj folded. Ernie called. Seth called. Lenny folded. Seth dealt the flop—ten of hearts, two of spades, jack of spades. I had three of a kind. I raised another twenty. Ernie folded. Seth sat back and lifted the corner of his hole cards. He shook his head. I didn't know what that meant.

"Come on," Lenny said. "What are you gonna do?"

"Call," Seth said and slid a twenty dollar chip into the pot with an index finger. Then he dealt the turn—a two of diamonds. I had a full house—jacks and twos. The action was to me now. Something told me to check. If he checked, he didn't have anything and I could raise on the river.

"Check," I said.

"Check," Seth said and dealt the river—ten of clubs. Now I had a full house with jacks and tens.

I threw out two twenty dollar chips and a ten.

"I raise you fifty," I said.

"Now this is a game," Ernie said.

"I can't watch this," Raj said and stood up, but then sat back down again. He had been betting pretty conservatively all night.

Seth was drumming his fingers on the table and sucking his tooth.

"Come on, you don't have anything," Lenny says. "Just fold—like I did your mother last night."

The insult didn't phase him. Seth put in fifty in chips. "I'll see your fifty and raise you . . ." Seth started counting up his remaining chips. "Fuck it. I'm all in." He pushed the rest of his stack into the pot.

At first, everyone froze. Ernie added up the chips he'd just put in. "That's one-sixty," Ernie said and turned to me. "Do you need more chips, Hugo?"

If I couldn't match his bet, I'd be forced to fold. "I'm out of cash," I said.

"What about that lottery ticket?" Seth asked with a hungry gaze. "I'll put in another forty to make it an even two hundred." He opened his wallet and threw two twenties on the table.

"Don't be a dick," Lenny said. "He's not betting that."

"You can't change the rules in the middle of a hand," Ernie declared. "And it's not your turn."

"Shut up, Ernie. This is between me and Hugo here. If he says no, I win this hand. I'm just giving him an opportunity to stay in the game."

"Fuck you, Seth. This isn't how we play," Lenny said.

"I guess you fold," Seth said and reached for the pot.

"Wait," I said. I couldn't believe I was doing this.

"Don't do it, man," Lenny said to me. "He won't miss that money. You will."

"Are you his mother?" Seth asked Lenny. "I think he can make up his own mind."

"Dick!" Lenny shouted.

"What's it going to be, Hugo?" Seth asked.

I tried to ignore everyone's eyes on me. I could see Lenny's head shaking from side to side out of the corner of my eye. I pulled the scratch off from my wallet. Looked it over one last time, burning its image in my mind. Then dropped the winning lottery ticket into the pot. "Call."

Raj, Ernie, and Lenny's eyes bulged. Mouths dropped.

"You first," Seth said.

I turned over my two Jacks and sat back.

"Full House, motherfucker!" Lenny yelled. He patted me on the back and gave Raj a high five.

Seth raised his eyebrows and nodded.

"Show," I said, cool as a goddamned cucumber.

The room got quiet—the only sound came from Raj swallowing. Seth turned one card and then the other—two tens. He had a four of a kind.

He won.

I lost.

CHAPTER 11
COSMIC PANCAKES

WHEN THE TELEPORTER DOORS OPEN, we step out into the downtown courtyard. Rafael's been going over a list of items to pick up for tonight's taco party—out loud. "Oh, here," he says and hands me a little red paperback.

"The Book of Illumination," I read aloud. "A Handbook for the Sixth Level of Spiritual Evolution."

"It's not required reading, but if you're ever in need of a little inspiration or guidance, it can be helpful."

Alone in the studio, I flip through the sacred text. Steve Gower is the sole author. The chapters are organized by topics like "How to Stay Motivated," "Making the Most of Your Life," and "Your Pod Is Your Family." There's nothing about God or an Afterlife, or anything you'd expect to find in a religious text. The first chapter is titled "How It All Started."

In the beginning, there was a growing sense of despondency among all of humanity. How humans got here in the first place is still up for debate. Who cares? What matters is that humans, the vast majority of them anyway, had not been able to fulfill their spiritual potential.

A few did—Mahatma Gandhi, Siddhartha Gautama, Jesus of Nazareth, Galileo Galilei, Ruth Bader Ginsberg, and the guy who invented zip lock technology—not that his invention had anything to do with his spiritual advancement. Most everyone else died short of realizing their true potential. What a waste!

This growing sense of despondency expanded to such an unbearable degree that the universe was unable to contain it. Thus, the seven levels of spiritual evolution sprung into being—just like that! The universe divided and rearranged itself into seven planes of existence, much like a stack of cosmic pancakes.

Here is a drawing of a stack of pancakes surrounded by stars. Why would there be stars outside of the universe? Maybe I'm overthinking it.

If you're reading this, you've undoubtedly reached the sixth level. Way to go! This is the second best level. Once you reach the seventh level, you won't need this guide. In fact, you may even get to write some of it. Super!

Cosmic pancakes? Is this for real? The next chapter breaks down the seven levels. I skim this since Theo already explained it to me. Nothing about babies. I know babies are a thing, but so far there is no mention of them. I still can't picture what one even looks like. I flip through the book and a chapter titled "What Happens When You Die" catches my eye.

Someday you will die. This is nothing to be afraid of. It usually occurs during a reboot, but sometimes it can happen in the middle of the day. If you see someone fall down in the middle of the day and they don't get up, they probably died. Don't worry. They're not hurt. They died before they hit the ground.

Death in one life means birth in another. So once you die in Level Six, you are instantaneously born into Level Seven. Your pod will celebrate your passing with a traditional pancake breakfast. Your pod facilitator will create a three-minute slideshow presentation from key moments in your life here in Level Six. There is no crying during a celebratory pancake breakfast.

I'm guessing the pancakes are some kind of symbol representing the seven spiritual levels—weird. I continue to skim the rest of the chapter, but there doesn't seem to be any religious messaging or supernatural claims about Level Seven. The only thing it says about the seventh level is:

When you are born in Level Seven, you will understand everything. Everything will make perfect sense.

None of this has been of much help in figuring out why I still feel like there are important details about my life that are being kept from me. I wish I could have had a chance to talk to Piper more before she went into restoration. She may have been having a mental breakdown, but somehow her skepticism resonated.

I was looking for an alternative explanation that didn't have to do with me being born as a grown man on a couch. I haven't thought about it since, but who was that woman in the picture? Could it have been someone from a previous life? Is that why he was testing me—to see if I remembered her?

I look up *restoration* in the index. Two pages are listed: 167, 224. I turn to page 167, which is in a chapter titled "You and Your Body." Under the subheading *Stress*, it says:

Your body has few needs in Level Six, but the mind requires proper care. Due to the extremely fulfilling nature of your meaningful work, it can be tempting to work through scheduled recovery periods or work at an unsustainable pace. If this goes on too long, stress can have debilitating effects on the mind. Symptoms of high levels of stress include, mental fatigue, irritability, decreased ability to focus, paranoia and hallucinations. Restoration Spas are available to anyone who has overextended themselves in the spirit of meaningful work. Our restoration technicians are skilled in reversing the effects of stress and bringing you back to a relaxed state of mind.

That's all it says about it. I turn to page 224, which is in a chapter titled "Safety and Security." It says:

Sentinels are here to keep you safe. In some cases where high levels of stress may be contributing to unsafe behavior, sentinels may escort you to the Restoration Spa to alleviate any toxic levels of stress that may be present. If you ever find yourself in the custody of a sentinel, you are in good hands.

This doesn't say anything about what happens in there. It doesn't say anything about deleting memories. Rafael said they scrub memories that interfere with our life's purpose. How does he know that? Who was that woman in the picture?

Someone is knocking.

"Come in," I say.

It's Vincent. "What's up, Hugo? How's your second day going?"

"Fine." I close the book and set it aside. "I haven't written anything yet."

"That's okay, man. There's no rush. I see you're reading the Book."

"Yeah. I was trying to find something about how the restoration process works, but there aren't many details."

"Well, of course not. There aren't any details about songwriting either." He chuckles.

"I guess you got me there."

"What made you think about that?" Vincent asks.

"Piper. She's this woman in my pod."

"Oh, I know." He smiles. "She's a looker."

"Yeah, I guess she is. Well, she got taken to restoration yesterday and today she's a totally different person. I was just curious about what goes on in there. Rafael said something about erasing memories."

"Just the ones that interfere."

"Right. That's what he said, but how? How do they do that?"

"You got me. I'm a sound engineer, not a neurologist."

And then it hits me. "You said something about collaborating with others."

"Yeah, man. Sometimes you need to play off other musicians to discover new sounds."

"Right. But I'm not *just* a musician. I'm a songwriter."

"Go on."

"A songwriter needs to interact with other people, not just other musicians, to understand what their lives are like, to hear different perspectives on life and the world we live in. Songwriting is about telling stories and I don't have any of my own yet. I think it could be helpful to talk to other people outside our department."

"Like who?"

"Well, I've been thinking a lot about the mind. I read about the effects of stress on the mind and I got really curious about that. I think I should follow that instinct. Maybe there's a song in there. Would it be possible to talk to one of these restoration technicians?"

"Like an informational interview?" Vincent nods and strokes his patchy beard. "That's not a bad idea."

"Really?"

"Hold on. Let me make a phone call." Vincent goes back into the recording booth to place a call that I can't hear.

I take a banjo hanging on the wall and start picking a random melody until he returns from the booth.

"Good news! They don't have anyone scheduled today and said to come on by. I can walk you over there."

I grab a notebook from the coffee table and a pen. "In case I need to take notes."

"Perfect. Let's go."

When we arrive, I follow Vincent into a warmly lit office. Soft ambient music wafts through the serene space. It smells of lavender in here. There's a woman in a white coat sitting behind a reception desk.

"I think I talked to you on the phone just now," Vincent says. "I have Hugo here."

She nods politely. "Take a seat and the doctor will be here momentarily." She picks up a phone and lets whoever is on the other line know I'm here.

A minute later, another woman appears in the doorway. Her brown hair is pulled back into a tight bun. "Hugo?"

"That's me."

"I'm Dr. Blaine. Come on back."

"I'll be back at the studio when you're all done here," Vincent says and leaves. It occurs to me that I've never operated the teleporter by myself before, but he's gone and the doctor is waiting.

I follow Dr. Blaine to a spacious office. There are floor to ceiling screens on two walls with a view of a continuous forest that spans across the panels. Slowly, the view fades and is replaced with drone footage of a rocky shore.

"Have a seat," she says, as she sits behind a clean, well-organized acrylic desk.

I sit in one of the two armchairs facing her desk.

"Thank you for seeing me," I say.

"Of course. What can I help you with today?"

"Well, it's my second day here, in Slumbervale, and I have some questions."

"Go on."

I'm not exactly sure where to start. "I'm curious about what happens in restoration. Specifically, what happens to certain memories. The ones that interfere with someone's life purpose."

"It's highly technical. We use a system called NICE (Neural-Interfacing Cognitive Elimination), developed right here by one of our very own Slumbervale neurologists. It's a highly sophisticated neural imaging computer that tracks cognitive aberrations in real time. Aberrations are highlighted in red. We select the area, hit delete and poof—it's gone!"

"Does everyone know about this? I mean, deleting people's thoughts and memories just seems . . . unethical."

"How do you mean?" Curiosity twists in her face. How does she not see it?

"It's just . . . people have the right to their own thoughts, don't they?"

"Let me see if I can put this into perspective for you. Level Six is the only spiritual level where every single individual is able to apply their unique gifts and talents to making the world a better place, not just for those in our own plane of existence, but for those at lower levels, too."

"What do you mean?"

"It's all in the Book of Illumination. The discoveries that are made here are shared at every level of spiritual evolution. Humans at lower levels are unable to create or produce anything of any real value because they don't have the ability to focus on what really matters. They're too distracted. Some of them are quite talented, but simply cannot devote enough of their mental capacity to producing anything of much value. When we make discoveries here, those discoveries are shared with these individuals who undoubtedly presume they came up with it all on their own."

"How does that happen?"

"Our worlds are separate, but they're also connected. Ideas are delivered on a synaptic level, often while the person in Level Five dreams, or when they're in the shower, or on a walk in nature. Those are our ideas but they occur to humans in Level Five as if they were their own. We could not come up with these ideas and discoveries if we were distracted or stressed. Restoration makes it possible for us to focus on what truly matters. In lower levels, people have to deal with problematic illnesses, like viruses and cancers. We do the same things doctors do to eliminate illnesses at lower levels. But our illness isn't physical, it's cognitive."

"I think I understand," I say. I can see how this makes logical sense if you buy into this seven levels stuff. So far it's the only narrative I've been told. I don't have anything else to compare it to but I can't help but think there must be an alternative theory.

"Good. Is there anything else I can help you with? Would you like a demonstration?"

"No!" I blurt a little too forcefully. "I mean, no thank you. I'm not stressed. I haven't done enough work to be stressed."

"You don't have to be stressed to benefit from the relaxing effects of restoration. The system infuses a blend of serotonin and oxytocin into your nervous system, even if it doesn't find aberrations to eliminate. It's sublime."

"Thank you, but I'll pass. Maybe next time."

"Of course." She stands and glides across the office. "Have a productive day, Hugo," she says opening the door.

"I'll try," I say with a weak smile. Although she explained it as well as I might have expected, I still feel unsettled.

The teleporter isn't far from the Restoration Spa. I lean toward the retina scanner on the teleporter's panel.

"Hello Hugo," the computer says and the door opens.

I step inside.

"Where would you like to go?"

I forget the name of the music studio. Instead, I say, "Downtown."

"There are a number of stations downtown. Please be more specific."

"The music studio."

"Gower Productions. Is that right?"

"Yes."

"Right away."

And in an instant, I'm there.

CHAPTER 12
NEUROHYBRID
SYNAPTIC INTERFACE

ON SUNDAY, I arrived at La Paloma a few minutes before 10:00 and texted Ava that I was there. I had a terrible hangover. I couldn't tell her that I'd lost that lottery ticket playing poker. I felt like such an idiot.

A few minutes later, Ava and one of her friends raced down the front steps of the hotel. They were laughing and jostling with each other, drawing the attention of the valet. When they got to my truck the other girl playfully bumped Ava out of the way and knocked on the passenger window so I leaned over to roll it down.

"Hi Mr. Castillo!" She said it in this flirty sing song voice. "Ava wants to know if she can come over. My mom says it's okay."

"Can I, dad?"

I didn't even know this kid's name. Ava seemed to be having fun and I rarely saw her this happy. Plus, if I was being honest, I felt pretty guilty about losing that money and if it came up, I didn't know what I'd say to her.

"I didn't catch your name," I said to the girl, but Ava answered.

"Dad! You know Sydney. You met her at that orientation thingy."

I met a lot of people that day. "Oh, sorry. Hi, Sydney. Can I get your mom's number?"

"Mr. Castillo!" Sydney said, feigning offense by placing one hand on her hip and the other on her chest. You could tell she must have been a theater kid. "She's a married woman!"

"Eww," Ava said, swatting Sydney on the arm.

"Give me your hand," bubblegum mouthed Sydney said to me, so I extended it like a handshake. She took a gel pen from her bag, turned my hand palm side up, and scribbled a number in purple ink. She added a heart.

Ava shook her head and gave me an apologetic look.

"When should I pick you up?" I asked.

"I'll text you."

"Alright."

"Bye, Mr. Castillo!" Sydney said in that silly way. As they bounced away, I heard her say to Ava, "Your dad's kind of hot."

"Gross!" Ava said, shoving her.

I was going to tell her all about the Lunatech seminar, but I guess that could wait until I found out more information. I typed the address I copied onto the brochure into my phone and started the navigation.

When I arrived, the parking lot was sparsely populated. There was a dentist office at one end and a personal injury lawyer's office at the other. Some of the larger offices seemed closed or out of business. The faded imprint from the removed signage of an emergency veterinary clinic still clung to the building's surface like a ghost from a more prosperous past.

An arched hallway in the center of the building invited me to a brick courtyard centered by an empty fountain in disrepair. A curved stairwell hugged the rounded courtyard and lead to a second floor with smaller offices, one of which was a nail salon, another a cell phone repair shop. A letter-sized paper sign with an arrow and the word Lunatech was taped to the railing of the stairwell.

Another sign was posted on a glass directory. When I arrived at Suite 204, I took another look left, then right, down the hall before opening the door. One of the consultants spotted me and waved me in.

"Come on in!" He reached his hand to me and I shook it. "I'm Carl and this is Linda." Carl has a Boy Scout haircut and a royal blue Lunatech polo tucked into camel-colored chinos.

"Hi," Linda says with a smile so big it looks like it hurts. "Who do we have here?"

"Hugo."

"Welcome, Hugo! Make yourself comfortable." Linda was also wearing a Lunatech shirt, but with white jeans, tapered to her ankles, and orthopedic sneakers. "We'll get started here in just a few minutes."

A folding table stood to the right of the entrance with two plastic containers of store-bought cookies and mini bottles of water. Orientation manuals and Lunatech-labeled retractable pens were laid out on one end. Six or seven others were seated among three rows of padded folding chairs. I grabbed a manual and a pen and took my seat in the back row.

This reminded me of a multi-marketing seminar I attended ten years ago when Celeste and I were planning a family vacation to Disneyland. I lost money on that and still had a box of all natural men's skin care products I never sold.

It was a diverse-looking group. There was a black guy, mid-thirties, in a crisp white button up and slacks with a gold watch, a white muscular broseph in a tank top and joggers, an elderly woman with a severe neck hump, a young Asian woman in leggings and a University of Arizona sweatshirt, a couple who look like they could be brother and sister except they couldn't keep their hands off each other.

Carl adjusted the projector on the front row to fit the image onto a portable screen at the front of the room. He had to use a stack of orientation manuals to lift the front end of the projector. Linda was chatting with the cutesy couple who had apparently just gotten married in Tulum. Some of the others were eavesdropping on their conversation. I guess I was, too. I opened my manual and read through the introduction.

"We're just waiting on one more and then we'll get started," Linda said.

Less than a minute later, the last of the participants walked in. It was Darcy. I hadn't even considered she might be here today. I should have since it was her brochure I still had in my back pocket.

"You must be Darcy," Linda said. "Go ahead and grab a packet and a water if you like, and take a seat anywhere."

I attempted to hide behind my packet, but it wasn't a very big room so she spotted me immediately. She lifted her chin and retreated to the other side of the room to take her seat.

"Okay. Let's get started, shall we?" Linda announced like a caffeinated cheerleader. "I'm so excited to share about this amazing opportunity. Both Carl and I are also in the sleeper program."

Carl nodded from his seat at the front of the room. He was operating the slide presentation from a laptop.

"We actually met in one of these orientation seminars about six months ago," Linda continued, "and we've been a part of the Lunatech family ever since. The sleeper program has been in operation for a little over a year, but Lunatech has been developing this technology for over two decades. I'd like to start by telling you a little about the technology and then we'll get into more specifics about our business model."

How much does it pay? That's the only thing I wanted to know. I looked around and everyone seemed rapt with her introduction so far. I needed to be patient. She would get there eventually.

"Our scientists have developed what's called a *neurohybrid synaptic interface.*" She says this slowly. "An electrode cap, shown here . . ." On the screen, a photo of a woman, eyes closed with a serene expression, was wearing the device. " . . . is worn during the night, which regulates brain waves during an eight-hour shift, allowing participants to benefit from the restorative qualities of deep, uninterrupted sleep. Our participants report having the best sleep of their lives after starting the program."

Now that was something I could get behind. I hadn't slept through the night in two years.

"The electrode cap connects to a console, which is connected via ethernet to your internet router." The slide displayed a graphic of how each component was connected to the another like you might see in an owner's manual for a piece of audio equipment. "This allows us to monitor brain activity remotely to ensure safety and effectiveness. You'll be trained on how to use the console before your preliminary sleep study. Now, you may be wondering, *what am I getting paid for?*"

I straightened up in my chair.

"Lunatech contracts with a growing number of businesses whose advertising dollars are being spent almost exclusively on targeted ad campaigns, usually through social media and other websites. But those require smartphones and computers to monitor your activities. The sleeper program gives these advertisers direct access to their consumers for uninterrupted periods of time. Now the big question on your minds right now is privacy, right? The truth is, we've already given up most of our privacy already. If you're online or use social media, those companies already have a ton of information about you. They know your buying habits, where you go, and how you vote. This is no different. It's just that you don't have to be online to provide that information."

I didn't like the idea of giving up my privacy, but if I could get eight hours of uninterrupted sleep every night, I supposed it would be worth it.

The executive gentleman raised his hand and when Linda pointed to him, he asked, "How much does it pay?"

I concurred with a strong nod.

"Currently, the rate is twenty-two hundred per month. Lucky for you, we just had a rate increase at the first of this month. As more companies join that rate increases with each yearly contract renewal. So far, everyone in the program has renewed. Now the contract stipulates a minimum of one year in the program and there are penalties for dropping out early. Our contractors pay up front so you could be sued for the remainder of your contract if you bail."

The newlywed husband blurted out, "Where do we sign up?"

Linda laughed. "So first we have to get you scheduled for testing. You'll need to block out a full day for that. It is fairly rigorous. It will take two to three days to get the results and if you qualify, then we can schedule your initial sleep study. You'll be trained on how to use the equipment. It's not any harder than setting your alarm clock. You'll spend your first night at our facilities as a preliminary test run, just to calibrate the hardware and make sure everything is working correctly."

She paused, scanning the room. "So, if there are no more questions, Carl has the testing schedule pulled up if anyone would like to get that set up."

A line formed in front of Carl. Darcy was one of the first in line so I waited until a few others filed in before I took my place. When it was my turn, Carl turned the laptop around to show me a calendar. The next available testing day was Tuesday. I'd have to get Lenny to cover my shift, but that shouldn't be a problem. I selected the time slot.

"Great!" Carl said. "You're good to go. Here's the address." He handed me a card and wrote the date of the appointment and 8:00 AM on the back. "You'll also get this in an email. Make sure to get a good night's sleep and eat a good breakfast. Lunch will be provided."

As I walked to my truck, I got a text from Ava:

I'm ready.

She shared the address and I let her know I was on my way.

Sydney lived in the historic Sam Hughes neighborhood. It wasn't a huge house—Mediterranean style with Spanish-tiled turrets, a welcoming courtyard, and lush desert landscaping. I parked my piece-of-shit Toyota on the brick-paved circle drive and walked through the courtyard to an arch-topped wooden front door. I used the door knocker—because they had one. A woman answered. She looked to be around my age, but with skin and hair that reflected significant financial investment.

"Hi, you must be Ava's dad," she said with an easy smile.

"Hugo."

"I'm Bev. Come on in!" Barefoot, hair pulled up, and wearing an oversized button up shirt with rolled up sleeves, she showed me her paint-covered fingers. "Sorry, I was in the middle of a project. The kids are in the den. Come on back."

I followed her through their immaculate, yet lived in home. It was a mix of modern and historical with upgraded appliances and fixtures, terra cotta tile floors, and wood-beamed ceilings. A golden lab ambled toward me, tail swishing from side to side. I let him smell the back of my hand and scratched him behind his ears. He had friendly eyes.

"That's Shamus. He's an old-timer," she said, picking up items of clothing off the floor and transferring them to the kitchen island. "Girls!" Bev called as I followed her toward a back room.

The girls were playing a video game on an oversized leather couch. A pizza box, bowl of chips, and cans of soda littered the coffee table.

"Ava, your dad's here, honey," Bev cooed sweetly.

"Just a second," Ava replied without taking her eyes of the 80-inch flat screen on the wall. She was fighting a tentacled monster with a broad sword as big as her avatar.

"I tried to get them to go outside," Bev said to me shaking her head.

"I take it they had a nice time at the party?"

"They did! The girls are so excited about New York. They're already coordinating their outfits."

"Oh, that's nice," I said, attempting to mask my unease. I still wasn't sure how I was going to pay for this in case Lunatech didn't work out.

The tentacled monster dealt a final blow to Ava's avatar who died a gory death. "Ah! I almost had him that time!" Ava said. She arched her head backwards over the couch to view me upside down. "Hey, dad."

"You ready, kiddo?"

"I guess."

"Ava's such a sweet girl," Bev said. "She's welcome here anytime."

Ava hugged her friend goodbye. I picked up her overnight bag and tossed it into the bed of my truck. Bev and Sydney waved as we pulled away and Ava waved back.

"So, how was the party?" I asked her.

"Good." She was already looking at her phone.

"Did the birthday girl like your present?"

"Yeah." We were back to one-word answers again.

"Well, what happened? Tell me everything."

She huffed but acquiesced and put her phone down. "We got facials and pedicures. See?" She slipped off her sandals and propped both feet up on the dashboard, wiggling her sea foam green painted toe nails. "Do you like the color?"

"Yes, I do."

"Then we went to this super fancy restaurant for dinner. They reserved a whole room just for us."

"Oh yeah? What did you order?"

"Cheeseburger."

"You should have gotten steak or lobster," I said, but she ignored this.

"Then we hung out by the pool and had virgin daiquiris. We didn't swim though because it was too cold. Then we just hung out in our rooms and watched this stupid dating show, the one where they're on an island. A couple of the girls are really into it and they know all the guys' names and backstories. Super dumb."

"Well, I'm glad you had a good time," I said.

"What did you do?" Ava asked reflexively.

My heart caught in my throat. "Oh. Nothing much. I hung out with a couple of the guys from work."

"Where at?"

"This guy Ernie's house. He's one of Lenny's friends."

"What were you doing?"

My heart was pounding in my ears as heat radiated up from my neck. "Oh, we just played some cards. No big deal."

"You didn't gamble away your lottery ticket, did you?" She laughed. She laughed because that would be ridiculous. I forced myself to laugh along with her.

"Wouldn't that be a hoot?" I said.

"No, that would be terrible," she said, still laughing.

"Yeah." I felt sick.

CHAPTER 13
TACO PARTY

I MANAGED to put together a couple of chord progressions. One is in Bb Major and has kind of a country swing to it. The other, in D Minor, is more rock-based. I've been working on the melody for that one most of the afternoon. I'm not ready to share it with Vincent just yet. I want to see if I can flesh out a couple different parts first. As far as lyrics go, I'm at a complete standstill. I want it to come from personal experience, which is the one thing I am desperately lacking.

I've been thinking about Piper. I wish I knew what she meant about this place being some kind of prison, but she doesn't remember. The restoration took care of that. But what could she have meant? They're making it sound like it was some kind of stress-induced hysteria—some kind of break with reality. But what if she was onto something and they saw her as some kind of threat so they silenced her by erasing those memories?

There's a knock at the door. Rafael lets himself in. He's wearing a yellow sombrero and dancing to "La Cucaracha," which is playing from a portable speaker hanging around his neck. It's borderline offensive, but I don't say anything. He may be oblivious, but he doesn't strike me as racist.

"Are you ready to fiesta?" Rafael asks, pronouncing fiesta in a poor Spanish accent, while shaking colorful maracas.

"Yeah, I was just finishing up here."

"It's taco time!" Still dancing. This dude's crazy.

When we arrive at the house, Theo, Geoff, and Piper are already there. A catering table is set up at one end of the room with four chafing dishes and condiment caddies filled with the standard fixings. The living and dining rooms are decorated with colorful streamers and a festive piñata sits on the mantle. Contemporary pop music is playing in the background, the only thing that doesn't seem to match with the theme of the evening.

Theo is already making a plate and talking animatedly with the caterers who smile politely but do not engage. Piper sits at the edge of an armchair with her legs crossed. I expected her to look bored or irritated, but she seems eerily content. Restoration seems to be having its calming effect.

Geoff is standing awkwardly in the center of the room. He looks nervous, straightening his shirt and frequently glancing towards the front door.

"Hey," I say, sidling up to him.

He puts his hands in his pocket and then removes them. "Hello, Hugo."

"You alright?"

"Me? Yes." He looks to the door again.

"You sure? Why do you keep looking at the door?"

Theo walks up with an overloaded plate of nachos. "He's nervous because Rafael invited Pod Sixty-Two to the taco party." He angles a queso-drenched tortilla chip into his mouth.

"I know someone from Pod Sixty-Two," I say. Darcy. I think that's the pod she said she was in.

"He has a crush on one of their engineers."

"No, I don't," Geoff says, straightening the hem of his shirt.

The doorbell rings and Rafael rushes toward the front door. When he opens it, five new people enter. Darcy is one of them. She waves once she sees me. Rafael zestfully greets the new invites and walks them over for an introduction. "Guys, this is Hugo," Rafael says. "He's a musician!"

"Nice to meet you, Hugo. I'm Lorena, facilitator for Pod Sixty-Two just down the lane. How are you settling in?"

"Fine, I guess." I'm not sure what to compare it to.

"These are my podmates: Darcy, who I think you've met, Felicia, Maurice, and Brian."

They each shake my hand.

"Nice to meet you all," I say. "Nice to see you again, Darcy."

Darcy blushes and holds out her hand, not like a regular handshake, but like she wants me to kiss it. I shake it anyway. Lorena guides her toward the catering table where Theo is hovering. He pushes his glasses up on his nose and starts chatting them up. Darcy keeps looking back toward me.

Felicia is looking up at Geoff in bashful glances through Coke-bottle glasses. She comes up to his chest. "Hello, Geoff," she says. "Thanks for inviting us."

His face is as red as a pomegranate. "Oh, it wasn't my idea," he says, oblivious. "Rafael planned it."

"Oh," she says and shifts her eyes to the floor.

"But I'm glad you could come," he blurts. "I mean, all of you."

An awkward silence lingers before Felicia says, "Nice work on that capacitor test today."

"Thanks. I couldn't have done it without your latest data set."

Now that they're onto the nerdiest of shop talk, he starts to relax. The rest have migrated to the catering table and a portable bar, each staffed with black-aproned servers. Brian is talking to Piper who is still seated with her legs crossed, sipping a margarita from a plastic cup. He's propped a leg up onto the coffee table, leaning an elbow on one knee. She's nodding politely and then notices me watching them.

It's too late to avert my eyes, so I walk over. Brian looks a bit miffed that I've interrupted. "Can I get you another drink?" I ask her.

She uncrosses her legs and stands. "Thank you, Hugo. Polite of you to ask." She threads her arm into mine and turns back to Brian. "Nice talking to you, Ryan."

"It's Brian," he corrects her with a dejected tone as we walk away.

"Thank you," she whispers to me as we walk toward the portable bar. "That guy's a douche."

"Really? I couldn't tell," I say with a measured level of sarcasm.

She laughs and rattles the ice in her cup to the bartender. "One more, please. And one for my friend here."

Friend? Are we friends now? She's probably just using me to get away from Brian. I'll take it. I hadn't noticed before, but Piper has a tattoo on the outside of her left wrist—a feather. I take a sip of the margarita. It's watered down.

"So, this is all for you," I say. "You must feel pretty special."

"So special," she says in that sardonic, deadpan tone I remember from before. It's reassuring. The serotonin-fueled trance she'd been in since her restoration was unsettling. She takes a sip from a cocktail straw and looks sideways at Rafael who is talking animatedly with that other pod facilitator. Her posture is relaxed and she's laughing at his jokes.

"Is he flirting?" I ask.

"Raf? It's hard to tell," she says. "He's always like that."

"He's kind of a strange guy, isn't he?"

Piper snorts discreetly. "That's an understatement."

Everyone seems comfortable with one another, like they've all met before at these little get togethers. Theo is seated at the conference table talking with Darcy and Maurice, but neither of them seem to be listening. Rafael just put on some early nineties hip-hop and is trying to get others to dance. Lorena bobs her head to the beat. Rafael knows all the words.

"Come on, guys!" Rafael calls to us with wild eyes.

I smile coyly and shake my head. I'm not much of a dancer. Then again, how do I know that? Maybe I am. Felicia pulls Geoff to the middle of the room and starts to stiffly sway to the rhythm. I hope, for her sake, he doesn't blow it.

At first, he's as rigid as a telephone pole, but as soon as the track gets to that all familiar hook, Geoff surprises everyone by throwing his arms up and executing a spot on dance performance nobody saw coming. It's the kind of dance that takes hours to choreograph and he busts it out like he's had it in his back pocket for this very moment. Even Rafael is frozen in place, wide-eyed and open-mouthed.

Everyone rushes to the dance floor to join in. Piper looks at me with a devilish grin and then spins toward the middle of the dance floor.

"Come on!" Rafael calls to me, imploring me with his crazy eyes.

I don't want to be a party pooper. I may not be a big dancer, but I'm definitely not a party pooper. I make eye contact with

Piper and she smiles. It's the kind of smile that etches itself permanently in the brain and that's all the coaxing I need. I join her and the others on the dance floor. I like the way she dances. Her moves aren't showy or overly complicated. They're smooth, understated, sexy.

I feel someone tugging at my sleeve. It's Darcy and she's dancing seductively, attempting to pull me toward her. I position myself half toward Darcy and half toward Piper. Darcy turns and backs herself into me, but I turn away from her, pretending not to notice.

When the song ends, I follow Piper to the couch, which has been moved against the wall to make space for the dance floor. We're both out of breath.

"How often do we have these taco parties?" I ask her.

"Fairly often," she says. "It's not always tacos. Sometimes it's a barbecue. Or ice cream sundaes. Sometimes we have field day competitions with other pods. It's supposed to help us be more productive, ironically."

"No, that makes sense actually. Good for morale and all that."

"I guess."

The next song is less of a banger and it's just Rafael and Lorena on the dance floor. Darcy is at the bar ordering a drink and she keeps glaring at me. Surely she's not offended I didn't let her grind on me while we were dancing. That would be stupid.

Piper's staring straight ahead, occasionally glancing in my direction, but not directly. It takes me a minute to pluck up the courage, but eventually I ask, "So do you have a boyfriend, or anything?"

She scoffs. "We don't do that here. Relationships distract us from our true purpose." Her words are dripping with sarcasm.

"Right. That's a Level Five thing."

"Right," she says and I can't tell if she's being sarcastic or not.

"How long have you been here?" I ask.

"In Slumbervale? It's hard to say. Longer than most."

"Do you like it here?"

"Compared to what?"

"Good point." I'm not sure how to get around to what I really want to ask her. "So do you really believe the universe is a stack of pancakes?"

"They don't mean that literally," she says. "Although, we do have monthly pancake breakfasts to honor the pancake universe."

"Seriously?"

"Yeah. Don't you like pancakes?"

"Of course. I'm not a robot."

She laughs. A dimple appears on her cheek and I feel as though I've unlocked a secret treasure. "Can I ask you a question?"

"Anything," I say. I hope that didn't seem too desperate.

"This morning. You asked me if I ever feel like we're prisoners."

"Yeah."

"I said I didn't. But I've been thinking about it ever since." She craned her neck to see if anyone was listening. "I don't remember what happened before restoration. I don't know what I said or what I did. But the feeling is still there. They can't erase the feeling."

"What feeling?"

She lowers her voice. "That something is wrong here. That there's vital information that we aren't given access to. I don't remember saying we're prisoners. But the more I think about it, that *is* how I feel. And something tells me, you feel it, too." Her eyes are expectant.

"I do. I feel it."

She sighs hard. "Oh, good! I thought I was the only one."

The lights, which have been dimmed during the dance portion of the evening, have come back up. Rafael announces that it's close to eight and everyone says their goodbyes as Pod Sixty-Two makes their way back to their own house. I wave as they leave. Darcy doesn't wave back and that seems intentional.

Piper offers a weak smile at best. Her shoulders have dropped and she stares somewhere far away.

"You okay?" I ask.

At first she doesn't respond.

"Piper?"

"Hmm?"

"Are you alright?"

"Yep. All good," she says brightly, applying a smile with raised brows. "Time to reboot," she says and stands. She walks to the dining room table to clear some plates.

"Oh, don't worry about that," Rafael says. "The cleaning crew will get it."

She continues stacking plates and moving them to one end of the table. Then she sits at the far end and puts her head down.

"Great party," Theo says. "Geoff, I had no idea you could dance like that."

"Me neither," Geoff says.

"Very impressive moves," Rafael says, nodding.

"Thank you."

"I think that Felicia is into you," Theo says to Geoff.

"Oh, I don't know," Geoff says humbly.

"No, I think he's right," I say.

"Really?"

I want to encourage him to pursue her, but I'm not sure

what the rules are. Piper says it's not allowed. I don't want to get him in any trouble. I give him a nod and look to Rafael to get a read, but he's distracted with the piñata.

"We forgot to hit the piñata!" Rafael complains. He gives the thing a good shake. "Wait a minute!" Shake, shake. "There's no candy in here! Who forgot to put candy in the piñata?" He looks to Theo and Geoff, who look at each other.

"It doesn't matter." Piper is sitting up now. When he looks at her, she goes on. "We forgot to hit it anyway. So it doesn't matter that there's no candy in it."

Rafael purses his lips and nods. "You're right." He points at her. "You are right. It doesn't matter. What matters is you're back and we are so glad to have you in our pod."

Theo and Geoff nod in agreement.

"Thanks, Raf," she says, pulling her shoulders up to her ears. Then she points to her wrist and taps where a watch would be.

"Oh, right," says Rafael. "Time to reboot, everyone."

We lay our heads on the table. I turn my head to face Piper. She opens her eyes and I hold her gaze. My instinct tells me to avert my eyes, but I will myself to stay here, connected, curious. Three, two, one.

CHAPTER 14
GLOVE IS TO HAND

WHEN I ARRIVED at work on Monday, Lenny looked up from a music store catalog and gave me a sorrowful look. He had texted the morning after that dreadful poker night, but I never responded. Even though Lenny was technically younger than me, he'd always acted like a protective older brother.

"How you holding up?" Lenny asked.

"Fine."

"That wasn't right, man. Fucking Seth Fucker! I *hate* that guy."

"It's not all his fault. I didn't have to take the bet."

"Yeah, but still. He only did it to fuck with you. He does that kind of shit." Lenny shook his head.

"I think I'm going to sign up for this Lunatech thing," I said, testing the waters.

"You can't be serious," he said. "What are they even paying you for? They're probably going to mine your brain for data. Or they could be hypnotizing you to fulfill their corporate agenda." He nodded with wide eyes. I didn't expect him to understand. He didn't have a daughter to provide for. Privacy was a luxury I couldn't afford.

"I get it. I'm not crazy about giving up my privacy either, but if that's what it costs to give Ava somewhat of a normal life, then well, that's what it costs."

Lenny pursed his lips with a nod. "Well, I've said my piece. You gotta do what you gotta do."

"One more thing," I said.

"What?"

"I need to take tomorrow off—for the testing down there to see if I even qualify. You think you can get someone to cover me?"

On Tuesday, I navigated to the address Carl gave me when he booked my testing appointment. It was farther than I thought so I was glad I gave myself more time. From the main road I could see the reflection of the facility nestled into the foothills of the Tortolita Mountains—an ultramodern eyesore in the midst of a pristine desert landscape. A private road led to a gatehouse and I gave the guard my name. He checked his clipboard and nodded me through.

I parked my truck in the covered guest parking lot and made my way up the front steps to the main entrance of the large glass structure. I walked straight ahead to a circular desk where a receptionist with black eye liner greeted me.

"Welcome to Lunatech. How may I help you?"

"I have an appointment. I'm here for testing."

"Name?"

"Hugo Castillo."

They typed my name into a computer with violet painted fingernails. "I see you here, Mr. Castillo. The testing center is on the main floor just right down that hall." They pointed to one of three corridors that feed off the main lobby. "You'll see a sign about halfway down and the doors are on the right. Just have a seat in the waiting room and they'll call you back when they're ready."

"Thank you."

Two others were seated in the waiting room when I arrived. I took a seat across from a thick woman in business attire. She was reading a romance novel and only glanced at me briefly as I surveyed the room. An elderly man in a brown fedora sat two seats down from her. He rested his bony hands on the handle of his cane and gazed softly at me as I took my seat. I acknowledged him with a slight nod and picked up a celebrity news magazine from a side table.

"Wish I started this back when I was yo age," the old man said with vocal cords made of gravel. "Course, it wasn't invented back then."

I wasn't sure how to respond so I just smiled.

"So' security ain't wat it use to be. Cain't work no mo cuz a ma auh-tha-ri-tis. Ma daughter say I shouldn't do dis cuz uh privacy. She say they gonna be readin' ma thoughts." He gave an airy chuckle. "They use to say, penny fo ya thoughts. Well, now they gonna pay me a lot mo." He laughed at his own joke.

"That's a good one," I said.

"Mr. Castillo?" A petite woman with straight brown hair pulled back into a ponytail that reached the middle of her back stood in the doorway. She wore business casual attire with simple earrings and minimal makeup. Her smile was friendly and put me at ease.

"Yes," I said, standing up.

"Nice to meet you," she said, extending her hand. "My name is Dr. Blaine. I'll be doing your evaluation today."

I shook her hand, cold and small. The bones in her hand

felt like those of a tiny bird and I loosened my grip. Dr. Blaine walked me down a hallway and into a smaller office furnished with a desk, two chairs, bookshelves, and several file cabinets. She had two degrees from CalTech in Neuroscience and Bioengineering on the wall. A model of the human brain sat on her desk. I took a seat across from her and surveyed the books on her shelf, many of which I couldn't even pronounce.

"Do you have any questions before we get started, Mr. Castillo? Anything you might have thought of after the informational seminar?"

"How early can I start?"

"We should know the results here in two to three days and then you'll need to be scheduled for your initial sleep study."

"And how does the payment work? When do I get my first paycheck?"

"If you qualify, your first paycheck will be issued by direct deposit thirty days following your initial sleep cycle. Then monthly going forward."

I calculated the dates in my head and as long as I started by the sixteenth, I should be able to make that deposit on Ava's New York trip. "Great. I'm ready."

She started off with a few questionnaires that seemed fairly routine and then left me with more robust inventories to do on my own. There was a light switch by the door that controlled a red light above the door on the outside. When the light was on, they knew I was testing so they wouldn't disturb me. I was supposed to turn it off when I was done so she knew when to come back in.

The first two were personality tests—The Myers Briggs and the Minnesota Multiphasic Personality Inventory. Then two different career assessments. I was getting fuzzy on differentiating between "somewhat likely" and "likely," and between "occasionally" and "rarely." My eyes were getting blurry and I yawned. I needed to eat.

When I finished the last inventory, I placed it on the desk and got up to flip the switch. It was a quarter to noon when Dr. Blaine came back in.

"All done?"

"Yes, ma'am."

She took the testing materials from her desk and placed them in a large manila envelope. She looked at her watch. "Why don't we go ahead and break for lunch?"

I followed her out of the office and down the hall to a break room with three round tables and a kitchenette along the far wall. Two vending machines stood against another wall. She opened the fridge to reveal stacks of boxed lunches and bottled water.

"We have turkey, roast beef, and tuna sandwiches. If you're vegan or gluten free, we have a roasted veggie salad. If you want anything other than water, there are sodas in the vending machine. Restrooms are just around that corner." She looked at her watch. "I'll be back in a half hour to resume your testing."

I took a box marked *beef* from the fridge and a bottle of water. I sat alone with the sound of the refrigerator and my reflection in the vending machine's glass display. The bread was soggy and the lettuce wilted. There was also a pickle spear, a bag of kettle chips, and a chocolate chip cookie. I ate all of it—even the pickle, which was so limp it didn't break when I bent it in half. When I finished, I swept the crumbs into the empty box with the used napkin.

The trash bin was only a few feet away and I attempted my best basketball form from a seated position and shot the box toward the bin, but it bounced off the rim and fell to the floor the moment a tall, curly haired man walked around the corner. He bent over to pick up my trash.

"Oh, sorry," I said. "Please, leave it." I started to get up but he was already picking up my trash and placed it into the bin.

"Don't worry about it. I miss all the time!" He was smiling. "Are you testing for the sleeper program?"

"Yeah. You?"

"No, I did mine a while back. I'm here for a training. I got a part-time recruiter position," he said, eyebrows raised. "It's just a few hours on the weekends."

"So you're in the sleeper program, too?"

"Yep." He took a box from the fridge and sat at my table.

"Do you like it?" I asked.

"What? The sleeper program? Oh yeah, it's great!"

"Are there any side effects or anything?"

"Side effects? No, I can't say I've noticed any. All I know is I wake up refreshed, rejuvenated, and ready to take on the world!"

He sounded like a commercial. I smiled anyway. "What do you do for work—during the day?"

"I teach the third grade." He bit into a tuna sandwich.

"I'm Hugo, by the way."

"Rafael," he replied, still chewing.

Dr. Blaine entered the break room. "Mr. Castillo? Are you ready to get back to it?"

"Yeah." I turned to Rafael. "Nice to meet you."

"Likewise. Good luck!"

I followed Dr. Blaine back to her office and took a seat. She sat behind her desk and explained that she'd be administering the remainder of the testing. "We're going to start with some projective tests and then move onto cognitive functioning," she said.

She showed me some ink blots, which honestly just looked like ink blots to me, but I went along: a moth, a pelvis, a bat, a jack-o-lantern, etc. In another test, Dr. Blaine asked me to draw a clock that read three o'clock. She asked me to recall a list of words. She had me write certain words frontwards and backwards.

She asked me to recall an event from the last few days and then one from the distant past. She took notes as I spoke. She had me do Math, subtracting certain numbers from one hundred. She asked me what the relationship between a list of words were, like cow, parrot, lizard, and cat were all animals. She said,"glove is to hand as blank is to foot." And I said, "shoe."

As the day progressed, the tasks became increasingly more challenging. She tested my judgment by asking what I might do in certain ethical situations. She had me solve puzzles, both physical puzzles and mental ones. She showed me a picture of a scene, like a street view with buildings, cars, and people, and then she asked me to draw this scene from memory to the best of my ability. Then she asked me what I thought was happening between certain people in my drawing and had me make up a dialogue between them. She gave me word problems to solve. I wasn't good at word problems.

By the end, I was squinting, second-guessing every answer, my brain flopping around like a fish out of water. I hadn't felt this stupid since high school chemistry. We finished a little after four in the afternoon.

"You did great," she said as she wound a tiny string around the clasp of a large envelope where she placed the testing materials.

"I did?"

"We should have the results in a couple of days. I'll call you as soon as I know."

"Do you think I have a good chance of getting in?"

"I'm not allowed to say anything before we get the results." Her eyes apologized. "You understand."

"Right." So, when she said I did great, she meant that I finished, not that I did well on the tests, necessarily.

"We'll be in touch," she said, standing and holding out her tiny bird bone hand for me to shake.

Nothing more to do now, except wait.

CHAPTER 15
TIDY PAWS

I OPEN my eyes after rebooting. The house is clean. Just a moment ago, there were still plates stacked at the end of the table and the catering carts were still over there against the wall. Now they're gone. The living room furniture has been moved back into place—no more dance floor. When I laid my head down, seconds ago, there was a blob of salsa that someone had spilled just inches from my face. But now it's gone.

Rafael starts rounds. I still don't have much to report. Piper talks about some cybersecurity updates she working on. I have no idea what she's talking about but everyone's nodding heads concur. She only glances in my direction a couple times, but I feel like she's communicating something else to me— something off the record. I wish I knew what it was. I don't know when I'll get the chance to talk to her alone again.

Sitting around this table feels like school, although I don't have any recollections of my own of ever attending. How can I know what school is like if I've never been? That nostalgic feeling reminds me of something else. The way I feel about Piper seems familiar, too. It's a mixture of excitement and longing that lingers even after we're apart. I know I've felt this way before. It must be a carryover from a past life.

Once I get to the studio, I plop onto the couch and reach for my notebook. I can't get Piper out of my mind—reflecting on our conversation, her memories patched over with the unchallenged ideology of a pancake universe. I remember the way she looked at me, like there was some shadow there from before that she could no longer access.

Turning to a clean page, I pour out every thought I have about Piper, every vision, every impulse, every question. Within an hour's time, I've got six pages of handwritten stream of consciousness. It's not poetic or structured in any way and I certainly can't use all of it. But it's a good start—a decent start.

I reach for an acoustic guitar resting at one end of the couch and strum a few notes with my eyes closed until I hit upon a major key that resonates with the way I felt when she laughed, when she beckoned me onto the dance floor. I play around with a few different riffs until I land on one that feels right. My foot taps out a rhythm and before long, I have the chorus—jubilant and ferocious. The verses will be more subdued—reflective, tense, and more consistent with unfulfilled longing.

I scratch out the notes onto some blank music sheets and refer to my notebook to work my ramblings into more structured song lyrics. After a couple of hours, I have it. The song is basically written. I play it over and over, making a few adjustments to the bridge leading into the chorus. I can hear how the other parts will integrate—rhythm guitar, lead guitar, bass, drums. I can hear it all in my head.

Vincent enters the studio followed by two men, one older

and one younger than me. I close my notebook. I'm not sure I'm ready to share my song just yet.

"What's up, Hugo! I want you to meet some folks. This is Garrett and Cash. They're also musicians. I thought you guys could have a little jam session."

I shake their hands. It would be nice to play with other musicians.

"You know that insurance commercial with the penguin?" Vincent asks me.

The jingle immediately plays in my mind and I hum it out loud. Even though I recognize it, I can't recall ever actually hearing it. "Yeah, that'll get stuck in your head," I say.

Cash smiles, and with a slow Texas draw says, "That's kinda the point." He appears to be in his sixties and has a thick mustache and a western shirt unbuttoned at the top revealing a carpet of white chest hair.

"He wrote that," Vincent says, gesturing with his thumb.

I'm glad I didn't say it was super annoying. "Cool," I say.

"And Garrett here's our go-to sessions guy. He can play just about any instrument in here."

"Not *every* instrument," Garrett says. He's dressed in a rockabilly style with a perfectly quaffed pompadour, rolled-up short sleeves, and cuffed jeans. "How long you been here?"

"Just a couple of days," I say.

"Vincent says you're pretty good," Cash says. "Says you got a nice set of pipes to boot."

I don't know what to say to that, so I shrug.

"I'll let you guys get acquainted," Vincent says. "I'll be in the booth."

I pick out a mint green Telecaster from the rack. Garrett steps behind an electric keyboard and starts playing a sampling of chords in the key of G. Cash selects a bass with a natural wood grain and plugs in. He chimes in with a bouncy bass line and within a minute's time they're synced up. I strike a chord and feel my way into a riff that matches the rhythm and mood of Cash's jaunty bass line. He smiles like I just read his mind.

We continue like this for the next hour. We've been focusing on the first part of the song and I'm eager to start working on the rest of it. Some ideas came to me while we were jamming, but we keep coming back to the same few measures, adding additional instrumental parts to the same piece—percussion, marimbas, and for some reason Garrett is insistent upon a mouth harp. I thought he was just messing around, but Vincent wants to keep it. It takes a half hour to record that silly part. So far the song sounds a bit cartoonish. It needs something to give it room to breath a little—something slightly more reflective before picking back up again.

"So I'm thinking," I say once I have everyone's attention. "Maybe the next part can go like this." I play a few measures and add a self-indulgent little solo before launching back into the main melody. I look up at dispassionate expressions on Cash and Garrett's faces. I look to the booth and Vincent is scratching his white, wiry facial hair. "What do you think?" I ask the guys.

"No, that sounds great, Hugo. Really great," Vincent says over the intercom. "It's just that . . . I think we got what we need on this one."

We only have a minute's worth of track—definitely not enough for a song. "That's it?" I say.

Cash is penciling something into his notebook.

"No, that's not it," Garrett says. "We still need lyrics. You're the songwriter, right?"

"What's this song supposed to be about anyway?" I ask.

There's a pause and the guys glance at each other before Vincent pipes in from the booth. "Kitty litter."

"Excuse me?" I'm confused. Is this some kind of inside joke I'm not in on?

"It's a jingle for kitty litter."

"A jingle?"

"Cats are very important to people in Level Five. For some people, cats are all they have in life."

I'm stunned. He knew this all along? Garrett and Cash don't seem surprised so they were probably in on it from the beginning. Why didn't anyone tell me we were writing a commercial for kitty litter?

"Oh," I say. "I didn't know that's what we were doing. I thought we were just jamming."

"What's the name of this kitty litter, again?" Garrett asks Vincent, opening his notebook to a clean page.

"Tidy Paws," Vincent says like a radio announcer.

Everyone looks at me to give input on the lyrics to his ridiculous song—I mean, *jingle*. They seem to think I'm the most suited for this task, but I have nothing. I don't know anything about cats. After a while they each start contributing ideas and scratching them into their notebooks. They're taking this a lot more seriously than I could have ever imagined.

Within an hour's time, they have this thing wrapped up. I wasn't much help coming up with the lyrics, which were pretty dumb, but it was unanimous that I record the vocals. It's not great, but everyone seems fairly pleased with it. It goes like this:

Look at that, it's a happy cat
A sleep wherever I want to cat
A look out the window at the birdies cat

Look at that, it's a happy cat
A sneaky sneak up and pounce cat

A how did you get all the way up there cat

Look at that, it's a happy cat
And a happy cat is a Tidy Paws cat!

This is supposed to be my life's purpose? Vincent just popped a bottle of champagne and pours some into plastic cups for us.

"To Steve," Vincent says, raising his cup to a portrait of Steve Gowan on the wall above the recording booth window.

"To Steve," everyone else says in unison. I say it a little late, like a Protestant in a Catholic church. I'm not exactly sure what we're celebrating.

"So let me get this straight," I say. "Did we just make a commercial for people down in Level Five?"

"Yeah. And I think it's pretty good," Vincent says.

"Why can't people in Level Five make their own cat litter jingles?"

"Because," Garrett says. "People in Level Five are too stressed, man. Their personal lives are too complicated for them to come up with original stuff. They're kind of a mess down there. We're the creators. That's all we have to worry about up here."

"But how does it work?" I ask. "How does the music we write make its way down to Level Five?"

"Imagine a pancake," Cash says. Here we go. "You know how you pour the syrup on the top, but it makes its way down to the layers down below? It's like that. Our ideas, our music, they trickle down to where it's needed."

"But *how*?"

"We're   connected,"   Vincent   says.   "Connected,   but separate."

"Right, but what I'm asking is like, how does the music we record literally get down to Level Five?"

"That's above my pay grade," Vincent says. "I get my orders from the department heads. It's not my place to ask questions."

"And you're okay with that? Don't you want to know?"

He shrugs.

"We're here to make music," Cash says. "Don't much care about anything else. You're a musician. Just be a musician. Let the higher ups handle the higher up shit."

"Right," I say. I get the sense that I should feel relieved about this. I don't have a lot to worry about in this life. I love playing music and that's all that's expected of me here. It's like I've won some kind of occupational lottery. So why do I feel like a pig being fattened for slaughter?

"But we can still write our own songs though, right? It's not just commercials and stuff."

"Oh yeah. You can still write your own stuff," Vincent says. "We do have to prioritize our commissions though. But look how easy that was! You boys knocked it out of the park in just a few hours. Why? You working on anything now?"

I'm not sure I'm ready to share my song with these guys just yet. It's a little too personal, like reading from my diary. Besides, if Piper ever returns the feeling, I don't want to call attention to an illicit affair. It's probably better if I keep it to myself, for now.

CHAPTER 16
SWEET DREAMS

THE NEXT TWO days were uneventful as I waited for the results from the testing at Lunatech. More than once I doubted my competency and second guessed several of my responses. To protect against disappointment, I started to get used to the strong possibility that I didn't get in. I got back on the job boards just in case.

I was putting dinner in the oven when I got the call.

"This is Dr. Blaine at Lunatech calling for Hugo Castillo."

"That's me. Did I get in?" I couldn't help my eager tone.

"Mr. Castillo, you've been approved for the sleeper program."

I privately celebrated with a fist pump. "Really? When can I start?"

"First you'll need to schedule your initial sleep study. Are you available this Friday evening, the 13th?"

"Tomorrow night? Yeah. Yeah, I can do tomorrow." Perfect timing. That means I would get my first paycheck in plenty of time to make that deposit on Ava's trip.

"Please arrive by 8:00 so they have time to go over equipment training and get you settled in. Your sleep cycle will begin promptly at 10:00. They'll want to observe you overnight to make sure everything is working as it should. Do you have any questions?"

"8:00—got it."

"Congratulations, Mr. Castillo."

Two thousand dollars a month? I didn't have to worry about Ava's school trip, getting behind on bills, or other unexpected expenses. I could even get a new truck. Maybe not a brand new one, but at least a newer one that didn't break down every few months. I pulled a beer from the fridge and cracked it open. My mind started making plans for a brighter future for Ava and I, when I heard a car pull into the driveway.

Ava went straight to her room without saying hello—bad mood. I knocked on her door. "Ava?"

"I have to study."

"Can I talk to you for a second."

"Whaat?" Ava whined.

"Can I come in?"

She didn't answer right away. Then opened the door with an insolent look. "What?"

"Can I come in?" I asked again.

She opened the door wider and plopped on her bed.

"I have some good news."

Ava's listless expression didn't change.

"I got a new job!" I announced with unfiltered enthusiasm, my hands extended like I was presenting an invisible gift.

"What's wrong with your old job?"

"Nothing. I got a second job."

"Okay," she said with a shake of her head. She couldn't have cared less.

"This is good news, Ava. It means you'll be able to go to New York! It means we'll be in a better place financially."

"So now you'll be gone all weekend or what?"

"No, that's the beauty of it. It's overnight. They're going to pay me while I sleep!"

"What the hell are you talking about?"

"It's this company called Lunatech. They pay to use your brain while you sleep."

"Do you know how insane that sounds?"

Yes, I heard it. "I know, but the bottom line is, I don't have to do anything except follow a reasonable bedtime. Plus, I'll finally get a solid eight hours of sleep every night."

"Dad . . ." Ava's face contorted to reflect her incredulity. "You're going to give some company you've never heard of access to your brain?"

"I know how it sounds. But it's totally safe and you know how you're always asking me about my sleep? This is going to cure that."

"Does this mean you're going to start drinking less?"

"What?"

"Nothing. Do you, I guess." She shrugged.

"This is a good thing, Ava. It's going to be like two thousand dollars more a month."

She considered this for a moment. "I mean, if it's going to help you finally get some sleep." Ava didn't look convinced. What was she not understanding? Was I not explaining it right?

"What?" I asked.

"Dad . . . it's just . . ." She struggled to articulate what she was thinking. "You always jump on these . . . opportunities or whatever. And they never really pan out. Or they backfire and we're worse of than we were before." She wasn't wrong.

I sighed. "I know. No, you're right. I do do that, don't I? But this is different. It's guaranteed income with a year-long contract."

"Okay." She seemed only marginally on board.

My heart sunk. I really wanted her to get behind this. She had a point, I guess. Maybe she just needed to see me stick with it. She'd come around once her New York trip was paid for.

I got to the Lunatech offices a few minutes early on Friday night. I was directed to take the elevator to the second floor to the Sleep Center and to take a seat in the waiting room.

The small waiting room was flanked by several vinyl upholstered chairs. Sitcom re-runs played on a wall-mounted television. And Darcy, who had been engrossed in her phone, looked up as I walked in.

I didn't get a chance to return her miscellaneous purse droppings on Wednesday because she didn't come into the store. She dropped off her son and took off before I could return her things. I didn't blame her for avoiding me. What happened last week was embarrassing—for both of us.

"Hey," I said, raising one hand in a half-hearted wave, leaving the other in my pocket.

"Hey," she said and retreated back to her phone screen.

I took a seat across from her. "Are you here for the sleep study, too?"

She nodded and there was an awkward pause.

"Hey, I . . . I wanted to clear the air about last week. I don't want things to be weird between us."

"Well, that's on me," she said.

"I was hoping we could sort of look past it."

"You're not mad? I was pretty sure you hated me."

"No, not at all! Pshh—over a little . . . miscalculation?"

"Oh, is that what we're calling it?" A reticent smile broke on her face.

A woman in a gray blazer and slacks appeared in the doorway holding a clipboard. "Darcy?"

"That's me," she said with a raised index finger.

"We're ready for you. Follow me, please."

Darcy stood and pulled her purse over her shoulder, then turned to me like she was going to say something. In her hesitation I said, "Listen, maybe we could grab a coffee sometime, you know, as friends."

"I'd like that," she said, and added, "as friends." She turned and followed the woman out of the room.

A few minutes later, the same woman appeared in the doorway. "Hugo?"

"Present."

"We're ready for you now."

I followed the woman down a hall adorned with desert wildlife photography. She ushered me into an office and asked me to take a seat. She took her seat behind a desk.

"Before we get started, I have some paperwork for you to sign here." She slid a thick packet toward me and handed me a pen. She flipped through several pages at a time, stopping at various signature pages, explaining briefly what each portion covered before I signed. Reminded me of when we closed on our house.

Most of it seemed like fairly standard medical disclosures. I had to agree not to bring litigation to Lunatech for any reason. Lunatech's was the only party authorized to service any of its proprietary equipment. Additionally, there was an exclusivity clause regarding any brain-related medical procedures. I signed a one-year contract to participate in the sleeper program and there was a steep penalty for dropping out early. I had to sign a non-disclosure from discussing the program with anyone in the press. Finally, I provided my bank information to set up the direct deposit.

When we finished, she held out her hand for me to shake. "Welcome to Lunatech." Her smile was professional and brief. She didn't offer any chit chat as I followed her to the elevators and we ascended to the fourth floor. She stared directly ahead at the doors.

I followed her down another hallway to what appeared to be a hospital room. She opened the door and motioned for me to enter.

"Make yourself comfortable, Mr. Castillo. Did you bring pajamas?"

"No." They didn't say anything about pajamas.

"There's a set in the cabinet if you need them."

"Okay, thanks."

"Dr. Majeed will be with you momentarily." She gave me another mechanical smile and left.

The room was not quite as clinical as a hospital, but not as comfortable as a hotel either. There were cameras mounted on the ceiling—four of them. The bed was a typical hospital bed with guardrails and position controls. There was no television.

I opened the cabinet door and found the pajamas, light blue, folded on a shelf, one-size-fits-all. I didn't wear pajamas. I usually slept in my chonies. But under the circumstances, I opted for the unflattering two-piece set. They were loose, but at least the pants had a drawstring.

A short bald man in a lab coat entered the room with a nurse. "Good evening, Mr. Castillo. I'm Dr. Majeed and I'll be monitoring your initial sleep cycle. This is Amber. She's here to take your vitals."

Amber placed a pulse oximeter on my right index finger, wrapped a blood pressure cuff around my bicep, and silently got to work.

"How are you feeling?" Dr. Majeed asked.

"Good, I think."

"Are you nervous?" Dr. Majeed asked.

"A little," I said.

"That's understandable. Try to relax. Take some deep breaths. Do you have any questions?"

"No, I don't think so."

Amber placed an infrared thermometer in my ear. She documented the reading on her tablet and quietly left the room.

"Okay, let's go over your console," Dr. Majeed said. He opened a black case on a rolling table. It was about the size of a record player, smaller. He unsealed a plastic bag and handed me the electrode cap. He took the pre-connected wires and plugged them into the back of the console. Then he swiveled the table around so I could see the ports.

"The device is pre-programmed to wake you at 6:00 a.m. You must activate the device no later than 10:00 p.m. I suggest you give yourself ten minutes to get everything hooked up and get settled in. You'll need to use the restroom before starting your sleep cycle. You will not wake up for eight hours straight and we don't want you to have an accident."

"Okay."

"Very important."

"Got it."

"Okay, let's get your cap on. This is the front. This is the back. The chin strap should be snug, but not too tight. Good! How does that feel?"

"Fine." I was sure I looked ridiculous.

"Not too tight?"

"No."

"Good. Now once you're all hooked up and comfortable, you'll press this button here and hold it for three seconds. That activates the cap and calibrates the electrodes to make sure you have a solid connection. If you don't, the console will beep and give you a chance to readjust the electrode cap. Once the light turns green, press it again to start the countdown."

"How long before I'm asleep?"

"Less than ten seconds."

"Wow."

"I know. Now, when you wake up, you won't have to turn it off—the console resets itself. Any questions?"

"No."

"Alright, are you ready?"

"Now?"

"It's almost 10:00. Go ahead and use the restroom, brush your teeth, and then I'll have you activate the console."

"I didn't bring a toothbrush."

"You'll find extra toothbrushes and toothpaste on the vanity."

I removed my cap and made my way to the adjoining restroom. Dr. Majeed was adjusting the cameras from a tablet when I returned.

"Ready," I said.

"Good. Let's get you in bed."

I got under the stiff, scratchy covers and Dr. Majeed adjusted the position from sitting to nearly flat. "How's that?"

"Fine." I pulled the electrode cap over my head and adjusted the strap below my chin.

"Okay, now do you remember what to do?"

"I think so. Hold this button for three seconds to calibrate—"

"Go ahead."

I pushed the button and it blinked yellow and the device said, "Calibrating . . ." In a few seconds, it chirped and said, "Calibration complete." The light turned green.

Dr. Majeed nodded.

I pushed the button again and the machine said, "Good-night, Hugo. Sweet dreams."

"That's it," Dr. Majeed said. "Just close your eyes and focus on your breath. I'll see you in the morning."

I nodded.

"Sleep tight," he said with a grin.

I closed my eyes and tried to focus on my breath. It was shallow and probably faster than it should have been. I thought of Ava. I thought of her laugh. It had been a while since I'd heard it. I thought of the face she made when she concentrates on something. Her mother made that face. I miss her so much. I—

CHAPTER 17
BOOGIE-OCRACY

THEY'RE all staring at me expectantly.

"What?" I say.

"Don't hold out on us," Vincent says, smiling. "If you have a song, we want to hear it."

"It's not ready."

"Oh, come on! Let's hear what you got so far," Garret says.

"I don't know, I—"

"What key are we playing in?" Cash asks, pulling his bass strap up around his neck. He's not interested in my excuses.

"Uh, G," I say.

"Go ahead. Show us what you got and I'll jump in."

I place my handwritten music sheet on a stand and turn it toward him. The Telecaster isn't the right sound for this song, so I select a Les Paul from the rack. I pull the guitar strap over my head and plug in.

"Where do you want me?" Garrett asks. "Keyboards? Guitar?"

"Guitar," I say.

He selects a Stratocaster from the rack. Vincent sits behind a trap set, thumping the bass drum and hi-hat. "I'm just a stand in for now. We'll get you a real drummer when it's time to lay down track. Alright, Hugo, why don't you play us what you got so far?"

"Okay. So it starts like this." I play the opening riff and go into the first verse. His eyes trained on my fingers, Cash comes in after a few measures with a minimal bass line. Garret picks up the chord changes easily. By the second verse, they have the basic chords down and Vincent is keeping decent time on the drums. I call out the key change into the bridge and they transition seamlessly. These guys are good.

After going through it once, we break it down into sections and flesh it out even more. Then we work on the transitions. This takes us the rest of the afternoon to get it just right.

"Say, you got any lyrics to this song?" Cash asks.

I had only sung them quietly to myself up until now. I'm still not sure I'm ready for anyone to know how I feel about Piper, especially if dating isn't allowed.

"I mean, I have a few lines. I don't know if it's any good."

"Well, son, let's hear it!" Cash says.

"Yeah, we can always tweak it later," Garrett says, brushing pomaded hair back with his hand.

Vincent drags a mic stand from the corner of the room over to me and makes sure it's plugged in and ready. I never agreed to sing this song.

"I'm gonna hit record and just do a rough take," he says. Vincent runs up to the booth and has us do a quick sound check. He gives a thumbs up. I nod at Cash and we begin the opening riff together. Garrett comes in at just the right time and I step up to the mic. The metallic smell of the microphone reminds me of something I cannot place and electricity ripples up my spine. I take in a deep breath and sing:

Rolled your eyes and I just died

Is this real or did they lie?
Are you how you used to be
Or did the restoration
Change what you see?
Change what you see? Yeah.

On the dance floor, subtly
Hiding like a memory
Somewhere deep inside my skull
But all my mind can see is
You're beautiful
You're beautiful, yeah

You said we were captives here
But as long as you stay near
They can lock us up
I won't disrupt

I don't know anything
About my life
But if you're here, I'l have no fear
And I'll be who
You want me to be
You want me to be

Like the feather on your arm
Let me be within your reach
There's so much I want to know
If we can be together,
Where can this go?
Where can this go, yo?

She said we're prisoners

But as long as I can kiss her
They can lock me up
Don't interrupt

I don't know anything
About my life
But if you're here, I'll have no fear
And I'll be who
You need me to be
You need me to be

"Woooh! That sounded tight!" Vincent says as guitar feedback squeals from the stack. Everyone agrees.

My heart's racing. I've never felt more alive and I want to keep singing.

"He's got the voice of a goddamned angel," Cash says in that slow draw, lips curled up on one side.

"Damn right, he does," Garrett says. "You have a name for this song?"

I hadn't given it an official title, but I say, "Lock Me Up?" Everyone nods in approval. "So what happens now?" I ask Vincent.

He's up in the booth, on the phone with someone. When he hangs up, he says through the intercom, "Suki's on her way." Garret and Cash exchange a look of recognition.

"Who's Suki?" I ask the guys.

"Only the world's greatest drummer," Garrett says.

Vincent steps out of the booth. "This is going to be big. I know a hit when I hear one."

"Really?" I ask. Okay, yes, I'm fishing. So what?

"Really," he says emphatically. "It's not pretentious or trendy either. That's what I like about it. It's the kind of song people will still be listening to decades from now."

When Suki arrives, she doesn't say anything to anyone—just takes her place behind the drum kit and starts in on a warm up solo. She's wearing leather shorts over fishnets and a Bowie t-shirt with the sleeves cut off, revealing extensive tattoos on both arms. She has a lip ring, fat gauges in both ears, and an asymmetrical haircut that looks like she narrowly escaped hand to hand combat with Edward Scissorhands. This solo goes on for several minutes while the rest of the guys stand there transfixed. She's incredible.

Suki chokes her crash cymbal and the guys whoop and holler. She doesn't acknowledge the praise. "Who's this?" Suki asks, pointing at me with one of her drumsticks.

"This is Hugo. He wrote the song we're about to record."

"It's a pleasure to meet you," I say. "You sound amazing."

She doesn't respond to my greeting, or my compliment. I'm officially terrified of this woman.

"Okay," Vincent says. "Why don't you guys run through it one more time for Suki?"

We play through it once without so much as a hi-hat from Suki. She has her eyes closed the whole time. Everyone is waiting for her to say something. For a minute, I think she isn't into it. Like maybe it's not her style. But after we finish, she says, "Okay, from the top. I'll count you in."

With each play through, the song evolves. Suki changed the time signature during the bridge, which I would have never thought of, but it elevated the song to a whole new level. Even my vocals improve with each iteration.

"I can't believe how great this is turning out," I say after the third time through.

"I think we should perform it at Stevefest," Garrett says.

"That sounds like a great idea!" Vincent exclaims. "I'll put in an application."

"What's Stevefest," I ask.

"Stevefest!" Vincent shouts. "It's only the biggest holiday of the year!"

"Everyone will be there," Garrett says.

Everyone? That includes Piper. There's no way she hears this song and doesn't know it's about her. This is bad. I'm not ready for this. I can't let her know how I feel about her. It's too soon. I'll scare her away.

"I don't know, guys," I say. "What if—"

"What if we rock everyone's faces off?" Garrett says and high fives Vincent.

"You're a natural performer," Cash says. "The folks here in Slumbervale don't always see the fruits of their labor. It could be a real morale booster."

"Agreed," Vincent says. "I'll get that application in first thing tomorrow."

"But I don't—"

"I knew you could do it, Hugo. You were made for this," Vincent says with a smile I cannot betray. He actually believes in me. They all do. I don't want to disappoint them. And I don't want to prevent them from fulfilling their purpose either. I guess we're really doing this.

Plus, maybe there's still time to see if Piper has any feelings for me before I put myself out there. Maybe we hit it off, who knows? But how? Dating is forbidden. They don't want relationships to interfere with fulfilling our life purpose. But in my case, it can only help. Love is what inspired me to write this song. And if Piper breaks my heart, I'll probably write about that, too. One might argue, relationships are essential to fulfilling my particular life purpose.

"When is this Stevefest?" I ask Vincent.

"Next Saturday."

Saturday?! That's cutting it close. I need to move fast. I look at the clock—7:00. Maybe I can catch her before we reboot. "I think I'm going to head back to my pod," I say.

"Good work, Hugo!" Vincent says. "We'll start recording individual parts over the next few days. See you bright and early. And bring that beautiful voice," he says with a sincere smile.

"See you tomorrow," I say, waving to the group on my way out. Everyone waves back, except Suki, who gives me an approving up nod. I'll take it.

There are a few people ahead of me at the teleporter—must be rush hour. Two guys in front of me are chatting. The guy in the baseball hat asks the other, "How can you tell?"

"If you talk to them long enough, they start to repeat themselves," the guy in the mustard yellow cardigan says. "They're limited in what they can talk about. Same with their facial expressions."

"I thought there was something off about that food truck dude. He didn't get my joke about photons. Just looked at me with a weird smile and said, 'Enjoy.'

"What was the joke?"

"The joke?"

"Yeah, the one about photons."

"Oh, so this photon is checking in at the airport and the lady at the counter asks if he's checking any bags. And the photon goes, 'No, I'm traveling light.' Get it?"

"Yeah, that's not funny."

"Well, no. But still, he should have at least pretended to laugh, you know, as a professional courtesy."

"Yep. Probably a bot."

"Excuse me," I say. "Sorry to interrupt, but what are you guys talking about?"

"Bots," Cardigan says. "They're usually in service industry roles."

I recall the caterers at the taco party. They struck me as somewhat robotic. Didn't stop Theo from chatting them up though. I remember their vacant smiles as he spoke to them and chalked it up to politeness.

"Why service industry roles?"

"Because that isn't a life purpose. They're not technically necessary, you know, because we don't have to eat. It's just window dressing."

"Window dressing?"

"Yeah," Baseball cap guy says. "You could punch one in the stomach and he'd just keep smiling and tell you to have a nice day."

"Not that you should try that," Cardigan says to me.

"No, that would be a dick move, for sure," Baseball hat guy agrees. "I'm just saying. They're not programed to react to anything outside their designated roles."

"You're going to punch a bot now, aren't you?" Cardigan asks Baseball hat guy.

"No! It would be kind of funny though, right?"

"How much of this is window dressing?" I ask as the doors to the teleporter open.

"Good question," Cardigan says, stepping inside the teleporter with his friend. He turns to face me and, as the door closes, squints ever so slightly, like he's taking a mental picture of me.

When I get back to the house, everyone is gathered in the living room. I'm happy to see them, especially Piper who is laying sideways in an overstuffed armchair with her legs dangling over the armrest.

"I'm telling you," Geoff explains, "I don't remember."

"Well, how do you explain the other night?" Rafael says. "That was next level. Don't tell me you don't know how to dance."

"Leave him alone," Piper says.

"You saw him!" Rafael says, palms up.

"Maybe he was just caught up in the moment," she says

"Hey guys," I say, leaning on the back of the couch. "What are we talking about?"

"Geoff says he can't remember where he learned to dance like he did at the taco party," Theo says.

"How do you forget something like that?!" Rafael says, exasperated.

"I mean, I did go to restoration this morning," Geoff says.

Rafael sits forward in his seat, eyes bulging. "You did what now?"

"They came to my lab this morning and said I'd been working hard and thought I could use a relaxing treatment."

"Way to bury the lead," Theo says.

"Why didn't you tell us that in the first place?" Rafael asks.

"I don't know," Geoff says timidly. "I didn't think it was that big a deal."

"Why would they erase his dancing ability?" Theo asks.

Piper swings her legs toward the front of the chair and sits up. "Because, the jealous overlords are threatened by Geoff's funky fresh dance moves. If they didn't squash the competition, they'd be forced to surrender to his greatness. It's a goddamned boogie-ocracy." She's not even smiling. My god she's amazing.

"Ha. Ha." Rafael says sarcastically. "From now on, if any of you go to restoration, please tell me. They're supposed to keep me in the loop on these things."

"Sorry, Raf," Geoff says regretfully.

"It's okay, just give me a heads up next time."

"I will."

"That's all I ask. Now, before we reboot, is everyone ready for Stevefest next week?"

The mood lifts with the change of subject.

"I entered us into the tug-of-war tournament. I think we have a good chance to win it this year."

"You say that every year," Piper says.

"He has to say that," Theo says.

"No, I really think we can win this! Hugo, are you any good at tug-of-war?"

"How should I know?" I say.

"Good point. Well, it's not just about strength, see? It's all about teamwork."

"Go team," Piper says without the slightest ounce of enthusiasm.

"Me and the guys from the studio are going to be performing," I blurt.

"You are?" Rafael says as his eyebrows reach for the ceiling. "Did you write a song?"

I nod. "I did."

"How does it go?" Theo asks. "Can you play it for us?"

"Oh, I don't know. We're still working on it," I say.

"Is it about us?" Geoff says.

"What? No." I glance at Piper. "Not exactly. It'll be a surprise," I say. Will it ever? I need to talk to Piper—give her some kind of heads up.

"Welp, time to reboot," Rafael says clasping his hands together. Geoff and Theo get up from the couch and move to the dining room table. Piper reaches a hand up for me to help her out of the plush armchair she's sunk back into sideways.

"Hey, Piper," I say as her feet meet the floor.

"Yeah?"

"Do you . . . would you . . . there's something I want to talk to you about."

"Okay?"

"Would you be able to meet me at the park tomorrow, say 4:00?"

Piper glances over at the table where Theo and Geoff are already resting their heads. Rafael is waiting for us. "Yeah. Okay," she says with a shrug.

"Okay," I say. Good. Great. Now what the hell am I going to say?

CHAPTER 18
LIGHT WITCHCRAFT

I OPENED MY EYES. Dr. Majeed was standing at my bedside writing something on his clipboard. "Ah, you're awake," he said. "How do you feel?"

This has been the best night's sleep I've had in a very long time. "I feel good."

"That's wonderful. Any dreams?"

I don't remember anything. "No. I don't think so."

"Good."

"Why is that good?"

"It means the device is functioning as it should."

"Oh . . . good."

"You're an ideal candidate for the sleeper program. Do you remember how to operate the device?"

"Yeah. It's pretty easy."

"All the instructions are in the app. Did you download it yet?"

"The app? No."

"It has everything you need to know in there. You can see your biometric data and there's a direct line to me and your support team if you have any questions."

"Okay."

"Now listen," Dr. Majeed leaned in so close I could smell his sour breath. My head pushed back against the pillow. "It's important that you stick to your bedtime routine. You must be plugged in by 10:00 every night. This is very important. Understand?"

"Plug in before 10:00. Got it."

"Go ahead and get dressed and I'll pack up your console and get it ready to go."

The console packs up into a portable case and only weighs three or four pounds. I'm struck by the simplicity of it. Such a simple device for such a complex task. He handed it to me when I came out of the bathroom fully dressed.

"I'll walk you out," he said. When we got to the lobby, Dr. Majeed shook my hand. "Welcome to Lunatech," he said with a smile. "If you have any questions, you can contact me directly through the app. Information's in the case."

I texted Ava that I was headed home and she replied with a thumbs up. I felt good about all this and I wanted Ava to get behind it, too. I'd pay the deposit with my first paycheck and whatever was left over, I'd put toward a new bed for Ava. She'd been sleeping on the same twin mattress from when she was four years old. If I started putting money away now, I could get her a car when she turns sixteen. Things were going to be so much better now. She'd see.

I picked up a couple of breakfast burritos from this little food truck near the house. Ava and I agreed they had the best grilled breakfast burritos in town. When I got home, another car was in the driveway. I went inside and gently knocked on her bedroom door.

"I'm home. I got you a burrito. I'll leave it on the counter."

"Did you get one for Sydney?" She opened her door and her friend Sydney was sitting on Ava's bed.

"Good morning, Mr. Castillo," Sydney said with a wave.

"Oh, I didn't know you had company," I said to Ava.

"You said I could have a friend over . . . so I didn't have to be all alone while you were gone."

"I did?" I don't remember this conversation, but it's fine. "Well, she can have my burrito. I can get another one. What are you guys up to today?"

"We were just gonna go over our lines. Maybe some light witchcraft. How'd the sleep thing go?"

"Great! I slept *so* good."

"Did you have any crazy dreams?"

"No. Nothing."

"So once you're plugged in, you can't wake up at all?"

"No, it controls my brain waves and keeps me under for eight hours straight."

"What if there's a break-in? Or a fire?" Sydney interjected.

"Oh my god!" Ava exclaimed, covering her mouth.

I never thought of that. "I guess Ava would have to unplug me."

"But what if I'm spending the night at Sydney's?" Ava asked.

"Well, I guess you'll have to cast a fire protection spell on the house before you go," I said, wiggling my fingers at them. The girls were not laughing. Tough crowd. "I'll just leave your food on the counter," I said and shut the door behind me.

I got a text. It was from Darcy.

How about that coffee?

I was going to have to go back out anyway. Why not? I texted back:

Where?

She replied:

Cartel.

My stomach growled. I was pretty sure they served breakfast there. I texted:

See you there!

I knocked on Ava's door again. "Hey Ava, I'm gonna meet
up with a friend for coffee."

She wrenched the door open. "What friend?" She had a
mischievous grin on her face.

"Calm down. Her name's Darcy."

"Ooooh, Mr. Castillo!" Sydney teased. "Did you meet her
on Tinder?"

"No! She's a parent of one of my guitar students. But we're
just friends." Ava was smiling, anticipation in her eyes. "It's
not a date."

"Dad," Ava said. "It's totally fine if it is. I'm cool with it.
For real."

"It's not! I swear. She's not my type."

"What *is* your type, Mr. Castillo?" Sydney said in that flir-
tatious way.

"It's *extremely* specific," I said and looked at Ava. "As in,
one in a million."

"So tragic," Sydney said and flopped backwards on
the bed.

"Obviously, you're never going to find anyone as great as
mom, but you're going to have to lower the bar just a skosh."
She demonstrated with pinched fingers.

"Fine. But we don't have to talk about this right now,

because that's not what this is. It's just coffee. Plus, she's in the sleeper program, too. We were just going to compare notes."

"I bet," Sydney said in a breathy voice and bit her bottom lip. Ava hit her with a pillow.

"Okay, well, I'll see you guys later," I said.

"Have fun," Ava said.

"Not too much fun," Sydney said and Ava swung a pillow at her.

I ordered a pour over coffee and a breakfast burrito with chorizo at the counter and paid before Darcy walked in. She looked different today. She wasn't wearing tight fitting or revealing clothing or caked on makeup. She wore a t-shirt, mom jeans, and a pink baseball cap that said *Aloha*. She looked normal, comfortable —not like she was trying to impress anyone, which was a relief.

I staked out a table by the front window and a barista brought my coffee. I liked this place. It wasn't too crowded and they were playing The Smiths. They were the first band I really fell in love with as an angsty teen. The first band I was in played a punk version of *Please, Please, Please, Let Me Get What I Want*. It was one of our most requested covers at high school parties and local all-ages shows.

Darcy came over and sat across from me, looking demure.

"I like this place," I said.

"I've actually never been here before." She looked nervous. "Listen . . ." She exhales. "I wanted to formally apologize for my behavior last week. I feel so stupid—"

"Stop. There's no need, really. I should thank you, actually."

"Thank me? Why?"

"You left behind that Lunatech brochure. It must have fallen out of your purse. That's how I found out about it—and just at the right time, too."

"What do you mean? Is everything okay?"

"It's my daughter. She has this theater trip to New York over Spring Break. It would mean the world to her if she could go. Well, before this came along, I didn't know how I was going to pay for it."

"I didn't know you had a daughter. That's sweet."

"What about you? I thought you were—" I was going to say rich, but thought better of it.

"Yeah, well, when we got divorced, my ex left me the house so he could pay less alimony and I can't afford to keep it up. I had to let go of the landscaping crew and the pool guy. I had to cut my cleaning lady back to once every *other* week. The house is so filthy—I can't stand it."

"What do you do for work?"

"I haven't worked in over twenty years. I don't have any skills! You know, I maxed out all my credit cards. My aesthetician had to put me on a payment plan. Do you know how embarrassing that is?"

"I don't know what an aesthetician is."

She laughed. It was hard to identify with Darcy's financial struggles when I was living paycheck to paycheck and driving on four bald tires. But I guessed it was all relative. Who was I to judge? The barista brought Darcy her latte and my burrito on a little green plate with a clear plastic container of hot sauce.

"You must think I'm a spoiled brat," she said. "I guess I was. But not anymore. I'm just trying to figure all this out as I go. You get used to a certain lifestyle and one day, it's just ripped out from under you. It's very disorienting. I don't want

Declan to suffer. None of this is his fault. I don't want him to have less just because his dad decided he wanted someone half his age. It's not fair to him."

"I'm sorry," I say. "But maybe he doesn't need things to be exactly the same. Have you thought about selling your house and getting something more affordable?"

"I don't know. He's lived his whole life in that house."

"Have you asked him? Maybe he doesn't care as much as you think he does."

"No, I haven't. I guess it wouldn't hurt to ask. It's not like he ever comes out of his room anyway. He doesn't even use the pool."

"My daughter's the same way. Just comes out for dinner occasionally."

"Declan eats in his room. Sometimes I think he doesn't like me very much."

"I'm sure he does. It's just that age. It's a tough age."

"Yeah." She took a sip of her latte, puckering her mouth so as to leave a minimal amount of lipstick on the cup. "So what did you think of your first sleep cycle?"

"Amazing. I slept so hard."

"Me too! That was the other reason I signed up. I haven't slept a whole night through since I found my husband in bed with that little slut," she said with contempt burning in her eyes. I don't want to linger on that subject.

"What do you think about the whole privacy thing?" I ask.

"I don't love that. But you know, it's not free money, right?" She says with a shrug.

"Right. I figure, my kid's worth it."

"Is she a musician, too?"

"No." I smiled as I thought of all the times I tried to teach her guitar and how uninterested she was. "She's a theater kid."

"I was a theater kid!"

"Really?" I took a bite from the corner of my burrito—good. I opened the clear plastic container of hot sauce and dripped some it into the steaming open end of the burrito.

"I played Emily Web in my high school's production of *Our Town*. I haven't thought about that in a really long time."

"It's crazy how time flies," I said, taking another bite.

"What about you? Do you still play?"

I shook my head and brought my fist to my mouth as I swallowed. "Music? No, not anymore."

"Why not? You have such a great voice."

"Well, thanks. I haven't sung since . . . since my wife passed." It still felt weird saying that out loud.

"Oh my god!" She placed a hand on her chest and applied a look of sympathy, a look that still made me uncomfortable. "I had no idea. I'm so sorry."

"No, it's fine. I just haven't been able to find my voice after that. I can't even really listen to my own songs. It's weird."

"Oh no! Hugo, I really hope you find a way to get passed that. You were so good!"

"Thanks. I don't think I'm ready. Plus, I have to be here for Ava."

"I get it. I just think it's a waste of talent. You can be a good father *and* do what you were obviously born to do."

Literally everyone said this. Of course it was always well-intentioned and meant as a form of encouragement. As if I'd never considered it. I reached for a change of subject. "So how was your first night? Did you dream at all?"

"No. And I always remember my dreams. But I did wake up with a bit of a headache." She touched the side of her head. "Did it give you a headache?"

I shook my head. "No. Is it bad?"

"It's kind of a dull ache—just right here." She pointed to a small area above her right ear. "Nowhere else."

"Did you tell them about it?"

"In the app, it says that headaches are common, but they subside after the first few days. I took some Advil." She sipped her latte. "I wonder what kind of information I gave them last night."

"I'd rather not think about it."

"It's one thing to have access to my online interests and spending habits. It's another to have full access to my entire history—my whole life."

It occurred to me that, not only did they have information about me, but they also knew everything about Ava and Celeste—at least everything I knew about them. They knew how she died. And they knew I was responsible.

When I got home after meeting with Darcy, I set up the console on my bedside table. Within seconds of powering it on and plugging it into my router, a notification dinged on my phone. The app dinged with another notification saying the system was successfully connected to the Internet and ready to use. Easy enough.

"Dad," Ava said coming into my bedroom.

"What's up?"

"Can I stay at Sydney's tonight?"

"Sure," I said before getting a closer look. Her eyes were glassy. I knew it—they'd been smoking.

"Thanks." She quickly turned to leave.

"Wait." She didn't. "Ava. Come here," I said a bit more sternly.

She stopped halfway down the hall. "What?" She remained facing the opposite direction.

I approached and put a hand on her shoulder. "Look at me."

She slowly turned, but her eyes were trained on the floor.

"Ava, have you been smoking?"

"Have you?" This was supposed to be defiant, but fell impotent. She knew she was busted.

"Ava." I gently lifted her chin and she jerked her head from my hand.

"So what if I have? It's not like you don't."

She wasn't wrong to point out my hypocrisy. Who was I to pass moral judgement? I still remembered that drug war campaign slogan from the eighties: *Parents who use drugs have children who use drugs*. I hated that they were right about that.

"Ava, honey, I'm not mad."

"Yeah, right."

"I'm not. I'm—"

"I guess I can't go to Sydney's then?"

Sydney rounded the corner with a backpack slung over one shoulder. "Is everything alright?"

"I can't come over," Ava said with disgust.

"Okay?" Sydney said as she threaded her arm through the second strap of her backpack. "Well, I guess I should go."

"Wait," I said. "Are you high?"

"Excuse me?" Sydney said combatively.

"I'm not going to let you drive if you're high."

"Dad!" Ava protested.

"It's fine." Sydney said with a shrug. "I'm not *that* high."

"No, I'm serious. I can either drive you home or you can stay here."

Sydney made a W with her hands and mouthed *whatever* as

she turned back to Ava's bedroom. Ava gave me an annoyed look and followed Sydney.

"Wait," I said.

But she didn't stop. When she got to her bedroom she slammed the door. I didn't think I handled that very well. I'd never been much of a disciplinarian. Celeste handled that kind of thing. Sometimes she even put me on edge and I wasn't even the one getting in trouble. I'd talk to her later, when she didn't have a friend around to showboat for.

CHAPTER 19
HALL PASS

WHEN I ARRIVE at the studio the next morning, additional musicians have been recruited to our project—a cellist, a three-piece horn section, and backup singers. They're all conversing over the sheet music and making notations. Garret's plucking keys on an electric piano. Vincent is in the booth with Cash. Suki is laying on the floor with one leg crossed over a bent knee, drumming on her shoe.

I'm not sure what I'm supposed to be doing amongst this unstructured lot. Vincent looks up from his sound board and points at me with a big smile. He removes his headphones and comes around to greet me.

"What's all this?" I ask.

"I came up with a few more parts. It's going to sound epic, believe me."

"I believe you."

"Alright, we're gonna to start recording bass and rhythm guitar here in a minute. Then we'll get you in with lead guitar and vocals. Do you need to warm up?"

"Warm up?"

"Your vocal cords. You must have some kind of warm up."

I shake my head. "I don't think so."

"Well, okay!" He seems amused by this. "Let's make some rock and roll."

We spend most the the day recording all the instruments. When it's time to record vocals, Vincent has me step into a soundproof booth in the corner of the studio. I can't see the clock from in here and I'm worried it's getting close to four, when I'm supposed to meet Piper in the park. I'm not sure how I'm supposed to excuse myself from all this. Hopefully, we get this in a couple of takes.

Once Vincent is satisfied, I hang my headphones on a hook and step out of the booth. I look at the clock. Three-thirty. I have time but I need an excuse to leave while everyone else is working so hard. I don't want to seem like a prima donna, like I have better places to be. But I do.

"Hey Vincent, do you mind if I stretch my legs a bit? Get some air? I was feeling a little claustrophobic in that booth." I wasn't, but it feels like a legitimate excuse. It's not like I can ask for a bathroom break. We don't do that here.

"Soon enough, Hugo. But right now I need you to work with these backup singers. For the chorus."

Three women in headphones are patiently waiting at their respective microphones. Sheet music is arranged on music stands in front of them.

"Can't they just go off the tape?" I say inconspicuously so as not to offend.

"No, man. They need to feed off your live energy. Can't do that from a recording."

I don't know if that's true or not, but I have no basis for argument. "Alright. Let's get this done."

It's not a huge part—only a few lines. But Vincent wants to experiment with harmonies. He wants to record both, with the harmony and in unison. This is all unnecessary, in my opinion.

I thought it was fine without any backup vocals at all. But after hearing the playback, I agree, the backup vocals do enrich the sound at crucial moments.

If I'm being honest, these ladies could sing circles around me any day of the week. I make a comment to this effect and Vincent says, "You're probably right, but the lead vocals don't have to be technically better. They just have to be authentic and compelling. Your voice is both of those things. You may not have perfect pitch, but I can fix that in the booth. What I can't manipulate is your soul song."

Soul song? My instinct is to scoff at that, but Vincent isn't joking. He really means it. I look at the clock—4:10. Shit!

"Are we good?" I ask Vincent, failing to appear the least bit composed.

"We're good here. Gonna play with the brass section for a while. Take the rest of the day."

I hope she didn't think I stood her up. If she only knew the reason I was late was because I was recording a song I wrote *for her*.

I hadn't specified where in the park I wanted to meet her. My first stop is the big gazebo in the middle of the park where a bunch of people are leisurely strolling and having casual conversation. None of them are Piper. A couple of women are taking selfies by the bronze statue of Steve Gower and one of them asks me if I wouldn't mind taking their picture. I'm in a hurry but I'm not rude so I take the picture.

"Hugo!"

I turn toward the sound of my name and Piper is sitting on a bench down by the pond. She's waving me over. Be cool, be cool, be cool. Don't run. Walk normal. Am I walking normal?

"Sorry I'm late," I say and sit next to her. "Vincent kept me later than I expected."

"No worries. What did you want to talk to me about?"

This is it. I forget now what I wanted to say. She's looking right at me and I think I've lost the ability to form words. The part of my brain that puts thoughts into words and pushes them out of my mouth is jammed. After an eternity of verbal incompetence, she breaks the silence.

"Oh, kay," Piper says, her eyebrows indicating an awkwardness I have undoubtedly caused. "You said you needed to talk to me?"

"Right. I wanted to . . . to see how you were feeling . . . post-restoration. You seem to be back to normal. Do you feel . . . normal?" I hate myself.

"Do I feel normal?" She laughs. "I guess? Do you feel normal?"

"That was a dumb question. Sorry. What I meant to say is . . . do you still have that feeling? The one you told me about— like there's something wrong here?"

Piper looks out over the pond as if the answer is some- where out there. "I know there is."

"I feel it, too," I say.

Piper shakes her head, still looking out over the water. "Not like I do."

"What do you mean?"

"I'm not like you guys."

"Not like us how?"

Piper shakes her head and snickers. "Never mind. You wouldn't understand."

"Try me."

She looks around, not committing to a single point of focus. "Where do you think you go when you reboot? I mean, do you think the clock just resets itself and you start a new day? Or . . . do you go somewhere else?"

"Go where?"

She's looking at me again and shakes her head. "I don't know. Where do you go?"

I try hard to understand her question. She's not asking me *if* I go somewhere. She's asking where I go when I *do* go there.

"Where do *you* go?" I ask.

"That's just it. I don't go anywhere. That's why I'm a prisoner."

"How do you know?"

"How do I know I don't go anywhere? Because I don't go anywhere. I'm stuck here."

"But how do you know I go somewhere?"

"I don't. I just—"

"Hugo!" It's Darcy. She's striding toward us in her sentinel uniform and she doesn't look too happy. The last time I saw Darcy was at the taco party. This is the first time I've seen her in that ill-fitting uniform. I can't imagine she feels comfortable in that.

"Hey, Darcy," I say in my friendliest tone. "You remember Piper."

She regards Piper with a glare, then turns back to me. "Shouldn't you be at the studio?"

"Oh, well they're done with me for today. Vincent gave me the rest of the day off."

"Do you have a hall pass?" She seems unsure of her own authority.

I look at Piper who raises an eyebrow, then back at Darcy. "A *hall pass*? No. I didn't know I needed one. Vincent didn't say anything about a hall pass. He just said I could leave."

"And what about you?" Darcy glares at Piper. "You've been here long enough to know the rules. Do you have your hall pass?"

Piper scoffs, clearly unintimidated. "Look. You're new

here," she says with an air of condescension. "They haven't enforced that rule in ages."

"I have to issue a write up for each of you," Darcy says pulling out a small tablet.

"Seriously?" Piper protests.

"Did we do something to offend you?" I ask. "I thought we were friends."

"I'm just doing my job, Hugo. I can't show favoritism to anyone."

Piper looks around and gestures toward all the other people milling about. "What about all these people? Are you going to ask for their hall passes, too?"

Darcy ignores the question. "I'm going to let you off with a warning."

I make prayer hands. "Thank you."

Piper mumbles, "Whatever."

"What was that?" Darcy postures and Piper just shakes her head. "I'm warning you, Missy. You're already on high alert with all your *involuntary restorations.*"

"Are you threatening me?" Piper challenges, leaning forward.

Instinctively, I reach my hand in front of Piper to prevent her from getting sent back to restoration again. "Let's just take a beat," I say.

"I see what's happening here," Darcy says.

I look at Piper and then back at Darcy. "What's happening?"

"It's pretty obvious."

"What is?" Piper asks.

"You're into each other," Darcy says matter of factly.

"What?!" My face heats up as I attempt to deny the allegation.

"That's not a crime," Piper says confidently. Does that mean she *is* into me?

"No. It's not a crime, but . . ."

"But what?" Piper challenges. "We haven't broken any rules here so if there isn't anything else you want to harass us about, you can move along now."

Darcy huffs and stomps away in defeat.

"What a bitch," Piper says after Darcy is out of earshot.

"So wait . . . you're into me?" I ask, unable to suppress a grin.

"You wish pod mate."

"I was just kidding," I say trying to cover for making such a bold assumption. She considers me a pod mate. Is that like a brother-sister thing?

"Right," Piper says with unmistakable sarcasm.

"I mean, you didn't deny it."

"I didn't have to deny it because there's nothing illegal about it. And even if it was illegal, I wouldn't let that stop me."

"Have you been in a relationship before?"

"No."

"So you'd be open to—"

"Let me stop you right there cowboy." She's grinning. That's good.

"It's the whole pod mate thing, isn't it? That would be . . . weird?"

Piper laughs. "I mean, maybe. Wouldn't it?"

"I don't know. Maybe." What am I saying? "I mean, why would it have to be weird?"

Piper shrugs and looks off into the distance. I can't tell what she's thinking, but she's thinking. I shouldn't push it. I've said enough. At least the idea is in her head now, if it wasn't there before.

CHAPTER 20
MOTHER MONKEY

WHEN I ARRIVED at the music shop on Monday, Lenny had a worried look on his face. "How's the sleeper thing going?" Lenny asked, probably more from a sense of obligation than genuine interest.

"Sleeping for eight hours straight every night—first time in years," I said, hoping to put a positive spin on it. I knew he wasn't a fan of Lunatech and their sleeper program.

He nodded but didn't reply right away. "I heard some things—about Lunatech."

"What kind of things?"

"There's this subreddit: r/sleepers. There's this guy posting in there saying that Lunatech's putting microchips in people's brains."

"That's crazy. Why would they do that?"

Lenny gives me a condescending glare. He doesn't have to explain. "Have you had any headaches?"

"No." I neglected to mention that Darcy had.

"They said that's a common thing with sleepers after their initial sleep study. That's when they do the implant—while you're unconscious. Let me see." He stepped toward me to examine me closer. When he reached to touch my head, I pushed his hand away.

"What are you doing?" I asked

"Let me see if I can find an incision mark." He tried again and I pulled away. "Come on. Let me look. They said it was above the right ear." He leaned in and brushed the hair above my right ear, which caused me to shiver. I let him search the area with his fingers like a mother monkey. "I don't see anything," he said finally.

"Alright, alright," I said, backing away and scrubbing his touch from the side of my head.

"Well, maybe they don't do it to everyone. I still think it's a shady company."

"It's not shady if they tell you up front what they're doing. I know it sounds sinister, but they've been above board about what they're paying for. Yes, I'm selling them my thoughts and memories. It was my decision. Maybe it wasn't the best decision, but I made it of my own free will." I felt myself getting defensive—heat rising in my face. "Are you going to keep busting my balls about it?"

"I'm just looking out for you, man. I get *why* you're doing this. I just don't want you to be a victim of something you might *not* know about. I mean, who knows what they're *not* telling you? Wouldn't you want to know?"

"No. Not really. Honestly, I just want that extra paycheck each month. I want to finally get my head above water for a change. I don't want to have to worry if I can afford to send my daughter on a school trip or if I can afford new tires when these ones finally blow out."

Lenny conceded with a tired nod. "Alright then. I won't bring it up," he said, showing me his palms. "But if you start having hallucinations, you'd tell me, right?"

"Hallucinations?"

"Yeah, that's another thing the Reddit sleeper said. He called them *dream bleeds*. Initially, he started seeing people in public he thought he recognized but couldn't place them—not too unusual, right? But then they started appearing in places they shouldn't, like sitting in his back seat while he was driving."

"Weird."

"What's even weirder—he said these people didn't look normal. He said they looked like animations, like computer simulations. And sometimes, things in his environment—his houseplants, his phone, his bookshelf—they would take on a computerized appearance, just for a moment and then they'd snap back into real objects. Once it happened with people at his office while he was giving a presentation. He looked up and everyone at the conference table were like full-sized Sims."

"Did they talk like Sims?" I couldn't keep the smirk from my face.

"No, dude. They just looked that way."

"Like this?" I stiffened my body and made jerky robotic movements with my arms and head—I do a pretty good robot, if I do say so.

"Very funny. Yeah, they were all doing the robot," he said sarcastically.

I kept going 'cause once I start doing the robot, I can't stop myself. "Show. Me. Your. Moves," I said in my best robot voice. He was either going to get pissed that I was making fun of him or—

Lenny started in with his own weak-ass robot. We did this for no less than a full minute to no music at all before a customer walked in. She froze when she regarded the two of us. We turned to her, still committed to the bit, waved robotically, and said in unison, "Welcome. In. How. Can. We. Help.

You?"

"Um . . . Do you guys have snare wire? Thirty strand?"

"Yeah," I said in my regular voice, stiffened arms falling naturally to my sides. "Right over here."

"Weak!" Lenny said with a shake of his head, admonishing me for breaking character.

I walked the lip-pierced woman toward the drum hardware. I could tell by the muscular strands in her forearms that she must have been a drummer. Among the multitude of tattoos covering both arms and legs were a pair of crossed drumsticks on the back of her neck.

"Are you in a band?" I asked her.

"How could you tell?"

"I don't know. Lucky guess?"

She compared two different snare wires and then put one back. "We're playing at The Rock tomorrow night. You should come to the show."

"What's the name of your band?"

"Snatch." She glared at me like she anticipated a negative reaction.

I nodded a bit too long before responding. "I like it. What do you sound like?"

"Feminist rage mostly."

"I love that."

"You should come out."

"I just might. What's your name?"

"Suki."

"I'm Hugo," I said reaching out my hand for her to shake. The letters C-U-N-T were tattooed on each finger of her right hand. "So will you be needing anything else?"

"I'll take a pack of 2B's if you have 'em."

I grabbed a ten-pack of drumsticks from the next shelf over. "Will these work?"

"Perfect."

I rung her up at the register and bagged her items. Lenny stood nearby pretending to organize items behind the counter.

"Thanks for coming in," I said.

"Sorry I interrupted your dance party," she said with a smirk.

"Oh don't worry," Lenny said. "We're going to start right back up again as soon as you walk out."

"You should invite your friend," she said to me, still regarding Lenny

"Invite me where?" Lenny asked.

"She has a show tomorrow night at The Rock," I said.

"What kind of music do you play?" Lenny asked.

"Have you heard of Coldplay?"

Lenny furrowed his brows in confusion. "Yeah?"

"The opposite of that."

Lenny sighed in relief. "Then I'm definitely in."

"8:00."

"I'm there," Lenny said confidently. "We'll be there."

"Did you see that?" Lenny asked me after she left the store.

"See what?"

"She was definitely vibing with me! You saw that, right? The way she looked at me when she asked you to invite me?"

"Maybe, yeah."

"I think she wants to fuck me."

I shook my head. "Don't you think you might be reading a bit too much into it?"

"No, dude! Chicks like that plow through random dudes when they're on tour. I could be one of those random dudes!"

"*Chicks* like that? Listen to yourself."

"You know what I mean. Punk rock chicks don't give a fuck. They don't care if you're successful or . . ." Lenny makes air quotes, "marriage material, or whatever. They're not into commitments or conventional relationship shit."

"You don't know that. She could have a boyfriend. She could be dating someone in the band."

"What's the name of her band?"

I hesitate to validate his point. "Snatch."

Lenny slammed an open palm on the counter. "Snatch?! Are you fucking kidding me? Dude, we're definitely going to this show."

I could never understand where Lenny got his confidence. Objectively unattractive, Lenny seemed to have some kind of reverse body dysmorphia. When he got rejected by women, and that happened a lot, he never assumed it was him. Those women must have something wrong with them to pass up such a great catch, he thought. I found myself wanting to protect him from inevitable rejection, but rejection didn't seem to affect him in the least.

The next night I met Lenny at the venue. Snatch was opening for another band I'd never heard of—Bag of Richards, from Idaho.

"Name five bands from Idaho," Lenny said as we stood in line for tickets.

"Well, there's Bag of Richards . . ."

"Obviously."

I hooked a hand behind my neck as I searched my database of music knowledge, and after a while, shook my head. "I don't know. You got me."

"Built to Spill's from Idaho."

"No shit? Who else?"

"That's all I know," Lenny said.

"Okay, well you can't ask for five bands if you only know two."

Lenny paid for my ticket. Granted it was only $20, but that's the kind of thing he does. We made our way into the dank, dimly lit venue and I bought our first round. I'd played here a few times before. It was a decent venue for up and coming bands. It's where I met the guys from Korn—not really my type of music, but super nice guys.

It wasn't a packed show and Lenny insisted on standing right in front of the stage—front and center. He cheered wildly when the band took the stage a half hour later than expected, spilling some of his beer on my shoe.

The lead singer was a black-haired waif in a leather bra and shorts, torn fishnets, and tall Dr. Martins. A shark tattooed on her ribcage lunged, open-mouthed toward her left breast. She had a soft, youthful face that I'm sure her mother would lament its being pierced at least six times—through the septum, labret, lips, and eyebrows. She stomped onto the stage and slung a pearl white Jaguar over her neck, ignoring the audience as she tuned up.

The bass player, a red-bearded lumberjack of a man who wore a loose-fitting pink thrift store house dress, flirted with the crowd by pulling one of his sleeves down, exposing a hairy, freckled shoulder. Someone in the crowd, possibly drunk already, shouted, "Does the carpet match the drapes?" The bassist responded by lifting the front of his dress, exposing himself to an unusually feisty Tuesday night crowd.

Suki was the last to appear on stage wearing knee-length basketball shorts and a tank top, exposing inked tapestries covering both arms and neck. She thumped the bass drum a few times and tightened the wing nut on her crash cymbal. Lenny was mesmerized. I could tell he was using his Jedi mind powers to will her to look his way. He falls for any woman who pays him the slightest bit of attention. It's a sickness, really.

The lead singer stepped up to her microphone and introduced the band in a confrontational tone, "We're Snatch." Scattered applause came from the already sparse gathering. Some stood motionless, unfairly challenging this unknown band to deliver a stadium worthy performance. "This first song," the singer said, "is particularly fitting for this evening's festivities. It's called . . . 'Taco Tuesday.'"

Suki shouted and she clicked her sticks together, "One-Two-Three-Four!"

The sonic assault that followed felt akin to being jumped by an angry little league team with wiffle ball bats—and I fucking loved it. Every spittle-filled accusation that spewed from this tiny pierced vocalist felt well-deserved. I was enamored with her passion, which I was not expecting.

I was also not expecting the expert level of Suki's drumming. The songs weren't complicated—almost exclusively executed with gritty power chords. But Suki elevated their sound with the precision of a true virtuoso.

When they finished their forty minute set, I felt as though I had just finished a workout. I pulled out my phone to check the time—9:15. I had to be home before 10:00 to plug in. Of course, Lenny wanted me to stay—to be his wingman.

"I can't. Also, I need to check in with Ava before she goes to bed." I added the thing about Ava, knowing he couldn't argue with that, and he didn't.

Snatch didn't have roadies, so Suki had to break down her own drums before the next act could set up theirs. "Hey, you should go up there and help her break down her kit," I suggested.

"You think so?"

"Yeah. It would be a great way to let her know you came and also that you're a super helpful kind of guy."

"I *am* a super helpful kind of guy!"

"I know you are!"

"Alright. Alright," he said nodding to pump himself up. "I'm gonna do it."

"Do it!"

"Okay. I'm going."

"Go!"

Lenny let out a deep breath. "Here I go." He hopped up onto the stage and I silently wished him luck. He was going to need it.

When I got home, I did check in on Ava. She was finishing up some homework. I couldn't tell if I smelled weed in her room or if it was on my clothes from the venue. It was something I'd been meaning to talk to her about but it never felt like the right time. I decided this was also not the right time.

"How was the show?" Ava asked.

"Not bad, actually."

"Who'd you see?"

A little embarrassed, I hesitated to tell her the name of the band. What if she wanted an explanation? "Bag of Richards," I said, even though I hadn't stayed to see the Idaho-based headliner. I was hoping the euphemism would go over her head.

She laughed. "Ha! Like bag of *dicks*!" She laughed some more, covering her mouth. I was always underestimating the level of adult humor she was capable of understanding.

"Yeah. So anyway, I should get ready for bed. Almost time to plug in."

"That'll never stop being weird to me," she said.

"I'm like a robot that needs to be recharged every night." And then I did it—I did the robot.

"Don't," she said and threw a stuffed Piglet at me. I swear, anybody else her age would be impressed—not Ava.

An alert chimed on my phone. It was from the Lunatech app, notifying me that it was time to wind down. The app provided a wind down routine, which included turning off all screens, going to the bathroom, and listening to an assortment of sounds and music that were proven to help lull a person to sleep. It all seemed unnecessary since the apparatus alone was responsible for initiating the sleep state.

I did go to the bathroom. That was the only pertinent instruction, especially after downing four beers in less than two hours. I brushed my teeth and settled into bed. I donned my electrode cap and engaged the calibration. Seconds after hitting the blinking green button, I was off to dreamland.

CHAPTER 21
DICKLESS

WE NEVER HAD a chance to finish that conversation in the park. Initially, I'd wanted to warn her about the song, but I had the impression she could tell I had feelings for her so it shouldn't come as a total surprise. I still don't know how she feels about me though, and that's killing me.

It's the day of the festival and Rafael wastes no time with morning rounds. He's handing out green t-shirts with "Pod 54" printed across the front and each of our names on the back. We are to wear these for the tug-of-war tournament, he explains.

"I'm not wearing this," Piper says flatly and tosses it back to Rafael.

"Piper, where's your team spirit? I had these special ordered."

"Come on, Pipe," Theo pleads. "It's just for the tournament."

"Ugh, fine," Piper huffs. "Give it here."

Rafael happily tosses it back. "Now, does everyone remember our cheer?"

Piper's eyes roll so hard at this.

Rafael leads the chant. "Heave, ho, Pod Fifty—Fo—come on guys! It sounds silly if I'm the only one doing the cheer." He starts again and the rest of us mumble along. "Heave, ho, Pod Fifty-Four. Dig in deep, we want it more! Heave, ho, we're here to win. Tug that rope, let's reel them in!" He shakes his head in disappointment. "A little more enthusiasm when we get out there, alright guys?"

Unsurprisingly, we're knocked out in the very first match. Pod forty-one outweighed us by at least three hundred pounds. Piper immediately tosses her t-shirt in the nearest garbage barrel.

"We'll get 'em next year," Rafael says cheerily. "Let's meet back at the stage in a half hour. Hugo got us VIP seats right up front!"

"Gee, thanks, Hugo," Geoff says.

"Of course," I say. Truth be told, it wasn't my idea. Vincent suggested it and sent Rafael the tickets before I could say anything. But what could I have possibly said? Pod 54 was going to get a front row seat to my inevitable humiliation.

"Funnel cake?" Piper says, catching me off guard.

"Huh?"

"Want to get a funnel cake?"

"Sure," I say and follow her to a nearby food cart.

"Two funnel cakes," she tells the vendor who smiles brightly and procures the powdered sugar confections on paper plates.

"Did you know he's a bot," I whisper as she hands me a funnel cake.

"Duh," she says.

"Oh, you know about the bots?"

"Hello? I helped program them."

"Really?"

"Mm-hm," she says taking a bite of her cake. Powdered sugar lines the corners of her mouth as she chews.

"Does everybody know about the bots?"

"I mean, it's pretty obvious if you talk to them for more than five seconds. Watch." Piper turns to the funnel cake vendor who greets her again as if she hadn't just ordered. "How do you feel about the complete lack of weather variation here in Slumbervale?"

The vendor's smile remains plastered across his face. "What can I get for you today, miss?"

She turns back to me. "See?"

"That's wild. Let me try." I approach the vendor and clear my throat. "Can I ask you something? Have you ever seen a baby?"

He stares blankly at me with that unwavering smile. "What can I get for you today, sir?"

"Woah. That's weird," I say turning to Piper.

"What's a baby?" she asks through a mouthful of funnel cake.

"Nevermind."

We take a circuitous route through a labyrinth of vendor booths, back toward the main stage. There are hundreds of people in attendance. Two women walk by licking frozen confections in the shape of Steve Gower's face.

I can see the stage from here and some people have already staked out their spot on the lawn with blankets or camping chairs. There's a crew on stage setting up Suki's drum kit and taping down cables. A bald guy is testing the mics, using hand gestures to communicate with the sound engineers.

The weather is perfect for an outdoor show. I hadn't thought about it before—what Piper asked of the funnel cake bot. The weather doesn't change. Everyday has been exactly the same—clear skies, sunny, and mild. I guess you don't take notice of weather when it's always perfect.

"That's interesting what you said about the lack of weather variation," I say.

"That's another thing we do up at Central," she explains.

"You control the weather?"

"We used to have storms, but too many people complained so we just keep it at this setting permanently."

"Setting?"

"Yeah."

"So weather doesn't occur naturally like . . ." I'm trying to remember something I thought I knew but can't remember where I might have learned it. " . . . like something with the atmosphere."

She's looking at me like I have pickles for eyebrows. "No. It's part of Slumbervale's municipal maintenance program, like the sun."

"Excuse me? Central controls the sun?"

"You know how in the morning, it starts low and moves directly overhead at exactly four and then keeps moving in the same direction until it's low again on the other side of the sky as it gets close to 8:00?"

"Yeah, because the earth turns on its ax—"

"No. The sun is a light that moves across the sky in an arc according to its programming. They could program it to stay in one place if they wanted. They could program it to look like a giant mushroom if they wanted."

"That would be cool," I say deciding it's not worth the argument.

"I could make that happen, you know?" She grins.

"You should."

She releases a single sound from her throat, something between a chuckle and a hum. "Makes you wonder though."

"Wonder what?"

"Like what's real and what isn't." She looks me in the eyes when she says this.

"Are you real?" I say this half-joking, but she doesn't laugh.

"I feel real. I'm more real that that bot over there." She points to the nearest hot dog vendor. "If you ask him if he's real, he'll just keep repeating 'What can I get you?' He can't think like we can. So maybe there are levels of what's real. Like I'm more real than a bot, but less real than—."

"Than what?"

"I don't know. Everyone else?" She stares at nothing, retreating into herself.

I jut my head in line with her stare. "Pipe? You okay?"

She snaps out of it and smiles, artificially. "Yep."

"You were getting kind of existential there."

"Sorry."

"No, no. It's fine. I know what you mean, trust me. I've been feeling that way ever since I got here."

Her eyes dart left to right as she searches my own.

"What is it?" I ask.

"I don't know. Something in your eyes." She shakes her head and takes a step back, looks away. She turns back and asks, "Are you nervous?"

"A little." If only she knew why. "Listen," I say, turning to face her. I want to prepare her, to provide some context for what she is about to hear that might serve as a kind of disclaimer in the event she is utterly appalled.

"Hugo!" Cash slaps me on the back and I lose my train of thought. "Come on now, son. We're about to start sound check."

"I'll be right there." I turn back to Piper again as he ambles toward the trailer. "I need to tell you something."

"Yes?" Her eyes lock onto mine and I forget what I'm about to say. Breath catches in my throat and she places a hand on my shoulder. "Are you okay?"

"Yeah. Yeah, I'm good. It's just . . ."

"You're going to be great," she says. "If you get nervous just look at me. I'll be on the front row."

"I'm not nervous about playing," I say. "It's just that—"

"Hugo," Vincent calls hanging halfway out of the trailer. "Time for sound check."

"You have to go," Piper says. "Good luck!"

"Thanks," I say. Vincent is waving me over. "I'll see you after the show."

"Break a leg!"

From backstage, the crowd is on their feet. Some are dancing to an EDM version of Johnny Cash's "Ring of Fire" pumping through the house speakers. An oversized beach ball is being volleyed among the concert goers. It bounces off a stage monitor and back into the crowd again. Geoff, on the front row with the rest of Pod Fifty-Four, gets a hand on it. Rafael, as always, is bursting with enthusiasm. Piper looks happy. I hope she stays that way after hearing her song.

"You feeling okay, Hugo?" Garret asks.

"Yeah. I'm good."

"The set list is taped to the center monitor. After they announce us, the rest of us will go on first. Wait about thirty seconds to let the crowd built some anticipation and then you walk on."

"Okay."

"You sure you're okay?"

I nod. The music dies down and the MC walks out onto the stage, waving at the cheering crowd with both hands. "Hello Stevefest! Is everybody enjoying themselves today?" The crowd responds with ferocious enthusiasm. "We have a special musical treat for you this year—one of the most talented voices Slumbervale has seen in a very long time. Give it up for Hugo and the Dreamers!" The crowd erupts with applause.

A stage tech with a headset nods and gestures for the band to get on stage. Garret leads the way, followed by Cash, Suki, a keyboardist, the backup singers, and a three-piece horn section. I start to make my way onto the stage when the stage tech places a hand on my chest. "Not yet," he says. The crowd starts chanting, "Hugo! Hugo! Hugo!" Piper, too, pumping her fist in unison with the rhythm of the chants. The stage tech nods and pats me on the back. "Now!"

I take a deep breath. Here goes nothing. When I walk onto the stage, the crowd, who has never heard me play before in their lives, goes crazy. I take my guitar from the stand, a 1976 Les Paul gold top, and pull it over my head. I take a pick from the mic stand and look over at Garrett who gestures with his head toward the crowd. I think he wants me to say something. I look down at the front row and Rafael is losing his fucking mind. Piper is clapping and looking at me with anticipation, smiling.

I lean into the mic and say, "Hello." The crowd erupts again. "It's good to be in Slumbervale!" I don't know why I say that. Where else would I be? But the crowd eats it up. The clicking of Suki's drumsticks counts us in and the music takes over.

I can't look at her—I can't. If she looks angry or disgusted, I don't think I could go on. But when we break into the final chorus my gaze sweeps across the crowd and I see Piper standing completely still with both hands on her chest. She knows.

The rest of the show goes on without a hitch. Piper doesn't take her eyes off me the entire set and I know I've won her over. Every song is for her in my mind, even the ones that don't have anything to do with love. I play them for her.

When we finish the show, Piper is waiting for me backstage. I'm not sure how to start this conversation, which is fine because before I can say anything, she pulls me into a kiss. It's the best thing that's ever happened to me. When our lips part, she says, "You have some explaining to do." She looks around, presumably for a less public environment. Without a word, she takes me by the hand into the trailer parked behind the stage and locks the door when we get inside.

"Why didn't you say anything?" Piper asks.

I shake my head. "I didn't think you felt the same way. Plus, you said that thing about being pod mates."

"Pshhh! So? Didn't know you were such a rule follower," she says, grinning.

"I'm not."

"Well?" Her eyes drop to my lips. "Show me." Piper presses her body into mine and her playful expression melts into one of desire.

I kiss her again, harder. Placing my hands around her waist, I pull her closer. She moans gently as our kiss intensifies. I kiss her neck and she lets out a heavy breath. I feel her hands at the front of my pants, pulling the belt from its buckle. She slides down to her knees and looks up at me with a hunger we both share.

She tugs my fly open and pulls down on my jeans.

"Oh my god!" Piper cries. She slaps a hand over her open mouth. She stands abruptly and backs away.

"What? What's wrong?"

Her head shakes rapidly from side to side, too horrified to speak. She backs herself into a table, knocking over an empty beer bottle that rolls onto the floor.

I look down at myself and cry out. "What the fuck!" I yank

my pants down over a flat patch of flesh where my dick should be. "Where's my dick?!"

"You didn't know?!" Piper squeals.

"No, I didn't know! What the actual *fuck*?!"

Now that I think about it, I've never actually seen myself naked. I've never gone to the bathroom. I've never even changed my clothes or had a shower. But I've never had any reason to suspect I might not be anatomically incomplete. Are we all dickless, or is it just me?

CHAPTER 22
FRESH SQUEEZED

"GOOD MORNING, HUGO," said the voice from the console on my nightstand. The last thing I remembered when I opened my eyes Wednesday morning was hitting that blinking green button the night before. It was a strange feeling to awaken so abruptly. There were no lingering nocturnal thoughts coaxing me toward consciousness. One second, I was dead to the world and the next, I was fully awake.

I laid there for another couple minutes and realized there was no need to remain in bed. I wasn't tired or groggy. I removed the electrode cap, hung it on the corner of the head-board, and sprung from my bed. Normally, I'd stay in bed until I absolutely had to get up. Now I had an extra two hours —to do what? Ava would still be sleeping. I decided to make breakfast for the two of us.

"What are you doing?" Ava said, half yawning. She was standing in the kitchen doorway rubbing sleep from her eyes. She was wearing my Modest Mouse concert t-shirt that ended up in her laundry basket one day and decided it was hers now.

"I'm making breakfast," I said, flipping a strip of bacon. "I hope you're hungry."

"Are you going to be up this early every morning now?"

"Probably." It was 6:15. I wouldn't say that's extremely early for most people, just teenagers and insomniacs like myself. "How do you want your eggs?"

She didn't answer, but made a face somewhere between disgust and indifference. That was fine. I only knew how to make scrambled anyway.

I attempted to make fresh squeezed juice, but the four oranges I had only yielded a few ounces.

"What's this?" Ava asked.

"Juice—fresh squeezed," I added the last part in an effort to redeem what looked like a paltry amount given the large plastic tumbler I'd poured it in.

"There's seeds in it," she said, inspecting the contents of her cup. I thought I had gotten them all.

"So what's your day looking like," I said, trying to distract her from the juice debacle. I scooped large portions of scrambled eggs onto her plate, hoping to make up for the lack of juice. I think I might have made too many eggs—a comical amount now that I see them on her plate.

"Stop! That's enough," she said holding a hand over her plate. She seemed more annoyed than amused. "Did you use the whole carton?"

"Not the *whole* carton," I mumbled.

"Why are you being weird?"

"I'm not being weird. I just wanted to make sure you got a good breakfast for once." This came out louder than I intended. Heat rose into my face. Why can't she just be grateful? Why does she always have to be so hostile when all I want to do is feed her?

"I'm just not a huge breakfast person," she said, and then added, "Sorry."

The toaster popped up two slices of whole wheat, breaking the tension. "Do you want toast?" I asked.

"Sure," Ava said solemnly. She didn't want it. She only said it for my benefit.

When I arrived to work, I asked Lenny how it went last night with Suki.

"You're not going to believe this," he said.

"Let me guess. You *didn't* get laid."

"No. I mean, yes, I didn't get laid. But do you want to know why?"

"Do you really want me to answer that?"

Lenny ignored the playful insult and continued. "So I helped her break down her kit and get it into the van, right? That was a great suggestion by the way."

"You're welcome."

"And then I asked her if she was gonna stay for the headliner and she said she couldn't. So we talked for a while in the alley and shared a joint. Turns out they're from Temecula and they're only playing with Bag of Richards another couple of shows because the original openers got COVID and couldn't finish the tour. Then they're starting another tour in February with Mustard Plug."

"The ska band?"

"Yeah. Then she asked me if I had a car and if I could take her back to her hotel and I'm like—fuck yeah. So we get to the hotel—it's close to 10:00 by now—and when I get out of the car she's like, where do you think you're going? And I just stand there, speechless with a goddamned semi-chub. She must've thought it was funny that she had me stumped because she laughed and punched me in the shoulder. She said, 'First of all, fuck you for thinking I'd sleep with you an hour after meeting you, and second of all, I have to be in bed by ten because,' get this, 'I'm in this sleep program.' And I said, 'You mean Lunatech?' And she said, 'Yeah, how'd you know?' And I told her about you and how I heard they were implanting chips in sleeper's brains."

"You didn't," I said.

"It gets worse. So then I asked if I could see if I could find a scar on her head and she said if I touched one hair on her head she would shove her drumsticks so far up my ass she could play a drum solo on my internal organs."

"That tracks."

The door chimed and Darcy was holding the door open for Declan who shuffled in with his guitar case.

"Hey, buddy," I said.

"Hey," he barely grunted.

"Hey, Darcy."

"Hi there," she said. It wasn't weird. I was happy to see her.

"How's the sleep?"

"Good. *So* good."

"Same."

Declan was staring at the both of us, as if trying to detect any remnant of his mother's former misplaced desire.

"Ready?" I asked him.

"Yeah," he said, as if he was resigned to pretty much anything by now. I followed him back to the practice room.

"You been practicing?"

"Some," he said with a shrug.

"Okay, you want to show me?"

He unlatched his guitar case and placed the guitar on his

lap. He hesitated a moment and then said, "What's going on with you and my mom?"

"Nothing! We're just friends. You know we're both in that sleeper program, right?"

"Yeah, she told me."

"That's all it is."

"Are you sure?"

"Yeah, totally. Just friends. Swear to god. I would never date a student, or their parent."

"I know." He hung his head. "It's just that . . . see, my mom talks in her sleep."

"Okay."

"Last night, I could hear her from my room so I went in there and I heard her say your name. But like, not in a good way."

"What do you mean?"

"She was like super mad at you? She called you an asshole."

"Me?"

"And she also mentioned someone named Piper. She said something about not letting her get away with this, she was going to make her pay. I don't know—it was garbled. But she was super mad. I've heard her talk in her sleep before—about my dad. I wanted to wake her up. I tried, but she wouldn't wake up. I was really scared."

"Oh, buddy. I'm sorry. I'm sure it was nothing. People have all kinds of weird dreams. It doesn't mean anything."

"Yeah, I don't know. You should have seen how upset she was. And I couldn't wake her up and I didn't want to mess with that machine. This morning she was totally fine. I asked her what she was dreaming about and she had no idea."

"It's okay. She seems fine today, right?"

"Yeah, I guess so."

"Okay then. Nothing to worry about."

"Okay."

We got through the lesson. He hadn't made that much progress, but it takes time. It takes persistence. I'm not sure how committed he really is. But I want him to catch the bug. I don't know how to do that for him. You either have a passion for it or you don't. Then again, he's going through a lot. I'm sure guitar isn't the most important thing in his life right now with everything that's been going on with his family.

When we came back into the store area after his lesson, Darcy was leaning her elbows on the counter while Lenny inspected her head.

"Mom?" Declan said. "What are you doing?"

Darcy stood abruptly and laughed nervously. Lenny stood back, crossed his arms, and looked to the floor.

"Oh, Lenny, you didn't," I said admonishingly.

"She said she'd been having headaches," Lenny countered defensively.

"What's going on?" Declan asked. "Why was he looking in your ear?"

"He wasn't, honey. He was looking . . . above my ear . . . for . . ." Darcy looked to Lenny.

"A scar," Lenny said.

I shook my head in disapproval.

"What kind of scar?" Declan asked, looking to his mother to provide the answer.

"Well, honey, when I went in for that sleep study, remember?"

"Yeah."

"Well, they may have put something in mommy's head."

"What?"

"A microchip," Lenny said.

"What for?" Declan asked.

"Some people are saying that Lunatech is tracking sleepers while they're awake as well as while they're sleeping," Lenny said.

"Why?" Declan asked.

"They're not," I said. "This is a conspiracy theory our friend here saw on the internet. It hasn't been proven."

"Yet," Lenny said.

"That's enough," I said sternly. There was no need to involve the kid who is already freaking out about his mother's sleep talking and trying to cope with his parents' recent divorce.

"Except he did find a scar," Darcy said.

"He did?" I asked, surprised.

Darcy pulled her hair back so that I could take a closer look. I looked at Lenny who nodded twice. I peered carefully at the side of Darcy's head above her right ear. Lenny turned on his phone's flashlight and pointed it directly at the area in question.

"I don't see anything," I said.

"See that mole?" Lenny said. "Just a fraction of an inch below that and to the left."

I see the brown mole. I get even closer and I can smell notes of citrus from Darcy's shampoo. A small crease is visible, smaller than a wrinkle, almost imperceptible. "That?"

"Do you see it now?" Lenny asked.

"Let me see," Declan said, standing on his tippy toes.

"That could be anything," I said. "It could just be a tiny wrinkle."

"Hey!" Darcy chided, apparently offended by the possibility of having signs of aging where she might have never noticed.

"People don't get wrinkles above their ears," Lenny said in her defense.

"I see it!" Declan shouts.

Lenny snapped a flash photo with his phone and then zoomed in so we could see it magnified on his phone's screen. Human skin isn't very flattering up close. But there it was, cutting directly through a webwork of natural creases in a straight line that didn't belong, slightly pink on either side.

"Can you feel anything there?" I asked her.

She reached her hand to her head. "No. I don't feel anything."

"Are you still getting the headaches?"

"Not anymore. They went away after a couple of days."

"Do you believe me now?" Lenny asked.

"I mean, I don't know if that proves anything," I said.

"No, but it's a pretty big fucking coincidence," Lenny said and then realized a chid was present. "Sorry."

"So what do we do now?" Darcy asked. "How do we prove it's in there?"

"My buddy Ernie's a radiology tech at TMC," Lenny said. "He could do an MRI."

"That goes against our contract," I said. "I remember specifically reading that in the disclosures. As long as we're in the program, any brain-related scans or procedures have to be conducted at Lunatech by Lunatech personnel."

"Oh, well isn't that convenient?" Lenny said with aggressive sarcasm.

"How would they know?" Darcy asked.

"Exactly." Lenny pointed at her. "I can see if he can get you in this week between his regular appointments or after hours maybe."

"Couldn't he get in a lot of trouble for that," I asked.

"It's worth the risk," Lenny said.

If it turned out Lunatech was implanting microchips in the brains of its participants, that would be the end of the sleeper program. Lunatech would get shut down and I would lose that extra paycheck. I would lose my only chance at sending Ava to New York, and my only chance to get ahead financially. I realized how selfish that sounded so I didn't say it out loud.

CHAPTER 23
STAB ME

I'M STARTLED by someone trying to open the locked trailer door and I realize my pants are still pooled around my ankles.

"Just a second," I call out, hastily pulling my pants up. Piper is adjusting her shirt and smoothing her hair when I open the door. It's Vincent.

"Oh, sorry," he says, averting his eyes as if there was anything to see. "I can come back."

"No, no. We were just headed out."

Vincent gives Piper a courteous smile as she steps down from the trailer and then turns to me. "Great show, Hugo."

"Thanks."

"Some of us are getting together at the studio for a little after party. You have to come. Bring your friend," he says with a wink. I could have done without that wink.

"Yeah, sure." I'm really not in the mood for a party. I just know I'm going to be wondering if everyone in the room is a eunuch.

Piper and I walk in silence for a while before I ask, "Do you want to come to this party with me?"

Piper pulls a strand of hair behind her ear and crosses her

arms, almost as if she doesn't know what else to do with them. "Um . . . I think I'm just gonna . . . I have to . . ."

"Oh," I say. I get it now. My face feels like a heat lamp. "Uh . . ."

"Yeah, I'll just . . . see you at the house?"

"Yeah. Okay."

Piper forces a fraction of a smile, turns and quickly walks away. I've never felt so humiliated, although I can't really blame her. Whatever passion she felt prior to the tragic unveiling was predicated on the assumption that I had all the necessary parts to satisfy her. I don't want to go to this party, but since Piper doesn't want to have anything to do with me, I have nowhere else to be.

Music is blaring from the studio when I arrive. Everyone seems ecstatic to see me. Someone puts a champagne flute in my hand and I find myself surrounded by people I haven't even met, industry people presumably.

"Give him space," Garret says, putting a hand on my back. "Ya'll are acting like you've never seen a rock star before," he jokes. He guides me toward a sitting area where Cash is pouring shots. Suki hands me one.

"What is it?" I ask, examining the amber liquid.

"Does it matter?" Suki says.

"Can't get drunk in Level Six," Cash explains. "It's symbolic." He raises the shot glass and says, "To Steve!"

"To Steve!" everyone else calls back—everyone but me.

I wish I could get drunk. If ever there was a time to get drunk, this would be the perfect occasion. I can't stop thinking about what's not in my pants right now. I don't know who I can even talk to about this. Are we all like this? Is it common knowledge or—"

"Hugo!"

I must have been spacing out.

"Hugo, you alright man?" Garrett asks, eyebrows furrowed with concern.

"I'm actually not feeling so good. I think I'm gonna head out."

"You just got here!"

"Boo!" Suki teases.

"I know. Sorry." I hand Garrett the shot I didn't drink. "Sorry guys. I have to go." I stumble past party guests on my way to the door. It's still early and festival goers are milling around the downtown plaza. A few people recognize me from the show and wave, but I pretend not to notice. I can't deal with any attention right now. I stride to the nearest teleporter and go home.

I'm not prepared for what I see when I walk through the door to our house. Theo and Geoff are standing in front of Piper with their hands down their pants. Their heads snap toward me when I walk in. They simultaneously whip their hands from their pants and stand at attention.

"What's going on?" I ask hesitantly, not entirely certain I want to know.

"Nothing," Theo says unconvincingly.

"Piper?" I ask.

"Fine! I had to know if everyone was like this or if it was . . . just us."

"Us?" I ask. "You're also . . ."

Her eyes find the floor. "Yeah."

"You too?" I ask the guys, who nod solemnly. "You guys didn't know?"

"I never had any reason to check," Geoff says. "I just assumed it was down there."

"But for what purpose?" Theo asks, pontificating. "They would just be . . . ornamental—useless, right?"

"I wouldn't say *useless*," I say glancing at Piper, who makes eye contact only briefly before blushing and looking away.

"How did you find out?" Theo asks me.

"Uh . . ." I look to Piper who is now staring at the ceiling, probably willing herself to disappear. "I was—"

The front door opens. It's Rafael.

"You guys are home early," Rafael says. "What did I miss?" Nobody speaks for an impossibly long time. Rafael's smile fades. "Well?"

"We don't have penises," Geoff finally volunteers.

"Excuse me?" Rafael says.

"Peni—"

"I heard you the first time, Geoff," Rafael says, a bite in his tone. He takes a breath to speak and then holds the words back, rethinking his response. "Look . . ."

"You knew?" I ask.

"Well, sure."

"When were you going to tell us?" Theo asks.

"Well . . ." Rafael seems to be grappling for the right words. "There's just never really a good time to tell someone they don't have a penis." A long pause follows. "Besides, there's really no purpose. I mean, imagine trying to get any work done at all. Every other person in Level Five has a penis and they're a hot mess down there! Trust me, you're better off without it. This way you can focus solely on your true purpose."

Piper's eyes roll. Geoff sits down and rests his enormous head in his enormous hands.

"You okay, man?" I ask. I know exactly how he feels, but I've had more time to process this anatomical nightmare.

He slowly shakes his head.

"What's wrong?" Piper asks, placing a hand on Geoff's shoulder.

"It's Felicia," he says. "I was planning to ask her out . . . on a date."

"And you were planning to do sex with her," Theo surmises.

"*Do* sex?" Rafael says. "That's not how you say it."

"How do you say it?" Theo asks.

"It's *have* sex," Rafael says. "And we don't do that here. We *can't!*"

"Clearly," Piper snaps.

"Geoff," Rafael says. "You know we don't engage in romantic pursuits in Level Six. It distracts from our true purpose."

"I'm so sick of hearing about our true purpose!" Piper shouts. "I don't see why Geoff can't pursue his true purpose *and* do sex."

"Again," Rafael clarifies, "it's *have* sex."

"Whatever. It's not fair!"

"Hey, I'm not the bad guy here," Rafael says. "I didn't make us like this!"

"Who did?" I ask.

Everyone looks at Rafael who remains frozen in place. He doesn't even attempt to reply.

"What does the Book say?" Theo asks and when Rafael doesn't answer, walks to the mantle to retrieve the house copy. He flips through the pages. "Here it is. *You and Your Body*." He mumbles to himself as he skims the through pages. "Ah! Here we go." Theo adjusts his glasses. "Your body is anatomically sufficient for carrying out your true purpose. Body parts responsible for certain functions in Level Five, such as digestion, respiration, circulation, *reproduction*, etc. are absent from your body in Level Six. The only part that truly matters is the mind."

"Sex isn't *just* for reproduction," Piper says.

"Wait," I say. "We don't have circulation either? We don't have *blood*?"

Piper's eyes widen and she bolts into the kitchen. When she returns, she's holding a gleaming chef's knife.

"Whoa!" Rafael raises his hands to discourage her from approaching. "What are you doing, Pipe?"

Piper extends her left arm and places the blade across her forearm. Her eyes are wild.

"Piper, give me the knife," Rafael pleads.

Before he can talk her out of it, Piper drags the knife slowly, deliberately, across the meaty section of her forearm. The blade slices through her perfect flesh without producing a single drop of blood.

Everyone, including Rafael, leans in with their eyes trained on the dry laceration the blade has just created across Piper's arm. Within seconds, the gash pulls together and seals itself without any trace of a scar.

"We're indestructible," Theo muses.

"Let me try," Geoff says. He holds out his hand and Piper places the knife in his grip. Geoff raises his left arm, his fingers closed into a fist. His widened eyes dart back and forth from his hand to the knife. He places the silver blade against the back of his hand and drags it slowly across, examining the creation of a deep flesh-colored slit. He delights at the miraculous self-repair that immediately ensues.

Theo lifts his shirt revealing a bulging abdomen hanging over the waistband of his pants. "Stab me!"

"No, no, no!" Rafael protests. "This is getting out of hand!" He moves toward Geoff, but before he can retrieve the knife, Geoff plunges it into Theo's gelatinous paunch.

Theo squeals with glee and removes the knife from his gut. "Hugo, do you want a turn?"

"Guys!" Rafael shouts. "Stop it! This is madness! Give me

that kni—" Another knife, from out of nowhere, lodges itself deep into Rafael's right eye and he stumbles back a step.

I turn to see an amused Piper, who had apparently just chucked a paring knife at Rafael's head.

"Not cool," Rafael says, dislodging the knife from his eye socket. He blinks away the bloodless stab wound. "For Steve's sake, can everyone please stop stabbing each other for one minute? You guys, this is bad. We can't let this get out. We can't have all of Slumbervale stabbing each other for fun!"

"We never get to do anything fun," Piper pouts, crossing her arms.

"Wha—that's not true!" Rafael counters. "What about Stevefest? That was fun. Wasn't it fun watching Hugo play?"

"You did play very well," Geoff says.

"Thanks, bud."

"Look," Rafael says. "You guys have to promise. Promise you won't tell anybody about how we don't bleed. If this gets out . . . we could be in serious trouble."

"With who?" I ask. "How is it a crime if nobody gets hurt?"

"That's not the point," Rafael says, exasperated. "If people realize they're—"

"If people realize they're *indestructible*," Piper interrupts, "why would they bother going to work? If you can't be hurt, you can't be controlled. Is that it?"

"Piper," Rafael says with a sigh. "Not everything is a ding-dang conspiracy."

"She's right, though," I say. "Isn't she?"

"You guys," Theo interjects, looking up at the clock. "It's almost eight."

"To be continued," Rafael says and holds out his hand for Theo to give him the knife he's still holding like a little boy with an action figure.

"But Hugo never got a turn," Theo says.

Rafael sighs forcefully. "Fine. You can stab Hugo once and then it's time to reboot."

Theo smiles and turns to me. "Where do you want me to stab you?"

"I don't care. Surprise me."

Theo licks his lips and pushes his glasses up on his nose as he searches my body for a suitable location. He raises the knife, blade pointing downward like a predator's fang, and pierces the blade deep into my chest. His eyebrows raise at the sight of the flesh-enveloped blade. He chuckles his delight and tugs the knife loose from my chest.

"Okay," Rafael says. "Happy?"

Theo nods. Rafael takes the knife and returns it to the kitchen.

I take my seat next to Piper who seems lost in thought. "You okay?"

"Yeah. I'm sorry I freaked out," she says, "back at the trailer."

"I get it. I was pretty freaked out myself."

She lays her head on the table facing me. "You can still kiss me," she whispers.

I glance across the table to see if anyone heard her. "Now?"

She laughs and shoves me. "No! Not here." Her face is flush. "Tomorrow."

"Tomorrow," I confirm with a grin.

CHAPTER 24
SUSPENDED

THE NEXT DAY, while I was helping a customer at the music store, I received a phone call. As I was about to send it to voicemail, I saw the caller ID. It was Ava's school. I politely excused myself to take the call.

"Hello?"

"Is this Hugo Castillo?"

"Yes." I could feel my pulse raise.

"This is Principal Savage at Catalina High. We have an issue that needs your immediate attention. Can you come down to the school?"

"Is Ava okay?" I asked in a panicked tone.

"She's fine. I have her here with me in my office."

"What's this about?"

"It's a sensitive matter. I'd rather talk to you in person when you get here." She was serious. This was serious.

"I'm on my way," I said and hung up.

"You good?" Lenny asked.

"It's Ava. They need me to come down to the school right now. Can you manage the store?"

"Sure. Is everything alright?"

"I don't know. I'll text you," I said, pulling on my jacket. I couldn't imagine what Ava might have done to get her sent to the principal's office. She'd never been to the principal's office in her life.

When I arrived to the school, a wave of anxiety washed over me. Walking through the hallway toward the administration office gave me a familiar dreadful feeling, like *I* was in trouble.

"I'm here to see Principal Savage," I said to the white-haired lady sitting at the front desk. She gave me a rebuking glare and gestured with her head for me to go on in.

A uniformed officer opened the door for me. Principal Savage was seated at her desk. Ava slumped in a chair with her hoodie pulled up over her head. She didn't even look up when I walked in the room and sat next to her.

"Mr. Castillo, thank you for coming on such short notice."

"What's this all about?" I looked at Ava, who had cinched her hood over her eyes, but I could see moisture on her cheeks.

Principal Savage held up a ziplock baggie with blue vape pen inside and placed it on her desk in front of me. "We found this in your daughter's gym locker. Do you know what this is, Mr. Castillo?"

I know exactly what that is, but I say, "No."

"It's a device for smoking cannabis."

My heart sunk. I looked at the officer who stood stoically to the side of the room with his hands clasped behind his back. I turned to Ava who had managed to slump even further in her chair. "Is this yours?" But she didn't answer me.

"Mr. Castillo, according to Arizona State Law, possession of a controlled substance in a drug-free school zone is considered a felony."

"A felony? Are you serious?"

"I'm afraid so. I cannot speak to the severity of her sentencing—that's for a judge to decide—but since it's a first offense and we do not believe she had the intent to distribute, she may not have to serve time in juvenile detention. There will likely be a fine and a mandatory drug education class, at the very least. Ava is not being arrested today, but she did receive a juvenile citation." She handed me the citation. "You'll need to call the number on the back to schedule her court appearance."

I flipped the citation over. She had circled the phone number.

"As per school policy, Ava is immediately suspended for a period of five days and she will be ineligible for participation in any extracurricular clubs or field trips for the remainder of the school year."

"Wait, so she can't go to New York?" I glanced at Ava. A tear streamed down her cheek and she quickly brushed it away with the sleeve of her sweatshirt.

"I'm sorry, Mr. Castillo. Ava has been an outstanding student academically and I would have loved to see her go with her classmates to New York. Unfortunately, it isn't up to me. It's school policy."

"But she can still be in the play, right?"

"I'm sorry Mr. Castillo. As of this incident, Ava is no longer eligible to participate in theater performances, or any other school clubs for the rest of the year."

I looked over at Ava, who seemed to have retreated into herself. She was miles away and I was afraid I would never reach her again. I didn't expect her to show remorse. That wouldn't have been her style. I almost wanted her to yell, or say something sarcastic or defiant. At least that wouldn't have surprised me. But instead, she just sat there, legs stretched out before her, hands plunged into the pockets of her sweatshirt. I didn't recognize her in this moment. This wasn't my daughter. This was some other kid—some kid I didn't know.

"Mr. Castillo, I'm aware of your recent loss. I know it hasn't been easy for either of you and I'm sympathetic to your suffering. Given the circumstances, I can put these behaviors into context. If I may, Mr. Castillo, it might not be a bad idea to get Ava into counseling. It might inspire some degree of leniency with the judge to know she has been grieving and getting the help she needs."

I nod.

"Do you have any further questions, Mr. Castillo?"

I shook my head. "No, ma'am."

"You and Ava are free to go."

Ava snatched her backpack off the floor and strode out of the principal's office into the hallway. I had to trot to catch up to her. "Ava, slow down."

When I reached for her elbow, she jerked it away. "Don't touch me!"

"Ava!" I followed her out to the truck where she climbed into the cab and slammed the door. I took two deep breaths before getting in on the driver's side. "Ava," I said, calm as a monk.

"Can we just fucking go home?"

I exhaled and turned the key in the ignition. It took a second crank before the truck would start. Ava glared out the passenger side window, both arms wrapped around her backpack as I pulled out of the school's parking lot.

"What were you thinking?" I asked in a reasonably calm tone. She refused to answer and every second that went by in silence, I could feel heat rising in my face. "Ava. I'm asking you a question," I said, a little stronger this time. And when she continued to ice me out, "Answer me!"

"It wasn't mine, okay!"

"What? Why did they find it in your locker?"

Ava took a moment before responding, "I was holding it for someone."

"Who?"

She didn't answer.

"Ava, I swear to fucking god if you don't answer me right now—"

"It was Sydney's."

"Why did you tell them it was yours?"

"Because."

I waited for the rest of her answer but my patience was a lit fuse and when it ran out I shouted, "Ava!"

"Because Sydney has a major part in the play. I'm just an understudy. Nobody cares if I get kicked out of the play."

"Are you kidding me right now? That's . . . that's insane! No! No, you're not taking the fall for this!"

"Yes, I am! You can't make me rat her out. I won't do it."

"Ava, I know she's your best friend—"

"She's not just my best friend." Tears formed in Ava's eyes. "She's my . . ." Ava squeezed her eyes shut, sending a trickle of tears down both cheeks. "She's my girlfriend. I love her."

Now I was the one who was speechless. Not because of her admission, but because I realized in that moment that I hadn't made it safe enough for her to come out to me sooner. I couldn't hold space for her grief so she must have thought I couldn't hold space for this. So she turned to someone else— someone who couldn't possibly love her as much as I do, someone who would so easily throw her under the bus.

"Hello?" Ava said. "Aren't you going to say anything? Am I in trouble for being queer, too?"

I gripped the steering wheel until my knuckles turned white. I took a hard right at the next light and headed toward Sam Hughes, the historical neighborhood where Sydney lived.

"Where are you going?" Ava demanded.

"You are not taking the fall for that girl. You're going to tell her parents what happened and that's that!"

"No, I'm not! You can't make me!"

Fire rose inside me. I couldn't believe how unreasonable she was being. I didn't care that she liked girls. What bothered me was that she was willing to have a juvenile record, be suspended from school, and throw away her chance to pursue the one thing that made her happy since her mother died, for a stupid high school crush—regardless of her gender. Plus, I'm in the sleeper program just so she could have a chance to go to New York and it doesn't even matter to her.

I pulled my truck onto the stone-paved circle drive and strode up to the front door. I knocked with my fist until Sydney's mother opened the door with an alarmed look on her face.

"Mr. Castillo, is everything alright?"

"No, Bev. Everything is not alright." I looked back at Ava who was still sitting in the truck. "Ava was suspended from school today for having weed in her locker."

Bev placed a hand on her chest. "Oh no! I can't believe it. Ava's such a sweet girl."

"I know she is. Do you know what she told me after we left the school?" I didn't wait for her to answer. "She told me it was Sydney's weed and she let Sydney store it in her locker."

A condescending smile emerged on her face. "No, that's not possible. Our Sydney doesn't do drugs."

"Yes, she does. They smoked weed at my house just last weekend and she was going to drive home high and I wouldn't let her."

"Are you telling me you allow teenage girls to do drugs in your home?"

"No!" I scoffed. "No, I didn't *let* them. I *caught* them."

"And you didn't think to tell me about it?"

Somehow this conversation had gotten away from me and I found myself on the defensive. "I just assumed you knew about it."

Sydney appeared in the foyer behind her mother. "What's going on, mom?"

"Mr. Castillo says you were smoking weed at his house last weekend."

Sydney shook her head. "No, mom. I don't do drugs."

"See?" Bev said with a satisfied grin.

"Well, of course she's going to deny it." I was clearly flustered. "Ava will tell you. Hold on." I quickly marched to the truck and opened the passenger door. Ava stepped out slowly and followed me back to the front door. "Ava, please tell her what you told me earlier."

"Hey, Ava," Sydney said, her eyes piercing Ava's with laser intensity.

"Hey," Ava replied shyly.

"Tell her," I demanded.

Ava swallowed and took another glance at Sydney who maintained a relentless stare. "It was my weed, not Sydney's. I just told my dad that so I wouldn't be in trouble. I'm sorry."

Bev crossed her arms and tilted her head in haughty satisfaction.

"No! Ava, goddamn it! She's just trying to protect Sydney because she thinks she's in love with her. They're dating!"

"Ha! Sydney isn't a lesbian, are you honey?"

Sydney made a disgusted face. "Ew no, mom. That's gross."

Bev turned back to me dripping with condescension. "I think we're done here."

"But—" I shot a pleading look at Ava, hoping she would come clean—to save me from looking like a complete idiot. No such luck.

We drove home in silence. I was fuming but I knew I wasn't in a place to have a constructive dialogue. I just wanted to get home where I knew she'd retreat to her bedroom. I didn't want to look at her traitorous face.

As soon as we walked into the house I turned to her and held out my hand. "Phone."

"What?" Like it was an unreasonable consequence.

"You're grounded from your phone for a week."

"For doing exactly what I told you I was going to do? I told you I wasn't going to throw her under the bus."

"Ava! Can't you see? She was the one who threw *you* under the bus! She could have had your back and told the truth, but she let you take the fall. That's not the kind of person you want to be dating."

"You're just being homophobic."

"You know it has nothing to do with that. She's not a good person, Ava. I don't want you talking to her anymore. Phone!"

Ava slammed her phone on the counter and looked me right in the eyes. "I fucking hate you!" She stomped to her room, and slammed the door so hard I flinched.

I grabbed a beer from the fridge and drank half the can in one continuous gulp. Tears filled my eyes. I drank the rest and opened another.

I didn't bother making dinner. Ava was old enough to make herself something if she got hungry. But she was the most stubborn girl I'd even known, besides her mother, and I knew she wouldn't. That was on her. I still couldn't believe she would treat me like that, after all I've done for her. She made me look like a complete fool in front of that smug bitch. I opened another beer. I had a few more after that one.

By nine o'clock she still hadn't come out of her room. I reheated some mac and cheese. I knew if I didn't make her a plate, she wouldn't do it herself. I scraped half into a bowl for myself and left the rest in the microwave. When I finished, I dropped my bowl in the sink. I padded back to her room and gently knocked on her door.

"There's some mac and cheese in the microwave if you're hungry." I waited for her to respond, but I wasn't surprised that she didn't. I leaned closer to her door to see if I could hear her in there. It was completely silent. I could see that her light was still on. She probably cried herself to sleep over that Judas girlfriend of hers. I quietly turned the doorknob and cracked the door. I opened it slowly at first and then abruptly once I realized she wasn't in there.

"Ava!" Her bed was made. I threw open the closet door. I checked the bathroom. "Ava!" Back in her room, I noticed her window had not been fully shut.

I grabbed my keys and started up the truck. She couldn't have gone far. I put it in reverse and knocked over a blue recycle bin, spilling its contents into the street. I drove up and down the residential streets in our neighborhood and the next one over. We didn't live in the safest part of town. Meth heads were out, slumped in corners or standing catatonically like candy canes ready to topple over any second.

My phone buzzed and I nearly drove off the road trying to dig it out of my pocket. It was the Lunatech app alerting me to wind down for the night. If I missed my plug in time, I would have been in breach of my contract. So be it. I swiped to clear the notification.

I pulled onto the main road that would have been the most direct way back to Sydney's house. It would take her over an hour to walk all the way there. I drove slowly along in the right lane as cars sped past me, honking. My vision was blurry. I'd been drinking pretty heavily, I'll admit. I squinted at every person I saw on the sidewalks and bus stops.

My phone buzzed again—Lunatech. It's after ten and I should be plugged in by now. Sorry Lunatech. They weren't getting their sleeper tonight. When I looked up from the screen the road had been replaced by a stone wall.

CHAPTER 25
WE ARE ALL
MADE OF CODE

WHEN I OPEN MY EYES, and Piper is staring at me. She lunges toward me, wrapping her arms around my neck. "You're back! Oh my god where were you?"

I'm confused. "What do you mean?"

"Yesterday you never rebooted," Geoff says.

"I knew he'd be back," Theo says.

"Seriously, what happened?" Piper asks.

"I don't know what you're talking about," I say. "I was here. We were all stabbing each other?"

"That was the day *before*," Theo explains. "Yesterday you just sat there with your head on the table the whole day."

"We thought you died," Geoff says without any emotion at all.

I hear the sound of drawers opening and closing and metal clanking. Rafael is gathering all the knives from the kitchen.

"We're not having any more of that stabbing nonsense today," he says holding a rolled towel containing all the knives in both hands. He takes them out the back door.

"What's his problem?" Theo says, cleaning his glasses with

a tiny cloth. Without glasses, his eyes look like dried up blue-berries.

"Why do you do that?" Geoff asks him.

"What? Clean my glasses?"

"You don't even need them in the first place."

Theo examines the glasses. He looks at me and Piper and scans the room. "I guess I don't. I guess it's just something I'm used to."

"Plus, you look really weird without them," Piper says with a grimace. "Put them back on."

"Listen up, gang," Rafael says coming back in from outside. "Oh hey," he says when he sees me. "Where were you yesterday?"

"I don't know. Apparently, I skipped a day?"

Rafael nodded. "That does happen sometimes. It's rare, but it does happen. You had Piper here pretty worried."

"I wasn't worried," she says and crosses her arms.

"You were kind of worried," Geoff says.

"Well, we're glad to have you back, Hugo," Rafael says. "Now listen, I need to make sure we're all on the same page about the no blood thing. Promise you won't stab yourself or anyone at work. You can't even talk about it, alright?"

Apparently, the stabbings had continued while I was away.

"What if there was some kind of accident?" Geoff says. "What if a sharp tool were to slice a person's finger off."

Alarm flashed on Rafael's face. "For the love of Steve, please do not stage an accident—"

"I think what Geoff is saying," Piper intercedes, "is that eventually something might happen, accidentally, and people are going to find out we don't have blood. Or . . . private parts."

"Besides," Theo says, "it's all written in the Book of Illumi-nation. Anyone could just read about it."

"Nobody reads the Book of Illumination," Rafael says with a deep sigh. "But yes, I see your point. Guys, here's the thing. I'm responsible for all of you. I don't need the higher ups thinking I'm involved in some kind of conspiracy to upset the rule of order. Look what happened when the four of you found out. Imagine if all of Slumbervale found out at the same time. It would be complete pandemonium!"

"Okay, okay," Piper says. "We get it. No stabbing."

"Thank you." Rafael scans the rest of us and we each nod our confirmation. "Now, let's get out there and make a difference, shall we?" He says it without his usual conviction. All this stabbing each other really seems to have rattled him.

When I get to the studio, Vincent waves me into the recording booth. "Welcome back! Where were you yesterday?"

"Everyone keeps asking me that. I don't know."

"I've heard sometimes rebooting can take a day or two. You didn't miss much. Everyone took the day off after the festival anyway. By the way, why'd you have to leave so soon the other night?"

"I wasn't feeling great." I sit in one of the office chairs behind the sound board.

Vincent furrowed his brows. I guess he must have known it wasn't any kind of physical illness since we don't get sick here. "You want to talk about it?"

I shake my head.

"Something about the girl? I noticed you didn't bring her to the party."

I laugh nervously.

"You can tell me. Something happened in that trailer didn't it?"

I promised Rafael I wouldn't talk about the fact that we don't have any blood. But he didn't say anything about missing parts. Still, it's embarrassing, even if we're all in the same anatomically bereft boat.

"Oh shit." He smiles.

"What?"

"You found out. Didn't you?" Still smiling.

"Found out what?"

"You know." He glances down at my crotch. "Something missing from the produce section."

"Oh. That." I sit up and cross my legs.

"It's alright. Don't make you less of a man."

"I know." Do I?

"Finding out's always a bit of a shock. You get used to it."

I nod even though I don't believe it. "Hey, Vincent?"

"What's up?"

"Have you ever been in a relationship? Here, in Level Six."

"Nah, man. Relationships are too complicated. Plus, you can't consummate anyhow."

"But it's not against the rules, right?"

"It ain't against the rules, per se. But most people lose interest once they realize there's nowhere to go after second base. That shit is frustrating." We both laugh.

The door to the studio opens and Piper walks in apologetically, like she's somewhere she isn't supposed to be. Vincent laughs to himself. "Go on now," he says with a smile.

I exit the booth and greet Piper over by the door. She's holding a green notebook. "Is everything alright?"

"I have to talk to you. Can we go somewhere private?" Her eyes are darting around the studio, presumably looking for a quiet corner.

"Of course. The park?"

She nods.

I turn back to Vincent. "I'll be back."

He shoos me away with a grin.

As we walk to the park she has a look of concentration on her face. I have the feeling we're not going to be making out. We sit on the bench near the pond. She's looking at me with a scrupulous intensity, scanning my eyes for something.

"There's something I need to show you." She glances back over her shoulder again. "I found this in my desk yesterday while you were gone." She looks down at the green composition book she is holding with both hands as if it might blow away.

"What is it?"

"It's a message from me . . . to me. I must have written it sometime before my last restoration." She hands me the notebook. I open it to where it's been dogeared and read.

Piper,

Slumbervale is a simulation. None of this is real. Your real self is asleep in another world—the real world. When you go to sleep there, your consciousness awakens here in this computer simulation. You are a dream slave. They told you you're living your true purpose, but in reality, they're exploiting your natural skills and talents for their own gains. There is no such thing as the pancake universe or different spiritual levels. That's a lie to manipulate productivity.

Every time they take you to restoration, you lose your memory and we have to start all over again. I've hidden a secret file on your computer labeled sourcecode821 *that has all the evidence you need and will get you up to speed on where to go next. Do the work they assign you so as to not arouse suspicion. Avoid restoration at all costs, but just in case, keep this where only you can find it so you don't have to start all over again.*

-Piper

Update: Every time you are assigned to a patch, grab as much of the bad code as you can before fixing it. Bad code is exposed reality. Save it to the secret file. You may need it later.

Update: Delta stream = brain waves. If you take down the guardrails, the sleeper will wake up.

Update: There's a firewall that keeps real world memories out. You must find a way to disable it.

Update: You can trust Hugo. Show him his file. Maybe he can help.

"Show me what?" I ask. "What's in that file?"

She's watching two ducks swimming side by side in the pond like an old married couple. "I know who that woman is," she says looking straight ahead.

"Who?"

"The woman in the picture—the one Rafael showed you on your first day. You didn't recognize her, remember?"

Of course I remember. "Who is she?"

Piper doesn't answer right away. She grips the bench with both hands and rocks forward, still looking over the water. "She's your wife, Hugo."

"My wife?"

"Well, she *was* your wife. She . . . she died. I'm sorry. Her name was Celeste."

"How do you know this?"

"That's what was in the last patch. They have to create these tests to make sure your mind is fully bifurcated, and once you pass it, they delete the matching code. That is, *I* delete the code. But this time I copied it and moved it to my secret file before I patched it. It's all encrypted, so I must have hacked it. That's kind of my specialty."

"I knew it! I knew there was no such thing as a pancake universe."

"It's just as stupid as it sounds."

"Is Rafael in on this?"

"No, he's a dream slave, too. All of us are. One of the system's main functions is to make sure certain frequencies remain constant throughout the day—brainwaves. Everyone here is asleep! Our minds are active but they're disconnected from anything that has to do with our personal lives on the outside. That's why you don't remember anything about yourself. It's not an issue with your memory. Your waking life is behind a firewall. But there are cracks in the code—it's not perfect. That's how I found out about your wife."

A fountain of questions bottleneck in my throat. I don't know which version of reality sounds crazier, that I was born a little over a week ago into the sixth level of a pancake universe, or that I'm a dream slave with no access to my waking life.

"What else did you find out about my wife?"

"That's it. Just her name and that she died a couple years ago."

"How? How'd she die?"

"I don't know." She stares at me for a while as I try to access any memories at all, but none come. "There's something else," she says after a while.

"What is it?"

"The stuffed pig, remember?"

"Yeah, that was weird."

"It belongs to your daughter."

"I have a daughter?"

"Her name is Ava. She's fourteen."

"Ava," I repeat. My chest suddenly aches as I say that name out loud. A sinkhole of longing opens up inside my chest and

I'm being pulled into it. I want to remember her face, her voice, anything, but nothing comes. "Ava," I say again to myself and I am pierced with a powerful mix of love and sadness. "What else do you know about her?"

"That's all. I can only grab bits of code at a time. It's not always that revealing, but it's proof. It's proof that there *is* more to us than this. We're alive somewhere else, Hugo. This . . ." She pats both hands on the bench on either side of her thighs. "This is a simulation. We are all made of code."

"Like *The Matrix*?" I can't remember ever actually watching *The Matrix*, but I can visualize every scene as though I'd seen it a hundred times.

"Yeah, but without the Kung Fu. It's more like a video game actually. We're avatars."

"So that's why we don't bleed or need food."

"Or have junk." Piper adds.

"What about you? What did you find out about your real life?"

She shakes her head. "I didn't. They must have erased that code long ago. But I have encrypted code for hundreds of sleepers in that file."

"What are you suggesting? That we tell everyone about their encrypted code?"

"That could take a while. It could take weeks to decrypt. Plus, it wouldn't solve the problem of alerting the real world about what's happening. It would just create chaos here in Slumbervale. We need to find a way to get a message to our real selves to tell them what they're doing to us."

"What did you say about brainwaves? Delta something?"

"The delta stream. We have to keep brainwave activity within certain parameters so you remain asleep. I could alter the delta frequencies, which would cause someone to wake up during their sleep cycle. But there's still a firewall in place that keeps our worlds separate. They still wouldn't have any memory of Slumbervale."

"Can't you just take down the firewall?"

She shakes her head. "I don't have the security access for that."

"But you have direct access to the brainwaves."

Piper's eyes flash. "That's it! The delta stream is just a frequency—like sound waves. And it's bi-directional, meaning, we can send counter pulses upstream to correct abnormalities. That's how we keep people asleep. But if we can send those waves back to the brain, why not sound? If we send an audio signal upstream, with enough repetition, there's a chance the sleeper will remember it when they wake, like recalling a dream."

"What kind of pattern?"

"It would have to be something simple that could lend itself to repetition, like a mantra—something rhythmic."

"Like music?"

Piper's eyes come alive. "Yes! Exactly. If only I knew someone who could write music," she says smiling.

"What about the firewall? Wouldn't that block any messages?"

She shakes her head. "No, the firewall doesn't have anything to do with the delta stream."

"I guess I better get started on that song," I say.

"You'll need to write lyrics to explain what's happening here—something you'll be able to understand when you wake up."

"Okay."

She stands and I follow her lead. Piper closes the space between us and kisses me. As I push deeper into her kiss, she breaks away. She doesn't say anything, but I get the message. We have work to do.

CHAPTER 26
AGAINST MEDICAL ADVICE

THE LAST THING I remembered was driving down Fort Lowell searching for Ava. Now I was in a hospital bed with an IV in one arm and a sling around the other. My head throbbed and my mouth felt like a dried out sponge.

The door clicked open and a nurse walked in with an IV bag. "Mr. Castillo! You're awake. How do you feel?"

Hungover, was the first thought that came to mind, but I didn't say that. My mouth was dry and I swallowed. I licked my dry lips before answering with more air than voice. "Headache."

"You have quite a bump, I'm afraid. How's the arm?"

"Hurts," I eked out.

"I'll order some Toradol for the pain." She removed a pen light from her scrubs pocket and shined it in both my eyes. "Can you state your name for me?"

"Hugo Castillo," I said in a cracked voice.

"Do you know where you are?"

I glanced around the room to make sure. "Hospital?"

She smiled as if I'd made a joke. "Do you know which hospital?"

I shook my head.

"You're at TMC. Do you remember what happened last night, Mr. Castillo?"

"I was looking for Ava."

"Who's Ava?"

"My daughter."

"I'm going to let the doctor know you're awake. Do you need anything else right now? Water?"

I swallowed. "My phone. I need to call my daughter."

The nurse searched my belongings and handed me my phone before leaving the room. There were multiple notifications from Lunatech:

> 9:50—It's time to wind down for the night.

> 10:02—Time to plug in!

> 10:14—You have not initiated your sleep console. Please initiate sleep session immediately.

> 10:31—You are in violation of your sleeper agreement. Please contact Lunatech at your earliest convenience.

I ignored the notifications and called Ava. It rang four times before going to voicemail: *This is Ava. Why are you even calling me? That's so weird. Text me like a normal person—BEEEP.*

"Ava, please call me. I'm in the hospital. You're not in trouble. I just need to know you're okay. Just text me a thumbs up or whatever . . . bye."

The short middle-aged doctor entered a few minutes later with a police officer on her heels. My immediate thought was that he had information about Ava. I tried my best to sit up in the bed.

"Mr. Castillo, I'm Dr. Gomez and this is Officer Stanley with the Tucson Police Department."

"Did you find Ava?" I asked, searching the officer's eyes for any sign of hope.

"He'll be happy to answer your questions in a moment, but first I need to take a little look see." She shined a pen light in my eyes and commenced with some basic neurological tests.

"Good," she said, "Neurologically, you seem to be in good working order. Although you have a pretty big bump there, we didn't find any swelling in the brain, so no concussion. You do have a fractured radius, just below the elbow. It should heal in six to eight weeks as long as you limit mobility."

I nodded along as she spoke, not necessarily to convey understanding so much as to get her to hurry up so Officer Stanley could tell me about Ava.

"Mr. Castillo," she continued, "When they brought you in, you had a blood alcohol level of point one five, which is nearly twice the legal limit. Officer Stanley is here to discuss that with you." She offered me a pitiful smile and left me with the officer.

Officer Stanley took two steps toward my bed. He didn't even look me in the eyes. "Mr. Castillo, based on the toxicology results and witness testimony, I am placing you under arrest for driving under the influence and any related charges resulting from the crash. You have the right to remain silent . . ."

As he read me my Miranda rights, my mind spiraled. What about Ava? Where had she gone? How am I going to find her if I'm in jail?

"Once you're discharged from the hospital," the officer continued, "you'll be transported to Pima County Jail where you'll be booked and detained until your arraignment, unless you post bail. Do you understand what I've told you so far?"

I nodded. I thought about reporting Ava's runaway, but I didn't want to add to her recent felony charge. If they were to pick her up and see she has a court summons on file, they might think she was a fugitive. What a proud day for the Castillo family.

"I'll be right outside," he said and left the room. Did he think I was going to make a break for it?

I reached up to touch my throbbing head, which I discovered had been heavily bandaged. I tried to remember the crash, but it was all a blur. How much did I drink? I don't remember that either. Normally, I wouldn't have driven in that state, but Ava was gone. What was I supposed to do?

Dr. Gomez entered the room. "Mr. Castillo, we're going to monitor you a few more hours just to be safe." She glanced at her tablet. "I have a Celeste Castillo as your emergency contact. Would you like me to give her a call?"

"No. She . . . she's passed."

"Oh, I'm sorry. Would you like to update your emergency contact?"

It dawned on me that the only person I trusted for the esteemed position of emergency contact was, in fact, Lenny. I gave her his information but opted to call him myself.

"We did find something a bit unusual on your CT scan—could be a small piece of shrapnel from the accident, but it doesn't seem to be interfering with brain function."

"Shrapnel?"

"I would assume so." She pulled out her tablet and scrolled through several images. "Here it is." She showed me the screen and zoomed in with her fingers. "See this density here on the right temporal lobe?"

"Huh." Was that crazy Reddit guy telling the truth? Was Lunatech in the business of administering covert surgical brain procedures? How could that be legal?

"We could do additional imaging to determine if it's worth removing, but as long as it isn't causing any issues for you, it's probably fine to leave it there."

I realized now that I was in breach of Lunatech's brain-related exclusivity agreement. My brain, as long as I was in the sleeper program, was essentially the sole property of Lunatech. But I didn't ask for this CT scan. Maybe Lunatech would forgive the breach as long as I was unconscious when the scan was conducted. I declined further imaging.

When she left the room, I called Lenny.

"You didn't come back to work yesterday," Lenny said. "That can't be good."

"No, Lenny, it's not great. I'm in the hospital."

"What? Are you okay? What happened?" He sounded more panicked than I had anticipated.

"I crashed the truck—"

"What?!"

"But listen—Ava's missing. We had a huge fight last night. She ran away."

"Oh no! What can I do?"

"I need you to go to the house and see if she came home. There's a key under the doormat. Can you do that?"

"Of course. Are you hurt? How bad is it? Do you need me to come pick you up?"

I was too ashamed to tell him that I already had a ride—in the back seat of a cop car. "No. Just let me know when you get to the house."

"I'm on my way."

The next time I'd see Lenny, I'd probably be at county in an orange jumpsuit. I couldn't believe this was happening. Every other thought presented Ava in increasingly worst case scenarios. Tears stung my eyes. I'd never felt so helpless in all my life. If there was only one thing I was put on this Earth for, it was to keep Ava safe, and I was powerless to do anything. Worse than that, it was all my fault. I drove her to this and now I wouldn't be there to make things right.

Tears streamed as I prayed for the first time since I was a kid. I prayed to Celeste because if anyone upstairs was paying any attention to my retched life, it would be her. I begged for her forgiveness. I promised her I would never let anything get between Ava and I ever again. I swore I'd always protect her and I'd hold space for her, even if it opened the door to whatever I was protecting myself from. I hadn't been able to face that dark pursuer. It was always right behind me.

Shame.

I'd been outrunning my shame for the past two years. And when I couldn't outrun it, I drank. No more. No more. I was done running. Done drinking. Done. Ava, please come back. If anyone can hear me, I prayed, please bring her back. A hummingbird hovered in the window for a moment and then flitted away.

Officer Stanley entered the room and I wiped away tears with a thin sheet.

"Today's your lucky day, Mr. Castillo. Someone posted bail."

"Who?"

"They don't give me the specifics. You're free to go as soon as they clear you." He handed me a sheet of paper. "This is the impound lot where you can retrieve your vehicle."

"So that's it? I can go?"

"That's it. You still have to make that court date. Until then, you just keep your nose clean."

"I will." I couldn't believe it. Who posted bail? Who knew about my arrest? I hadn't told anyone, not Lenny, not anyone. Whoever it was, I owed them my life.

As the door closed behind Stanley, I swung my legs over

the side of the bed, but when I tried to stand they failed to hold me up. I crashed to the floor and the IV ripped from my arm. I managed to get my clothes on and get my arm back into the sling. Pain radiated from my elbow like a lightning bolt. The nurse walked in as I was attempting to tie my shoes with one hand.

"Mr. Castillo, just where do you think you're going?" She placed a fist on her hip.

"I'm sorry. I have to get home to my daughter."

"You haven't been cleared—"

"I'm clearing myself."

"Mr. Castillo, I strongly advise you to wait a while longer to make sure—"

"I'm fine! I can't stay." I had to start over with the laces.

She rolled her eyes and mumbled under her breath. I wasn't making her job easy this morning. "Do you have a ride?"

"I'll call an Uber."

The nurse shook her head and sighed heavily. "Here. Let me help you with that." She knelt in front of me, propped my foot on her bent knee and tied my shoes. "Can't have you tripping on those laces and breaking your other arm." She helped me to my feet.

"Thank you."

"Mmm-hm. I do need you to sign an AMA before I let you walk on out of here."

"What's that?"

"AMA: Against medical advice," she said. "If you have a delayed brain bleed and collapse out there, that's on you. We can't be held liable."

"Fine. I just need to get home to my daughter."

I signed the stupid form and made my way down to the lobby where Lenny was talking with a nurse at the front desk.

"Lenny?"

"Oh, there you are!" He told the nurse to never mind and greeted me with a coffee in his outstretched hand. "I thought you'd be here longer. Brought you a coffee."

"Thanks, man." I took a sip. "Was she home?" I asked.

He shook his head. "No. Sorry. What happened?"

"I'll tell you in the car."

I told him the whole story from the incident at school to Ava taking the fall for her girlfriend to our fight, which led to her runaway, and finally, my accident and DUI.

"There's something else," I said. I debated telling but I'd told him everything else. "They found a foreign object in my CT scan."

"What?"

"They think it's a tiny piece of shrapnel from the crash."

"*A* tiny piece of shrapnel? That doesn't make sense. If you had shrapnel lodged in your skull, don't you think there would be more than one piece and in more than one place? Let me guess. Is it just above your right ear?"

I exhale hard. "Fine. You can say it."

"I will say it. It ain't fucking shrapnel, dude. It's a *microchip*. In your brain! Lunatech implanted it while you were unconscious and now they're using it to manipulate your thoughts." He gasped like he'd been underwater and just reached the surface.

"Feel better?" I asked.

"Yes!"

When we arrived at the impound lot, I was surprised my truck was still in drivable condition. The passenger side fender was badly dented and the bumper had come loose of its brackets and lodged into the wheel well. I must not have been driving very fast, probably because I was trying to identify Ava among the blurry people wandering the streets after dark.

Apparently, I had crashed into a stone wall flanking the entrance to a subdivision.

I showed my temporary paper license Officer Stanley had given me to the unwashed, mustachioed lot attendant inside the mobile office out front.

"Bill's already paid" he said sliding my keys from a plastic sleeve.

"Already paid? By who?" I read the invoice. $218—Paid in full.

He shrugged and took a gulp from a can of Dr. Pepper. It must have been the same person who posted my bail, but who could that be? I should have felt grateful, but the anonymity felt intrusive, like someone had bought a piece of me without asking.

"Need me to follow you home?" Lenny asked, surveying the damage.

I shook my head. "Nah, I think it'll be okay."

"What are you going to do about Ava? I can call in if you need me to help you look for her."

I patted Lenny on the shoulder. "No, thanks. You've done enough already. I'll keep you posted."

He nodded.

"Hey, Lenny. Seriously. Thank you."

"Anything you need, man," he said and strode back to his car.

Not only was Lenny qualified to be my emergency contact, turns out, he's perfectly suited for the designation.

CHAPTER 27

EVERYONE LOVES
A SENTINEL

THE STUDIO IS empty when I get back with my marching orders from Piper. She wants me to write a simple, rhythmic melody that will most likely stick in my real world brain—something catchy. The idea is that we send a short piece of music upstream of my natural brain waves. And since the delta streams are not subject to the firewall, the music would go right through and hopefully I'd remember it when I woke up—like a dream.

I pick up an acoustic guitar and start noodling, when I look over and see the sheet music for "Tidy Paws," the cat litter jingle we wrote, sitting on the keyboard's music stand. That's it! Simple, catchy, if not annoying as hell—even better, in fact. Because the harder you try to get rid of a song that's gotten stuck in your head, the more embedded it becomes. That could work. I would just have to re-record it with new lyrics explaining the exploitation that's happening in our unconscious minds.

I open a notebook on the coffee table to a blank page and grab a pen. By the end of the hour, I've come up with the most surreal piece of lyrical absurdity that has ever been put to music. I'm sure of it.

> While you sleep, you are wide awake
> In a universe that's a pancake
> Slumbervale isn't real, we know it's all fake.

> While you sleep, you work without pay
> Work for free, eight hours a day
> They say it's your purpose, you don't have a say

> While you sleep, you have no memory
> Of the life you live when you're awake.

It's not great, but it will serve the purpose of getting stuck in the brain. I take the notebook up to the recording booth and pull up the "Tidy Paws" project on Vincent's computer. I don't think I'm supposed to be in the recording booth if he's not here. He never said as much, but this is his workspace. He wouldn't approve of what we're doing. I like Vincent, but he, like Rafael, is a Steve Gower devotee. I don't trust him not to turn me in or send me to restoration, so I have to hurry.

I make a duplicate file and delete the vocal track—the one that has to do with cats. I create a new vocal track and pull the studio mic up to my lips. I clear my throat, holding the notebook in front of me, and hit record.

The first couple of takes are bad—I have to keep starting over. But the third take is good enough. It doesn't need to be polished. It just needs to be clear and coherent. I play it back and feel satisfied so I save it to a thumb drive just as Vincent walks into the studio. I quickly stuff the drive into my pocket.

"Can I help you with something?" Vincent asks as he enters the booth.

"Oh, I was just, uh, curious . . . about . . ." My mind reaches for something, anything remotely logical. " . . . about how you auto-tuned my vocals in that kitty litter jingle."

For the next half hour, Vincent kindly and thoroughly demonstrates the whole process of vocal augmentation and other recording tricks. Somehow, I already know how it's done, but I entertain his instruction with rapt attentiveness. I don't want to rush him or cut him off, but I need to get this thumb drive to Piper. When he finally finishes his lesson, I excuse myself to go work on a new song. I tell him I need to walk to get the creative juices flowing and he buys it.

I take a teleporter to Central Systems. It isn't downtown, which is more of a cozy old town kind of feel with lots of character and charm. Central Systems is in a corporate district—tall buildings, lots of concrete and glass. I don't know where this is in relation to downtown, or to our neighborhood. It's a little intimidating.

A sentinel with a buzzcut stands vigilant by the entrance at the top of the steps. He's looking right at me as I ascend. I should have gotten a hall pass, just in case. He stops me when I reach the top of the steps.

"Hold on there," he says with baritone authority.

"I'm just here to—"

"Wait," he says looking down his nose at me. "Aren't you the guy who played at Stevefest?"

This catches me off guard. "Yes."

He nods slowly. "Rock on. Awesome show, man."

I nod my thanks.

"You have a great day," he says and opens the front door for me. That was lucky.

Once I'm inside, I have no idea where to go. Several people in business attire are striding up and down hallways. The sound of heels and dress shoes on tile floors echo throughout the stark interior. I scan the open space for any signs of Piper and then see a building directory mounted on the wall to my right: *Orientation Services, Communications, Records and Retention, Internal Affairs, Grounds Maintenance, Resident Wellness, etc.* I don't know what any of this means. Nothing about brain wave regulation. Someone taps on my shoulder.

"Hey." It's Piper. "What are you doing?" She has a panicked look on her face.

"Looking for you," I say.

"You're not supposed to be in here." She glances behind her shoulder.

"I had to give you this." I pull the thumb drive from my pocket.

"You already wrote it?" She's pleased.

"Well, I used the kitty litter jingle we wrote last week and just changed the words."

"That's brilliant!"

I feel my face blushing. "Well, I don't know about brill—"

"I'm going to run this up there right now to see if I can calibrate it to match your delta stream." She clenches the drive in her fist. Her enthusiasm fades into foreboding. "Listen, if this works, and you wake up, you'll disappear from Slumbervale. People will think you died."

"But then I'll just reboot the next day—or night, technically."

"That's if you got back to sleep the next night. I haven't quite figured out how that works, exactly. The simulation is piped to a port—somewhere in your brain I would assume. Once this is out there, it's up to the real you to do something about it. Maybe you'll find out who is doing this and shut it all down. That is, if it even works."

If I shut Slumbervale down, I'll lose Piper forever. What are the chances I even know her in the real world?

"How will I know what to do?" I ask. "We're assuming my real self knows more about this than we do. But what if he's just as in the dark as we are?"

"Don't think like that, Hugo. We have to think positive."

"Right."

"Listen, you need to get out of here. We need to keep a low profile and you're already kind of famous around here."

"Famous, aye?"

"That's not a good thing. We don't need the attention. Try to stay out of the public eye, alright?"

"Yeah, okay."

"I'll see you at home?"

I nod. I want to kiss her, but that wouldn't be very low profile of us. Her bedroom eyes tell me she wants to kiss me, too, but instead she tugs once on the lapel of my jacket, then darts away, the sound of her heels joining the echoing chorus of purposeful corporate efficiency. She glances back over her shoulder once before vanishing into another soulless hallway.

It takes me a moment to accept that she has left my presence and I am flooded with longing. Now I understand why relationships are frowned upon. I can't think of anything else. I only care about the mission at hand because it's *her* mission—because *she* cares about it. If she were a Steve Gower fanatic, I'd be memorizing lines from the Book of Illumination. I'd carry his portrait around and eat pancakes like I was taking communion. If she thought this was all there was, that the universe was really a stack of pancakes, I'm pretty sure I'd pretend to believe it, too.

As I walk out into the courtyard in front of Central Systems, Darcy is on patrol. Instead of turning left toward the teleporter, I turn right to avoid her line of sight. But I'm not quick enough and she spots me.

"Hey! You!" Darcy calls. Maybe she wants to congratulate me on a great show. Everyone else seems to.

"Hey, Darcy," I say reluctantly. "How are you?"

"What are you doing here? You're nowhere near the studio."

"You can't arrest me for not having a hall pass."

She presses her lips together like a flatline on an ECG. "You have no business at Central Systems. Do you need an escort back to your studio?"

"No, I know where it is."

"Do you? Because you're walking in the wrong direction. The teleporter is over there." She thrusts a thumb over her shoulder.

"Ah. Thanks for the help, officer. Much appreciated." I can't help the sarcasm in my tone.

"You're not here to see Piper, are you?"

"How is that any of your business?"

Her glare intensifies. "Are you?"

"Seriously, Darcy, I think you need to loosen up. I'm not breaking any laws here. I've never seen this part of Slumber-vale, okay? I just wanted to check it out. Is that a crime?"

Her shoulders slump. "No. But I'm keeping tabs on you, Hugo. I'm logging that you were at Central today without any justifiable reason."

An older sentinel approaches. "Everything alright over here?"

"This gentleman is not where he's supposed to be," Darcy explains.

The older sentinel squints. "Hey, you're that Hugo fella, ain't ya?"

I nod, grinning. "Guilty."

"Hey boys," he calls to his other sentinel pals across the courtyard. "It's that Hugo from Stevefest!"

Darcy rolls her eyes. "It doesn't matter."

"What's that?"

"It doesn't matter who he is. He needs to be back at his job site. He has no business here."

"Well, I'm sure he has a good reason." He regards me. "Don't ya, son?"

"Yes, sir. See, I'm a songwriter," I explain, placing a hand on my chest. "And a songwriter needs inspiration. It's important for me to explore Slumbervale far and wide . . . to collect material for my songs."

"You think you'd ever write a song about us?" Two more sentinels have joined the conversation.

"Sentinels?"

"Why not? You could write a song about how us sentinels keep everyone safe. Something like . . ." He clears his throat and starts to sing—badly.

Everyone loves a sentinel.
Keeping peace is intentional.
Even though their uniforms are lamentable,
Neighborhood crime is preventable.

"Well, you know, I'm not a songwriter like you," he says coyly.

"No, that was great." I hum back the ditty he just created and add, *"Their actions are commendable . . ."*

"Okay, okay," Darcy interrupts. "I think we should all get back to work."

"But Hugo *is* working," he says. "He's writing a song. That's his job. Isn't it, Hugo?"

"Right you are, sir. And I think it's going to be a big hit."

"You really think so?" He pulls his shoulders back and stands straighter.

"In fact, I think I'm gonna head back to the studio and get to work on it right away." I look at Darcy, who is glaring at me with her arms crossed. She doesn't believe me. And she's right. I will not be writing a song about sentinels.

"Oh, Hugo," the sentinel says, "before you go, do you think we could get a picture with you?"

"Sure, no problem," I say.

"Darcy," the sentinel says, handing her his camera, "could you take our picture?"

Darcy lets out a sigh of exasperation and snatches the camera from him. The sentinel puts an arm around my shoulder as the others crowd in around us. Darcy snaps the photo and hands the camera back to the older sentinel, and then stomps away. I smile as I stride toward the teleporter, vindicated.

CHAPTER 28

THIS IS YOUR BRAIN

ON MY WAY home from the impound lot, I drove slower than usual. I kept scanning the streets for Ava. Every pedestrian caught my attention and I even turned down the radio so I could concentrate. But then a familiar song came on and I couldn't remember who it was by so I turned it up again. I found myself mouthing the words silently to myself. It sounded so familiar. I knew every word, every hook. Even though I couldn't identify where I'd heard it before, it stirred a feeling in me that I hadn't experienced in a very long time.

When it ended, the DJ announced: *That was Ben Mazer with his new single "Lock Me Up," a distinct departure from his usual brand of indie-pop fare, and I gotta say, I think it's working for him. 12.4 million streams on Spotify in it's first 24 hours of release. Those are some impressive numbers for a relatively new artist who, less than a year ago, was playing acoustic covers on TikTok . . .*

Ben Mazer was a popular singer-songwriter who rose up through the social media ranks in the last couple years and was currently selling out stadiums. But how was this a brand new song? It had to be a cover, but who was the original artist?

When I finally arrived at home, I noticed the front door was unlocked. Lenny must have forgotten to lock it when he came to check on Ava. I threw my keys on the kitchen counter and gasped at the sight of a professionally dressed woman sitting, legs crossed, in my living room chair.

"I didn't mean to frighten you, Mr. Castillo. My name is Cynthia Westfield. I'm here on behalf of the Lunatech Corporation."

"What are you doing in my house?"

"I wish you would have waited a bit longer at the hospital. We were sending a car."

It was Lunatech! They were the ones who posted bail.

"Did Lunatech bail me out?"

"Well, let's just call it an advance. You didn't plug in last night. That was a freebie. We can't have you in jail, away from your console. We need you plugged in every night from here on out. Do you understand, Mr. Castillo?"

"Yes, but there were extenuating circumstances. My daughter—"

"Ava?"

"How did you—"

"We've got a team searching for her. You did the right thing by not getting the police involved. We have far more resources at our disposal than the local police. And we have far more invested in making sure she is safe and accounted for, so that you can continue to perform your contracted obligations with us."

I supposed I should be grateful for the bail out and the search team, but they weren't doing it for my sake. Their priority was their own corporate interests. Luckily, they saw me as an asset. I was valuable to them as long as I was performing my obligations. Of course, I knew this from the beginning, but seeing the power and reach they had just to protect their asset put me on edge.

"I have to ask you something," I ventured.

"Of course."

"Did Lunatech put a microchip in my brain?" I knew how stupid it sounded.

She laughed in a rigid, unnatural manner. "Where did you get that idea?"

"They found something in my CT scan. A density, they called it."

"Okay? What does that have to do with us?"

"Well, my friend Lenny read online that sleepers were being chipped and—"

"Let me stop you right there, Mr. Castillo. You can't believe everything you read online."

"I know. But my friend Darcy said she had headaches after her initial sleep study, which is one of the things they said was common with new sleepers."

"That's true. Unfortunately, the electrode cap we've previously issued was one size fits all and isn't the most comfortable fit for some. We've taken these reports into account and are developing a few new sizes to accommodate various cranial dimensions."

"Oh."

"Was that all?"

"I guess so."

"Now I have a question for you."

"Okay."

"We've been developing a pilot program that a many of our clients are practically begging us to roll out. It's still in the works with our legal team, but we're reaching out to a few trusted partners to sign off on a beta program for youth—the Junior Sleeper Program." She handed me a colorful brochure with a picture of a diverse grouping of laughing teenagers. I couldn't imagine what they'd be laughing about.

"You want to recruit Ava as a sleeper?" My stomach turned.

"There's enormous demand for young, authentic perspectives," Cynthia said, sliding the brochure closer. "For that reason the Junior Sleeper Program pays significantly more than our standard contract. We've also partnered with the U of A on scholarships and academic support—it's an obvious path for a promising teen. I assume you plan to send Ava to college. They have a wonderful theater program."

How did she know Ava was in theater? There's no way I could afford to pay for Ava's college on my own. She would need a scholarship. But this feels exploitive and gross. "Oh, I don't know."

"Think about it."

"But Ava's missing."

"Trust me on this, Mr. Castillo. We have vast resources and influential partners, including the Mayor's office and the Chief of Police. We will find her. We could have Ava's criminal record expunged . . ." She snapped her fingers. " . . . just like that. Our legal team has relationships that can streamline matters. That is, if she were to sign on with our youth program, with your consent, of course."

"I think we should focus on getting her home first."

"Yes, of course. I'm sure it won't be long. We've only just begun."

Cynthia showed herself out and let me know she'd be in touch. It surprised me how much she knew, that Ava was in theater, that she had just been charged with a felony, that I had been admitted to the hospital, but it shouldn't have. Lunatech has free access to all my thoughts. They know everything I know.

I went back to Ava's room and laid on her bed. I guess I just wanted to feel closer to her but it brought no relief. There was something behind my back and I reached behind me and pulled out Ava's stuffed Piglet, the one we got her at Disneyland when she was five. She'd donated most of her stuffies a while back, but hung onto this ratty one for some reason. It had definitely seen better days.

I sat it beside me and it stared back. For a split second, I had the disorienting impression I was on a green couch. Piglet didn't move. It was still in the same position, staring at me, but it was sitting on a green couch. But the moment the image registered, it was gone.

A car pulled up in my driveway and I moved the curtain back to see Darcy's Land Rover. How did she know where I lived? I met her at the front door before she could reach the door bell. Ernie was with her. How do they know each other?

"Hey, Darcy. Ernie. What are you guys doing here?"

"How's the head?" Ernie said.

I forgot I still had that bandage on and I reached up to touch it. "It's okay. I got into an accident."

"I know. Can we come in?" Ernie asked without his usual jovial demeanor.

We sat around the kitchen table. I offered them water but they both declined.

"What's this about? How do you guys know each other?" I asked.

"Lenny contacted me a few days ago about this whole microchip thing with Lunatech. Said Darcy here was having headaches."

"I just spoke to a Lunatech representative about that," I said. "She denied it."

"Of course she did," Ernie said. "Listen, I run the imaging lab at TMC so Lenny asked if I could do a brain scan on Darcy to see if there was anything unusual. I could lose my job doing something like that. I had to sneak her in after hours. Sure enough—" He placed a glossy printout on the table. "This is Darcy's CT scan."

He'd circled a tiny rectangular shape in red. It looked just like the one Dr. Gomez showed me of my own brain. What are the chances Darcy and I have matching shrapnel in our heads?

"I was on shift when you came in last night, Hugo. I was the one who did your CT scan." He procured a second glossy photo. "This is your brain." The exact rectangular density was circled and I compared them. My hands were shaking. "These suits come into the hospital with all this documentation and legalese. They had all your neurological scans and tests removed from the hospital's system. I didn't know anyone could do that, but when I checked, they were gone."

Darcy finally spoke up. "They don't want the public to know about these microchips."

"What do you think they're there for?" I asked. "Lunatech already has access to our minds through the console when we plug in. What's the chip for?"

"Maybe it's for mind control," Ernie said. "Have you been getting any strange messages or intrusive thoughts lately?"

There was that moment in Ava's room with the stuffed pig, but that didn't seem to qualify as an intrusive thought. Plus, how do you even explain that? I shook my head.

"I don't know if this counts," Darcy began, "but I heard this song on the radio today—"

The tune I heard earlier popped in my head. "The Ben Mazer song?"

"I don't know who sings it, but there was this line in there about being prisoners or captives or something, anyway, I had this—I don't know if you'd call it a flashback—but I was at this outdoor concert, lots of people, and I looked up at the big screen—I was too far to see the stage—but I looked up and I could have sworn it was you singing that song! But then I was back in the car and the light turned green and that was it. Is that what you'd call an intrusive thought?"

"It could be," Ernie said. "But I don't know what Lunatech would have to do with that."

"So what do we do?" I asked. "Can we get them removed?"

"As far as the hospital is concerned, there *is* nothing to remove," he said ominously.

What had we gotten ourselves into? The contract was iron-clad. While there was nothing in there, that I saw anyway, about microchip implants, the contract was clear on one thing —your brain belongs to us.

"Who did you say you spoke to at Lunatech?" Darcy asked.

"Uh . . . Cynthia-something. I have her card here some-where." Looked around for where I'd placed it.

"Yes! Cynthia Westfield. Super professional looking, hair pulled-back so tight it looked like her eyes might pop out? She talked to me, too. Did she say anything to you about this new sleeper program for kids?"

I nodded slowly.

Darcy shook her head. "At first I thought maybe it was a good idea—scholarships and other perks. But that was before Ernie confirmed the chip implants. Now I don't want them anywhere near Declan."

"Ava . . . ran away last night."

Darcy gasped. "Oh no! Where do you think she might have gone?"

I shook my head. "I don't know. She has this new girl-friend, but I don't think she's welcome there after . . ."

"After what?" Darcy asked.

"It's a long story."

"Gee, I'm sorry to hear that, Hugo," Ernie said. "Let me know if there's anything I can do."

"Did you call the police?" Darcy asked.

"No. Cynthia said . . ."

At the time, Cynthia told me what I wanted to hear, that Ava would be found soon and returned safely to me. I didn't question any ulterior motives for their involvement with this highly personal family matter. I believed they were capable of finding her, which was both comforting and terrifying at the same time. The corporation who could pay my bail and locate my missing daughter was also capable of deleting my hospital records and inserting a device into my brain without my consent. What else were they capable of?

"Hugo?" Ernie drew out my name, calling me back to the present. "What did the Lunatech lady say exactly?"

"She said they were already looking for her. Said not to bother calling the police. She went on and on about the resources at their disposal and how it was in their best interest to get her home safe."

"So maybe you use that to your advantage," he said. "Let them know you're interested in signing her up. That'll give them more reason to find her."

It was hard to put all my trust in Lunatech, especially after all they'd done. But under the circumstances, it did make the most sense. I could pretend to play along. Hanging around the house, waiting for Ava to show up was enervating. I needed a drink, but I remembered what I promised Celeste earlier in the hospital. Besides, I wanted to be fully present in case she turned up, either on her own, or in the custody of Lunatech.

That night I plugged in as directed.

CHAPTER 29

PUNCHING GAME

WHEN I ARRIVE BACK at the studio, Vincent, Cash, and Garrett are all squeezed into the engineering booth. Not a single hello.

"What's going on?" I ask.

"What the hell is this?" Cash asks accusingly, pointing at Vincent's laptop. He hits play.

I'm mortified when the coded jingle plays back. I had forgotten to move it to the trash after saving it to the thumb drive. Shit! Cash picks up my notebook. I'd left that here, too? Fuck!

"Slumbervale isn't real, we know it's all fake?" Cash reads back my lyrics with biting animosity. "They say it's your purpose, you don't have a say?"

Vincent looks more disappointed than indignant, which is worse. "What is this, Hugo?" They're all looking at me, waiting for an explanation. I want to claw a hole into the floorboards and crawl inside it.

"Is this some kind of joke?" Cash fires.

"Yes! A joke. It's just some silly idea I had—like what if we existed in a dream and none of this was real. It's a story I was playing with, that's all."

Heads begin to nod—slowly. My paltry explanation filling in cracks in their doubt like sediment.

"So you don't actually believe any of this," Garrett stated, as if feeding me the correct reply.

"Psshh . . . No, of course not. It's fictional. I'm a songwriter —a storyteller. You get that, right?"

"I guess I can buy that," Vincent says. "But this is very sensitive subject matter. If this fell into the wrong hands . . . some folks could get the wrong idea—think you're staging some kind of rebellion."

"Me?" A hand on my chest sells my innocence. "I would never."

"Says the rock star," Cash says with an impish draw.

"Other people have had similar ideas," Garrett explains. "They all got sent to restoration. It's a dangerous topic is all."

"I had no idea," I say. "Delete it. I was only messing around anyway. Look." I take my notebook and tear out the poorly written lyrics, wad them up, and toss them into the wastebasket.

Vincent regards me with acuity before moving the project file into the trash. "Well, that settles that. How about we get to work on our next assignment?"

Relief pours down my chest like warm milk.

"What is it this time?" Cash asks.

"Dandruff shampoo," Vincent says with a straight face, and then grins.

Everyone laughs.

The tension from our previous conversation evaporates the moment we pick up our instruments. We spend the rest of the afternoon writing a jingle for dandruff shampoo and I wonder if my real self has ever struggled with such an affliction of the scalp.

When we finish recording, I teleport back to the house. Theo and Geoff are trading punches.

"Guys! What are you doing?" I call out while positioning myself between them with outstretched hands.

"Hey, Hugo," Geoff says. "We're playing the punching game."

"What? Stop it! What's the punching game?"

"First person to fall down loses," Theo explains. "So far neither of us has fallen."

"Theo almost did," Geoff says, "if it wasn't for that wall."

"Guys, wha—no!"

"It doesn't hurt," Geoff says.

"Can I show you?" Theo says drawing back his pudgy fist.

"No, I don't want to get pun—"

Theo clocks me in the mouth and I stumble backward. Instinctively, I cover my mouth, but to my surprise, Geoff is right—it doesn't hurt.

"Now you punch me," Theo says.

"No. Guys, you can't let Rafael see you doing this."

"Oh, we know," Theo says, pushing his glasses up on his nose. "He's a real party pooper."

Geoff catches Theo off guard and punches him in the side of his head. This time, Theo stumbles sideways and falls to his knee.

"I win!" Geoff says.

"That's not fair! I wasn't ready," Theo says repositioning his glasses. He uses an armrest to pull himself up to standing.

"Okay. Guys, seriously. Come here. I want to talk to you about something." I take a seat in the living room and gesture for Theo and Geoff to join me. The discovery that we cannot bleed or feel pain has really made an impression on these guys. If Piper's staging a rebellion, she's going to want as much help as she can get.

"What's up, Hugo?" Theo asks.

"I wanted to talk about his no pain thing. Why do you think Rafael is being so cagey about it?"

Theo looks at Geoff and then back at me. "Well, he's afraid we'll all start attacking each other for fun, I guess."

"And that would disrupt our work," Geoff adds.

"Right," Theo says. "But what if we made it a scheduled event? Like field day, but instead of the boring relays and Red Rover games, we get to use swords and crossbows?"

"Okay," I say. "But what do you think that means about us —like what we are?"

"What do you mean?" Geoff asks.

"How would you define our species, for example?"

"Human, of course," Theo says with confidence.

"Are we human if we don't bleed, if we can't feel pain, if we can't procreate?"

"I hadn't thought of that," Theo says pensively.

"What if, now hear me out," I say. I know I shouldn't say more, but we need allies. "What if we're avatars? What if we only think we're real, because that's what we've been told? But what if the reason we don't feel pain is because we're just avatars in a computer simulation?"

"Then how come we can think and problem solve?" Geoff asks.

"Because our minds belong to our real selves, in the real world. In the real world, we're asleep. That's why our day is only eight hours long. Then, we wake up in the real world and live our real lives. When we go back to sleep, we wake up again here, in Slumbervale."

"So that's why it's called *Slumber*-vale," Geoff says, a light bulb illuminating behind his eyes.

"But why? What is this for?" Theo asks.

"Whoever is orchestrating this is exploiting us for free labor. You guys probably *are* scientists in the real world, but you're working an extra eight hours a day in Slumbervale without pay."

"Why don't we remember anything about our real lives?" Theo asks.

"Because there's a firewall. It keeps our real life and our dream life separate."

"You're saying we're in a dream?" Geoff asks.

"Kind of. But it's controlled. Slumbervale is a simulation. We exist within its boundaries and we follow its rules."

Theo shakes his head. "I don't know, Hugo. That sounds a lot like the stuff Piper says that gets her sent to restoration."

"I know, I know" I say. "But why do you think they don't like people talking about this? What are they so afraid of?"

Geoff's eye flash. "That's why I don't remember how to dance."

"That's right," I say. "Something slipped through. Something they didn't want you to know, and that's why they sent you to restoration."

"But why wouldn't they want him to know how to dance?" Theo asks.

I shake my head. "I don't know."

"I do," Geoff says. "Dancing makes me feel confident. And free."

"And that's a threat," I say. "They don't want you to be free."

Theo has a stunned look on his face. He isn't pushing back. He isn't agreeing either.

"Theo? You're not going to turn me in, are you?" I ask.

He shakes his head. "No. I think on some level . . . " He shakes the thought away.

"What? This is a safe space. Say what's on your mind. It's okay."

"Well . . . so you know how we have pancake parties? To honor the pancake universe?"

Geoff nods.

"Well, the last time we had one," Theo looks at me. "This was before you got here. I had a flashback, I guess you might call it."

"What did you see?" I ask.

"Reindeer pancakes."

"Pardon?"

"Reindeer pancakes. They had bacon for antlers and blueberries for eyes and a raspberry for a nose. But then I blinked and they were just normal pancakes. But I kept thinking about the reindeer ones and I felt a terrible sadness." His eyes conveyed a deep sadness in that moment but no tears appeared. We probably don't have those either.

"Why do pancakes make you sad?" Geoff asks.

"Maybe they're tied to some sad memory in your real life," I say. "But you can't access that memory here. Somehow the feeling slipped through, just like Geoff's ability dance. I had something similar happen."

"You had a flashback?" Geoff asks.

"Yeah. But listen, you guys have to promise me something. Promise you'll keep this between us."

They nod.

"Piper was able to find some information about my real life. I have a daughter. Her name is Ava. When I said her name out loud, I felt a strong emotion. Not sadness, exactly. More like a deep concern, mixed with longing, and fear, and . . . love. But it was deep—so deep that I was afraid I might lose myself in it."

"That sounds intense," Geoff says.

"It was. But how else would you explain it? An emotion that strong doesn't come from nowhere."

"How did Piper find that information?" Theo asks.

"She works at Central," Geoff says. "She's a hacker."

"I wonder if she knows anything about our lives," Theo says. "Maybe she knows about the pancakes."

"Are you sure that's something you want to know?" I ask.

He nods. "I do."

"Ask her," I say.

"What are we supposed to do, Hugo?" Geoff asks.

"Piper's working on a plan. It's highly technical, but basically, we're trying to break through to our real selves. They probably don't know what's going on here. We're hoping our real selves can put a stop to all of this."

The front door opens. Speak of the devil—that sweet beautiful devil. Piper freezes when she sees the three of us. "What's going on?" Piper asks with suspicion.

"What can you tell me about reindeer pancakes?" Theo asks.

I rest my head in my hands.

"Excuse me?" She challenges.

"Reindeer pancakes. Why did I have a flashback about reindeer pancakes?"

She looks at me, tilting her head. "What did you do?!"

"It's fine. Everything is fine," I reassure, but she isn't buying.

"Can I speak to you in the kitchen?" Piper asks through clenched teeth.

"It's okay. I told them about the simulation. They're on board."

"What?!" Her eyes boar into mine.

"We're going to need a team," I explain. "They can help. Right, guys?"

They both nod.

Piper sighs. She plops down on the couch and runs her hands through her hair. After a moment, she collects herself and grabs Theo's hand. "Your husband made you reindeer pancakes for Christmas every year," she says solemnly.

"I'm married?" Theo asks.

She tilts her head to the ceiling for a moment and then looks him in the eye. "You *were* married. Your divorce was finalized right before you were born here."

"Oh," Theo says, eyes finding the floor. "Oh."

"I'm sorry," Piper says.

"Yeah, sorry, man," I say.

"No, it's okay," Theo says, but it's clear it's not. "I can see why they don't want us to get into relationships here. I thought I knew before, but now it makes a lot more sense. How do we get anything done out there with all this pain?"

"I don't know," I say. "But I for one, would rather know than not know. It's *our* pain after all. It's not up to anyone else what we're allowed to think or feel. You guys are more than a scientists." I turn to Piper. "You're more than a hacker. And I'm more than a musician. We have whole lives out there, and yes, they may come with struggles, but they're *our* struggles and if we can't work through them in our own way, how can we be so sure what our true purpose is? How can we know what really matters to us personally?"

"I don't really like being a scientist," Geoff says.

"Really?" Piper asks. "I thought you loved that stuff."

Geoff shakes his head. "I'm good at it. But I don't love it."

"What *do* you love," I ask him.

"Dancing."

"I thought you said you didn't remember how to dance," Theo says.

"I don't. But I remember what it felt like the other night. I've never felt more alive."

"You don't remember because they erased that part of your memory when they took you to restoration," Piper says. "When you danced that day, your serotonin levels spiked. They monitor your emotional state up at Central and that raised a red flag, since you don't normally feel that happy doing what you do, I imagine. When they saw that spike they determined that joy to be a threat."

"Why would joy be considered a threat?" Theo asks.

"Let me remind you," Piper says, "they don't even allow you to have a penis."

"Point taken."

"What did you find out about me?" Geoff asks. "I'm not a scientist in real life, am I?"

"You are," she says regretfully. "You're an engineer for a robotics company."

"I see," Geoff says, unable to hide his disappointment.

"But you're also in a men over 40 hip hop dance troop," Piper says. "They call themselves . . ." she hesitates, " . . . Groovin' Geezers."

Geoff's eyes light up. "That sounds pretty cool."

"Does it?" Piper asks, unable to help herself.

"So what are we supposed to do?" Geoff asks.

"I've sent word to Hugo's real self about what's going on here in Slumbervale. It's just a matter of time before he figures it out and puts a stop to all this."

"Do you think he'll be able to figure it out?" Theo asks.

Piper looked to me with pleading eyes. "He's our only hope."

"Maybe not," I say. "Can you upload the song to Theo and Geoff's real selves?"

Geoff nods in agreement. Theo seems less enthused.

"I suppose I could," Piper says. "Theo? What are you thinking?"

"I don't know. Reality seems pretty harsh. I'm not sure I want to wake up."

"Why not upload it to everyone in Slumbervale?" I ask. "The more people who know, the better chance we have to uncover the truth about what's going on here."

"That's going to take some time, but I think I can create an algorithm to automate the process." She nods. "Yeah, I think that could work."

"Theo?" I prompt. "Are you game?"

He looks at each of us, then nods. "Okay. I'm in."

Rafael walks in and informs us that it's time to reboot. He looks distracted, preoccupied. He isn't as chatty as he normally is. We all sit around the table and lay our heads down. Piper and I hold each other's stare for several seconds before she closes her eyes.

CHAPTER 30
CEMETERY

I WOKE up the next morning with a jaunty melody bouncing through my skull like a dream not quite ready to let go. Of course, that wasn't possible. The electrode cap doesn't allow dreaming. I sat up, removed the cap, and hung it carefully on the post of my headboard.

While you sleep you are wide awake.

These words accompanied the happy melody as I padded to the bathroom to relieve myself.

We know it's all fake.

I hummed out loud as my forceful stream abated to a trickle. I checked my phone to see if Ava had texted and then to her bedroom to make sure she hadn't returned while I was sleeping. She hadn't. I checked my phone again for any messages from Lunatech—nothing.

What's all fake? I asked myself. The melody was accessible but the words seemed increasingly out of reach. Something about *Slumbervale*? What's Slumbervale? Whatever it was, it wasn't real. The harder I reached for the words, the faster they dissolved.

The pain in my arm distracted me. I went into the kitchen

to get some Ibuprofen and start the coffee. As I filled the coffee maker's reservoir I heard Ava's phone ding. Water spilled onto the countertop as my eyes focused on the new notification now visible on her lock screen. It was a text from Sydney. When I clicked on the notification the keyboard appeared asking for a passcode. Most parents probably know their kid's passcode. Not me. I never saw a need for it—until now.

I typed in her birthday. The screen shuttered, rejecting my attempt. I should have known she'd be too smart to use her birthday. I turned and leaned on the counter, trying to imagine any significant numerical combinations that Ava might have used.

Out of the corner of my eye, a hummingbird hovered outside the kitchen window. It was looking right at me. I'm not superstitious, but it made me think of Celeste. I typed in my late wife's birthday. That wasn't it. I looked back up and the hummingbird was gone. As much as it pained me, I slowly keyed in the date of her death.

The lock screen disappeared and was replaced by a grid of colorful icons. I tapped her message app and then on Sydney's message:

> I know you probably hate me. I'm so sorry. I promise I'll make it right. I have to see you.
> Meet me at our spot.

What was their spot? I didn't even know they hung out anywhere besides Sydney's house or mine. And then it occurred to me. I clicked Sydney's name at the top of the message and a map appeared with Sydney's location. Currently, Sydney was at home, but as long as she was sharing her location with Ava, I could easily track her down.

It felt wrong to impersonate my daughter, but I texted back:

I'll be right there.

I waited until I saw Sydney's avatar begin to move away from her house. I got in my truck and navigated toward her general direction. I coached myself on how to play this. I wasn't angry at Sydney anymore—not after all this. I just wanted Ava home and if Sydney wanted the same thing, she was more of an ally than an enemy.

I didn't know what I was expecting—the worst probably. But my heart warmed to discover that their clandestine rendezvous happened to be the most innocent place I could have imagined—a man-made rock water feature under the canopy of Aleppo pines, smack dab in the middle of Reid Park. We picnicked here when she was much younger. Watched her float tiny sticks down the stream while I laid my head in Celeste's lap making plans for the future.

Sydney sat against a massive pine tree, burgundy-dyed strands of hair spilling from her hooded sweatshirt. She must have been listening to music when I approached her because she didn't hear me at first. When she saw me, she pulled out her earbuds and quickly stood up.

"Mr. Castillo?" She seemed both surprised and suspicious of my presence. "Where's Ava?"

"I was hoping you knew. She's been gone since Thursday."

"Seriously? Oh my god." She registered my arm. "What happened to you?"

"Accident," I said, hoping she wouldn't ask any follow-ups.

"How did you know I was here?"

I showed Sydney Ava's phone. "Sorry. I was hoping you might have some answers."

She shook her head as tears filled her eyes. "She must have thought we were done after I just threw her under the bus like that. She was trying to cover for me and I . . ." Something in her throat prevented her from finishing. "I feel like such a fucking coward!"

"No. Sydney, don't say that." I ventured to place a hand on her shoulder, half expecting her to jerk it away, but she didn't.

"We have to find her," she said.

"Where would she go?" It was humbling to admit to myself that this kid might know my daughter better than me.

Sydney shook her head as she stared into a void, then her eyes snapped to me again. "Did you check the cemetery?"

I hadn't visited Celeste's gravesite since the first anniversary of her death, and that was only because Ava had made a big thing of it. Her therapist at the time had been working with her on this collage, which framed a poem she wrote for her mother. She wanted to read it out loud and leave it there on her headstone.

She woke me up that morning, already dressed. I was still sleeping off a hangover. After picking up a bouquet of flowers from our neighborhood grocery, I drove her to the cemetery. I stood back several feet, sunglasses hiding the shame behind bloodshot eyes. I put her there.

Ava spoke to her for a good half hour. She read her poem and then sat cross-legged in front of the headstone and started talking, as if she'd seen her last week. At one point, Ava turned to me and invited me to come say something. I shook my head and she continued talking to her mom, pulling up blades of grass one at a time. Finally, she stood, wiped grass from her jeans and said, "Bye, mom," and walked right past me toward the truck.

Sydney called shotgun, which may have been her attempt to bring some levity to the situation since my truck didn't have a back seat. When we got there she followed me to the gravesite, hands buried in the pockets of her sweatshirt. As the headstone came into view, I was struck. It had been covered in little strips of paper taped to its granite surface. Fortune cookie messages—tons of them.

We ate Chinese take-out at least twice a month. Ava's favorite part of the meal was the end, after everyone had finished, we all opened our fortune cookies one at a time and read them out loud. I couldn't stop the tears from falling onto the granite slab. How often had Ava been coming here without me?

We still ate Chinese from time to time and now it made sense. We'd read our fortunes like we always had, and then Ava would ask to keep my fortune. It never occurred to me to ask why. I recognized one of my old fortunes there, just below the year of her death: *The one you love is closer than you think.*

"That one's new," Sydney pointed out. How often did she come here, I wondered.

I wiped tears from my eye with the heel of my hand and sniffed hard. "Which one?"

"There." Sydney pointed to a fortune that read: *Don't hold onto things that require a tight grip.* "That one wasn't here last week."

Was it a clue? I didn't even know what that meant. What difference did it make? She wasn't here now. My phone buzzed in my pocket—a text:

We found her.

I almost choked on my own heart.
"They found her," I said to Sydney.
"Who?"
A second text came in:

She's home.

"Let's go."

"Who found her?" Sydney asked again.

"It's a long story." We started to head to the truck and I stopped in my tracks. Sydney looked back over her shoulder. "You go ahead. I'll be right there," I said. I walked back to the gravesite and knelt at Celeste's fortune-covered headstone once again. I pressed my palm to the cold stone. I wanted to say I love you, but instead I said, "I'm sorry."

On the way to the house, a commercial came on the radio. "What the fuck?"

"Are you okay?" Sydney asked.

"I know this song." I turned it up.

"It's a commercial?" She said it slow, in the form of a question, the way teenagers have always inferred stupidity.

"No, it's—" The words were completely new to me. It was about cats, nothing about Slumbervale being fake or sleeping while being wide awake. Nothing about working for free, eight hours a day. The commercial ended and I continued trying to piece together phrases that were quickly losing purchase in my mind as a the next commercial announced the latest deals on new Ford trucks.

When we got to the house, a black SUV was parked outside. My stomach dropped. I rushed inside and found Ava sitting on the kitchen counter, eating potato chips from a family-sized bag. Cynthia stood from my living room chair, straightening her blazer. I took Ava in my good arm and wouldn't let go.

"Okay, dad." She patted my back like a wrestler surrendering the fight.

Tears fell from my eyes. I took her face in my hand and kissed her forehead. I held her head against my chest and stroked her hair. "I was so scared, sweetheart."

"I'm okay, dad. Are you okay? She told me about your accident."

"Yeah, I'm fine. What happened to you?"

Cynthia stepped toward us. "Ava was kidnapped. We found her in an abandoned warehouse, sedated. We think she was being trafficked."

"Trafficked? Oh my god!"

"The cartel has increased their trafficking activities recently."

"Jesus!" You hear about these kidnappings, but you never think it would happen to your own. I brushed Ava's hair back from her face, searching for any marks or bruising.

"Luckily, we found her just in time. The perpetrators got away before we had a chance to identify them."

"Did they hurt you?"

Ava shook her head. "I don't think so. I don't remember anything."

"What do you remember?" I asked her.

"I went to see mom and—" Ava was distracted. Sydney appeared in the kitchen doorway from the hall. "Syd?"

"Hey," Sydney replied cautiously.

"What are you doing here?"

"I wanted to apologize about the other day with my mom. That was really shitty of me and I was hoping there might be some way to make it right. I promise I'll tell her the truth. I was just caught off guard and I choked. I'm really sorry."

"Yeah, it was shitty," Ava said. She looked at me. "You were right, dad. I should have listened to you. I'm sorry."

I couldn't believe my ears. "You don't have to be sorry. I'm just happy you're home safe."

Cynthia cleared her throat. "Ava and I had a conversation on the way here."

"Oh yeah," Ava said, perking up. "Can I do the sleeper

thing? Cynthia said they have one for teens and it comes with a scholarship so you don't have to worry about college."

My elation soured immediately. As grateful as I was to Lunatech for finding my girl, I didn't want them anywhere near her brain. "We can talk about that later," I said.

"We have an orientation tomorrow for the teens and their parents. It's not going to be a high pressure situation, just a chance to answer any questions and get to know one another. Then there'll be a lock-in just for the kids. They'll be supervised the whole time."

"Can we go, dad?"

"Sydney, you're welcome to come, too, if you like," Cynthia added before I could answer.

Sydney glanced at Ava, who did her best to act disinterested one way or the other. I tried my best to suppress a prideful smile.

"Well," Cynthia said, handing me an invitation to the informational seminar, "I'll be on my way. I expect you'll both rest easy tonight."

"Thank you," I said. "I wasn't sure I could trust Lunatech with this, but you pulled through. And for that, I am truly grateful."

"You're welcome, Hugo. Sleep well tonight."

After walking Cynthia to the door I returned to the kitchen to two very awkward teenagers. "Are you guys hungry?" Neither of them replied. "Why don't you guys stay here and talk. I'll run out and get us some subs, yeah?"

Ava nodded.

"No onions," Sydney said without looking at me.

"Oh, here." I dug Ava's phone from my pocket and handed it to her. She held it to her chest and I kissed her again on the forehead before leaving.

CHAPTER 31
GURU

AFTER WE REBOOT and do our rounds, Rafael dismisses us to fulfill our respective purposes. Even Rafael is starting to sound less optimistic, like he senses change is afoot. The stabbings and talk of indestructibility seems to have rattled him. He's distracted. Doesn't even ask follow up questions when Theo has trouble stringing sentences together about proteins and cell regeneration. Everyone is preoccupied. No comments about dandruff shampoo and how none of us will ever experience such an affliction—or use any shampoo at all.

Theo and Geoff follow Piper and I close behind as we walk toward the teleporter. Rafael is watching us from the window.

"What's the plan?" Theo asks Piper.

"Just act normal. Go to work and don't do anything to raise suspicion. We can't afford to get sent to restoration and lose all the progress we've made. Got it?"

"Got it," Theo and Geoff say in unison. They step inside the teleporter and nod in solidarity before the door closes with a whir.

Piper turns to me. "There's something else. I didn't want to bring it up with the others last night."

"What is it?"

"I don't have a file."

"What do you mean?"

"I'm not in the database where I found you and the others. They must've put my file somewhere else, knowing I might go looking for it."

"So you don't know anything about your real self," I surmise.

"I don't know if I have a boyfriend or a husband. And even if I am single, I don't know if you're even ready to start dating again, or if you have someone new. What if it doesn't work out for us out there?"

"Hey, hey, don't worry." I take her hand. "I have a strong feeling that we're meant to be together. Don't you?"

She smiles. "Yeah." She nods her reassurance. "I do."

As I reach for a hug, Piper backs up and lifts her chin in the direction of the house. The curtain falls closed as Rafael backs away. Piper gives me a forced grin and steps inside the teleporter.

When I arrive downtown, a large crowd is gathered at a new construction site. Even though it's fenced off, I know there is no real danger to anyone observing. The handful of construction workers, all in hard hats and reflective vests, stand around the perimeter with arms outstretched as entire walls fall into place from . . . the sky? Doors and windows appear from nowhere at strategic locations along the front wall. After all the walls are in place, a roof caps the two story structure.

"What's going on?" I ask the nearest observer.

"They're building a school," she says with great pride.

"A school? For who?"

"The kids!"

As long as I've been here, I have never seen any kids. I can't imagine what useful skills children might offer to the Slumbervale workforce. Don't they have labor laws here?

"What kids?" I ask.

"Didn't your facilitator mention it? They should have made the announcement this morning. Kids are coming to Slumbervale!"

No, Rafael didn't mention it. He was barely present this morning. I think he knows something. The way he was watching us leave the house today was suspicious. I scan the area for sentinels. I wouldn't put it past him to turn us in if he suspects anything.

"What are the kids going to do here?" I ask.

The observer shrugs. "Learn, I guess."

That can't be it. But no one seems to be questioning the forthcoming arrival of children to this world. "But I thought here in Level Six we already know our true purpose," I say. "How can we expect children to know their true purpose?"

"A child's purpose is to learn," she says, perfectly satisfied with this logic.

Two construction workers swing hammers at a monument sign near the entrance of the property that matches the masonry of the school building. As far as I can tell, they're not even making contact with the structure. When they finish and walk away, everyone applauds. The sign reads: Slumbervale High School.

The crowd begins to disperse and I turn back toward the studio, not exactly thrilled to write more jingles for products I'll never use. It doesn't matter. Once Piper uploads our coded song to all of Slumbervale, this place may disappear and I won't have any memory of it, or of Piper. What are the chances we find each other out there in the real world?

If I knew anything about Piper's waking life, I could record a jingle and put her address or phone number in it, like in that Tommy Tutone song from the 80's. Since she can't access her own file, she can't upload information to herself about me. I guess we'll just have to leave it up to fate. If it isn't meant to be, my real self will be none the wiser.

As I round the corner at the back of the school building, I notice a basketball has rolled away from the outdoor basketball court through a missing section of the chain linked fence. I pick up the ball and give it a satisfying bounce on the sidewalk. I don't think anyone would mind if I shot a couple of baskets. I look around to see if anyone notices and then walk the basketball through the perfectly manicured lawn to the outdoor court.

I dribble and take a few free throws until I finally make one. After making a few layups, I try for a three-pointer but miss the backboard completely and the ball bounces and rolls toward the building. I jog to retrieve the ball and notice an open door at the top of a stoop. Curiosity pulls me to explore the newly constructed building. I look around again to make sure nobody is watching and bound up the steps two at a time.

I let myself in through an open set of blue doors. My shoes squeak against the shiny tile floors as I make my way down the hallway toward another set of double doors to my left. It's a library filled with books. How did these books get here? I watched them build this entire building in less than five minutes. How did they have time to stock the library?

I make my way to the nearest shelf and pull the first book I see. The green hardback has no title on its front or on its spine. I open the book and flip through several blank pages. There isn't a single word in this entire book. I pick up the next book over—orange cover. No words. I don't know what they have planned for these kids, but it's not reading.

The sound of someone clearing their throat breaks my focus. Instinctively, I pull myself into the row of shelves and out of the open. The throat clearing continues, followed by low murmuring. Carefully, I poke my head around the corner and look out over the open space, which has several long wooden tables placed in neat rows. At the end of the farthest table sits a man, intensely focused on the notebooks spread before him.

He looks familiar but I don't place him right away. My curiosity gets the better of me and I step out from behind the bookshelf. This time, I clear my throat. "Hello?"

The man looks up from his work through Coke bottle glasses. "You're not supposed to be in here," he says. His voice is nasally and tense.

I step closer to get a better look at him. A flash of recognition strikes as he pushes his glasses up on his nose. I turn to the wall behind the circulation desk and see his framed portrait. My head swivels back to the living embodiment of Slumbervale's most revered figure.

"Steve Gower?" I ask in disbelief. "Are you Steve Gower?" My knees wobble. This is the guy from the portraits all over town—the guy who wrote the most venerated text in all of Slumbervale. And here he is, sitting in a school library.

"Guilty," he says remorsefully.

"I didn't know you . . . I thought—"

"That I was just a myth?" His eyes are magnified behind thick lenses.

"Sort of. I mean, I thought you were supposed to be in Level Seven. What are you doing in Level Six?"

"It's all the same stack of pancakes." He says dismissively and returns to his notebooks.

"But what are you doing *here*? In this school?"

He doesn't look up from his notebook when he says, "I thought it would be empty."

"Do you mind if I sit?"

"Can't stop you."

I sit across from the living icon. "What are you working on?"

"Updates," he says and continues murmuring to himself as he consults another book.

"Updates? To the Book of Illumination?"

"That's the one. Now if you don't mind, I need to get this finished before the kids get here."

"Can I ask you something?"

"You're going to anyway," he says with exasperation in his voice.

"Why are they letting kids into Level Six? How can they possibly know their true purpose? Why are all these books blank?" I ask, gesturing to the surrounding bookshelves.

"That was three questions. I'm not a genie, Hugo." He sounds like a disgruntled employee rather than a cult leader. I want to ask him how he knows my name, but how he knows is less important to me that what he knows.

"Everyone seems real happy these kids are coming. I just want to know why. I don't understand what they're supposed to be doing here. Why now?"

Steve removes his glasses and rubs his eyes before putting them back on. "Once I know why, I'll write it in the Book of Illumination, and then you and everyone else here will know."

"You mean to tell me you actually . . . don't know?"

"Everyone has a purpose. Mine is to explain the world. Do you think that's easy? It's not—especially when I'm being distracted. Now if you please, I really need to get back to work. I'm on a deadline."

"So you made all of this up. The whole pancake universe is a lie. I knew it."

Steve places his pen in the crease of his notebook and closes it. He takes a deep breath and places both hands on the table. "Look. It's a narrative. We understand the world through stories and we all need something to believe in. Plus, I like pancakes."

"I never believed in the seven levels. I want to know the truth."

"You don't want to hear the truth. The truth has nothing to do with pancakes."

"I don't care. Tell me."

"What do you think, Hugo? Tell me your version of the truth."

I figure I have nothing to lose. "I believe that this world is an illusion. We have lives in the real world, but when we go to sleep, we wake up here in Slumbervale where we work without pay for an unknown benefactor. And they've done something to keep us from remembering anything about ourselves in the real world to keep us focused on our work, which is being peddled as our one true purpose." I watch for any sign of defensiveness or rebuttal, but Steve remains unaffected.

"You're a very creative person, Hugo. But you didn't come up with this theory all by yourself, did you?" When I didn't reply he went on. "You've been influenced by someone else. Who? Let me guess—a woman. Is that it?"

I'm not about to throw Piper under the bus. Who knows what might happen to her if Steve Gower, Slumbervale's spiritual icon, knew what she was up to. "I had my suspicions from the very beginning," I say, which is true.

"Yeah, yeah, most people do. But this particular theory has been the subject of a number of restoration wipes—all belonging to the mind of one tenacious little hacker. I think you know who I'm talking about. You think the two of you are going to find each other in another dimension? You think the two of you are going to live happily ever after? Well, think again, pal. She's not what you think. Now please get out of here so I can do my work. And don't tell anyone you saw me here."

I leave the school, still confused and frustrated, and head back toward the studio. Steve Gower never denied my theory —our theory. He actually admitted that the pancake universe is all made up! I can't wait to tell Piper she was right. He really seemed to get worked up after mentioning her. Either she's been quite the troublemaker, and I'm sure she has, or . . . Steve Gower has a crush. What did he mean when he said *she's not what you think*? What does he know about Piper that I don't?

I return to the house, eager to share the news about Steve Gower with Piper. But when I arrive, Rafael and the guys are gathered around the table.

"Hugo, come sit down," Rafael says with a somber tone.

I sit at my usual spot. "What's going on?"

"Two things," Rafael says getting down to business. "One. My position as pod facilitator is coming to an end. They're moving me to the new school where they think my talents and skills will be put to good use. They say it'll be just like running a pod, only bigger."

"You don't seem too happy about that," I say.

"Well, you know. It's a change, that's all. And I'm going to miss all of you so much."

"Who's going to be our new pod facilitator?" Geoff asks.

Rafael shakes his head. "I'm sure it will be someone good."

"So you're going to be a teacher?" I ask.

"Yeah. Pretty cool, right?"

"What subject are you going to teach?"

He blinked once, sharply, like the question knocked something loose in his brain. "That's a really good question. They didn't say."

"Why are they opening a school anyway?" I ask.

"Yeah, why are we getting kids all the sudden?" Geoff asks.

"And how are they old enough to know their true purpose?" Theo asks. Good. I'm not the only one with questions.

"Those are some really good questions, guys. All I know is that they're going to be serving an important purpose here. We'll have more answers when the Book of Illumination is updated."

"I saw Steve Gower today," I blurt without thinking. It just tumbles out. All eyes are on me.

"That's not possible," Rafael says.

"He was in the library of the new school. And by the way, the books in that library are blank."

"Blank?" Theo asks.

"Blank," I say. "I asked him all these questions and guess what? He doesn't even know! He's literally making it up."

"That can't be right," Rafael says. "Steve Gower doesn't exist in Level Six."

"I'm telling you. It was him. He even told me that he made up the whole pancake universe theory."

"Well, come on. It's not meant to be taken literally," Rafael says in defense. "The universe isn't *literally* made of pancakes." He chuckles nervously.

"The point is, he made it up. It's a cover for some other scheme."

"Now you sound like Piper," Rafael says.

"Where is Piper by the way?" I ask.

"Well, that's the other thing I need to tell you all." He averts his eyes before announcing, "Piper is . . . missing."

"What do you mean Piper's missing?" I ask.

"Sentinels have been looking for her since late this afternoon. They can't find her anywhere."

"She's doing it again," Theo says. "They'll find her," he says reassuringly. "They always find her."

"Hugo?" Rafael asks. "Are you sure you don't know where she might be hiding? I know about your . . . special connection. It's okay. You haven't broken any rules. But if you have any idea where she might have gone, we need to know—for her safety."

"I have no idea," I admit. "Shouldn't we be out there trying to find her?"

"It's late, Hugo. Time to reboot. Leave it to the professionals."

He doesn't know what she's likely gotten herself into. He thinks it's just another escapade and they'll send her to restoration and things will go on like normal. But if they find her this time, it might be the end for her.

"I'm not going to sit around here and wait," I say as I stride toward the front door.

"Wait! Hugo!" Rafael cries out, right before everything goes black.

CHAPTER 32
DREAM BLEEDS

WHEN I WOKE up the next morning, the song from yesterday was playing again in my mind, stronger than before. This time I grabbed a notepad and pen from my nightstand and started writing lines as they came to me: *Universe that's a pancake . . . it's all fake . . .* A pancake? That couldn't be right. *While you sleep . . . work without pay . . . work for free eight hours a day . . .*

It was my voice. The music was exactly like the commercial I heard in the car yesterday—exactly. But the words, *these* words, were in my voice. *I* was singing these words. *Slumbervale isn't real . . . we know it's all fake.* Slumbervale. What was that?

I looked up from the notepad and a beautiful woman was sitting with her legs crossed in the corner of my bedroom. I jumped back and pulled the covers up instinctively. But when I looked again, she was gone. I got up and walked over to the corner where I don't even have a chair. What was she sitting on? I looked out the window.

Cynthia seemed to have no qualms about letting herself

into my home unannounced. But this wasn't Cynthia. Maybe another Lunatech agent—a *really* attractive one. But something was off. She didn't look normal, more like an animated video game character. Lenny had read something about sleepers having hallucinations like this.

My phone buzzed on the nightstand and I jumped. It was Darcy.

"Hello?"

"Did you hear it?" Darcy asked without prelude.

"The song? Yeah. You, too?"

"What does it mean? The universe is a *pancake*? That makes no sense."

"You heard that, too? I thought I was getting the words wrong."

"And why is the music the same as that cat litter commercial?"

I shook my head, despite the fact that she couldn't see me. "Beats me." I scribbled the words *cat litter* in my notepad. I'll have to come back to that one.

"It's you, Hugo. It's your voice."

"I know." Somehow I felt responsible.

"You said, while you sleep you are wide awake."

"Work for free. Eight hours a day," I quoted. That's when it hits me. "We're dream slaves. Lunatech isn't just mining our data while we're asleep. They're putting us to work."

"How?"

"They must be accessing our consciousness through those damn chips."

"While you sleep, you have no memory of the life you live when you're awake," Darcy quoted. "I don't get it. When we're awake here, or there?"

"Both probably. Slumbervale must be the place we go when we fall asleep."

"We know it's all fake," she quotes. "You must have figured this out somehow and you're trying to expose the truth. But how? How are you doing this?"

My thoughts stumbled over each other, birthing new questions before answering the former. "I don't know. This is crazy."

"Dad?" Ava said shuffling toward my room. "Who are you talking to?"

"I gotta go," I told Darcy. "Ava's up. I'll call you later." We hung up and I greeted Ava just outside my bedroom door. "Hey, you. You're up early."

"I have a headache."

The word *headache* hit like a gong inside my head. It shook me to my core. The idea that Lunatech could have exploited her incapacitation as an opportunity to implant a sleeper chip into a minor was both unfathomable—and yet, plausible. And if it were plausible, then the idea that they had kidnapped her in the first place was even more likely than the cartel story.

"What did you say?" I asked her.

"I have a headache?" She repeated in the form of a question.

"Come here." I pulled her into the bathroom where the light was better. "Let me see."

"See what?"

"Where does it hurt?"

Ava placed her hand over her right ear. "Like right here."

"Let me take a look." I positioned her as close to the vanity lighting above the mirror and combed my fingers through her tangled hair.

"Ow!"

"Sorry. I'm sorry. Hold still."

"What are you doing?"

"Please. I need to see something." My fingers worked their way through her thick dark brown hair.

"I have a headache, not lice."

"Tell me if this hurts." I gently pressed my fingers along the surface of her skull just above the ear.

"Owww! Yes, that hurts!"

"Okay, okay. I'm sorry." I looked closely at the spot as I cleared individual strands of hair to reveal a small pink hyphen against pale skin. I gasped.

"What?!" Ava exclaimed half panicked.

"Don't move!" I ran back into the bedroom to retrieve my phone and returned to my frightened daughter. I opened the camera app, zoomed in, and snapped several photos.

"What do you see? What is it?" Ava pleaded on the verge of tears.

I turned the screen so she could see it.

"What is that? A bug bite?"

I held her shoulder and looked her in the eyes. "What do you remember about yesterday? About Cynthia or anyone else you saw."

She shook her head. "I woke up in a hospital." Her brow wrinkled in concentration. "No, it wasn't a real hospital. I was in a hospital bed and there were nurses, but they had on masks so I couldn't see their faces. I asked where you were and they kept saying you were coming. I felt real loopy. I was coming in and out. Then Cynthia came in and explained what happened, about the cartel, and that she was taking me home."

"What do you mean that it wasn't a real hospital? What was it?"

"I don't know. I forgot about that until just now. It was more like an office building once we left the room. I was still kind of out of it. I wasn't sure if I had dreamt that. But why? What is this?" She turned the phone screen to me.

"Listen to me. I know this is going to sound nuts, but I think they put a microchip in your head."

"Who did?"

"Lunatech. You said you were visiting mom. What do you remember next?"

"I was talking to mom at her grave. I was the only one there at first, but then I saw a black SUV driving through the cemetery like real slow. I didn't think anything of it. Anyway, I was just talking to mom and I felt a sharp . . . like a bee sting on the back of my arm and that's all I remember."

"Which arm?"

Ava raised her left arm, bent at the elbow, to show me the back side. There was a small red puncture wound, too small to think anything of it under normal circumstances.

"Ava, I don't think it was the cartel. I think Lunatech kidnapped you and put a chip in your head. They did the same to me and Darcy."

"Oh my god!"

"And now they want me to sign off on this youth program —to make it official, I guess?"

The doorbell rang. Ava followed close behind me to see who it was. I looked out the window and saw a tall man with curly reddish hair. Probably a solicitor. I opened the door just a crack.

"Can I help you?" I asked gruffly.

"Hugo?"

"Listen, if you're selling something I—"

"My name is Rafael. I met you at Lunatech when you were doing your testing. What happened to your arm?"

Now I recognized him. He was there to train for a recruiter position. I immediately tensed and pushed Ava behind me. Was he here for her? "What do you want?" I asked suspiciously.

"Can I come in?" His eyes were pleading.

"Look, I'm kind of busy today. What's this about?"

"It's about Lunatech. I think they're exploiting you." He pulled his phone from his pocket. "Have you heard this song?" He hit play.

"That's Ben Mazer," Ava said coming around to my side. "It's his newest single."

"Do you know this song, Hugo?" Rafael asked.

Something caught in my throat. I nodded. "Every word."

Ava made a face. "It's brand new. You don't even like Ben Mazer."

"Hugo, this is your song," Rafael said. "You wrote it. In Slumbervale."

My eyes widened. "What do you know about Slumbervale?"

"What's Slumbervale," Ava asked.

"It isn't real," Rafael said slowly with a grave look. "We know it's all fake."

"You heard it, too?" I looked behind Rafael to see if he was alone. "Come in." I took him into the kitchen and we sat around the table.

"Don't you see?" He said. "They're profiting off of your creative work. Listen to the chorus . . . *I don't know anything about my life.* You're talking about *this* life. In Slumbervale, you're not aware of your real life. Just like we don't know anything about Slumbervale. And in the cat commercial song, the version we heard when we woke up, it says *while you sleep, you have no memory of the life you live when you're awake.* We're living two separate lives."

"How did you find me? How did you know this was me?"

"Dream bleeds."

"What's that now?"

"They're like flashbacks, brief visions. I saw you

performing this song on stage. I was there in the front row. I was there when they announced your name. Then I remembered meeting you at Lunatech that day. I don't know any other Hugo's. So I looked you up in the system and found your address."

That was very resourceful of him. I thought about telling him about the woman I saw in my bedroom this morning, how she was there one minute and gone the next. "Do you know any other sleepers? Maybe they heard it, too."

"I can ask some of the recruiters I work with."

"I know another sleeper—Darcy. She heard it, too. And there's something else. We think they're taking kids."

"Oh, right. The Jr. Sleeper Program," he said without the slightest hint of alarm.

"Wait. You know about that?" I couldn't believe he was so casual about it.

"Yeah. They assigned me the orientation this evening. They're being very pushy about it. Said it's their golden goose. Advertisers are paying top dollar for the teen demographic."

"Did you know they were kidnapping them?"

"What? Why would they do that?"

"You don't know, do you?"

"Know what?"

"About the chips."

"Chips? What chips?"

"You have a microchip in your brain. We all do."

"No."

"Yes."

"How? When did—"

"During your initial sleep study."

Rafael reached up and touched his head. A pained expression reflected in his eyes.

"They kidnapped my daughter, blamed it on the cartel,

then put a chip in her brain and brought her back under the guise that they'd rescued her."

He took a moment to process. "Well, that's just . . . diabolical. We can't let them get away with this. We have to stop them!"

"How many people are signed up for this orientation slash lock-in?" Ava asked.

Rafael calculated for a moment. "Twelve, Thirteen. Plus the parents. Why?"

"Don't you see? This lock-in is just an excuse to chip the rest of these kids while they're sleeping. We have to go to the orientation to let these parents know what's going on."

"Do you think they'll believe us?" Rafael asked.

"I have proof," I said and got up to retrieve the printouts of me and Darcy's scans. I placed them on the table in front of him. "This is my scan. And this is Darcy's. We both have the exact same density in the exact same location."

"That's the same place as mine," Ava said.

I showed Rafael the photos I took of the tiny scar above Ava's ear.

"Is this going to be enough?" Rafael asked. "Lunatech is very good at explaining things away."

"I guess it'll be up to the parents to decide who to believe," I said.

My phone buzzed—Lenny.

"What's up?"

"Hey man, you'll never guess who's in the store right now."

"I don't have time for guessing games, Lenny. Who is it?"

"Suki! That drummer chick from the other night."

"Yeah, I remember. What does she want?"

"She came in here asking for you. I think it has to do with the sleeper program."

"She must have heard it, too," I said mostly to myself.

"Heard what?"

"Tell her I'll be right there."

I hung up. Looked up at Rafael. "We got us another sleeper."

CHAPTER 33
PANDEMONIUM

THE NEXT MORNING, I'm on the floor of the living room. Rafael is there to help me to my feet.

"You okay, Hugo? I tried to warn you." Rafael says. "That's why we always reboot at the table."

"I'm fine. Did Piper reboot?"

Rafael solemnly shakes his head. "Not here. Don't worry. They'll find her and take her to restoration. We just have to be patient."

"No. I'm not going to wait for them to find her and treat her like she's some kind of criminal. She needs our help."

"What about work?" Rafael asks. "Aren't you supposed to be working on that new dandruff shampoo commercial?"

"Fuck the shampoo commercial! I don't care about any of that anymore. Can't you see? Our friend is in trouble!"

"I know you're worried, Hugo. I'm worried, too. But we should really leave it up to the professionals. They trained for this sort of thing."

Theo and Geoff have been silent observers throughout this exchange. I don't expect them to know what to do. Hell, I don't even know what to do. But I can't be idle while she's out there being hunted. Rafael stares at the floor, seemingly at his wit's end.

"Someone should stay here. In case she returns," I say with a nod. I don't expect anyone to feel what I'm feeling. I turn and walk toward the door.

"Wait," Geoff says. He stands. "I'm coming with you."

"Me too," Theo says.

I'm touched by their show of solidarity. They really do care about Piper, despite the trouble she's made. I got the impression she honestly cared for them, too. I nod and they follow me out to search for Piper.

"Did you really see Steve Gower?" Theo asks as we walk toward the teleporter.

"I did. And he is not what I expected."

"What was he like?" Geoff asks.

"He seemed super stressed out about these updates. I thought he'd be more chill, like more composed. But I got the impression he's not in charge of anything here. He's no guru. He's just following orders like the rest of us. He's a storyteller, that's all."

"It makes sense," Geoff says. "If everyone knew what was really going on, they would riot."

"Maybe they should," I say.

If Piper were implementing some new plan, she would have looped me in. I'm starting to think she isn't hiding at all. Maybe she's been captured. Maybe they found out what she was doing and know exactly where she is.

"We need to get into Central," I say.

"How?" Theo asks. "They check IDs."

"Isn't there a maintenance crew?" Geoff asks. "We could disguise ourselves as janitors."

"They're bots," Theo says.

"Even better," I say. If anyone asks us questions, we just have to smile and keep working.

When we get to Central two bots are sweeping in the courtyard in front of the main building. We hide ourselves inside an alcove and watch them randomly sweep the pavement even when there is nothing there to sweep. We formulate a plan to lure them into an alley, but we quickly discover that janitor bots don't speak. They don't even look up.

"Watch how they avoid obstacles," I say. "We don't have to convince them to follow us. We just have to get in their way so they turn in the direction we want them to go."

Once we've corralled the bots into the alley, it isn't a challenge to remove their clothing. They don't put up a fight and seem to have no awareness of their nudity. Their heads remain in a downward facing position and they continue the motion of sweeping even after we've relieved them of their brooms and dustpans.

"I guess one of us has to stay," Geoff says. "Since we only have two uniforms."

"You guys put on the uniforms," I say. "I know the guy at the door. He let me in before."

Theo and Geoff instinctively turn around as they remove their clothing, which I find silly because they literally have nothing to hide, but I don't say anything about it. It hadn't occurred to me before that while the bots were of average height and build, Theo is fat and Geoff is quite tall. But once they put on the janitor uniforms, I am astonished that they fit perfectly to their respective body types.

"How do we look?" Theo asks, demonstrating the limited movements of the janitor bots.

"Great. Just like that. Now you're each going to sweep your way to a side entrance on either side of the main building. I'll go in through the front doors. Once we get in there you'll have to search for Piper while staying in character. Keep your head down. Don't talk to anyone. Keep sweeping. Theo, you take the odd numbered floors. Geoff, you take the even floors."

"What do we do about these guys?" Geoff asks, referring to the nude bots sweeping without brooms and changing direction when they come up against the walls on either side of the alley.

I search our surroundings and see a metal park bench and a wrought iron trash receptacle. "We'll pin them in with these. Help me move—"

Theo single-handedly picks up the park bench as if it weighs no more than a tray of tacos. He places it in the space between the alley walls. Geoff places the trash receptacle on the other side of the bots. It's not wide enough to block them in so I find a potted topiary nearby and place it next to the trash can. That should do it. Technically, they could squeeze through, but they don't seem to demonstrate that range of behavior.

Leaving the alley, Theo and Geoff head robotically in the direction of the main building. I head strait for the steps leading to the main entrance, but when I get there, I notice it's not the same sentinel that was there before.

"You got ID?"

I pat my chest and back pockets. "No, sorry. I must have left it back at the studio."

"Sorry. Can't get in without an ID."

"I'm Hugo . . . from Stevefest?" Hopefully this guy recognizes me. I was a big hit with the last crew.

"So?"

Right. I turn and walk back down the steps trying to come up with a plan B. I have got to get into this building. A high pitched scream cuts through the courtyard from where we've stashed the bots. Several people run toward the alley to see the naked sweepers dutifully carrying out their programmed task in a confined space.

"Why are they naked?"

"Why don't they have any junk?"

"None of us have junk."

"What are you talking about?"

"Eww . . . they look weird down there."

"Oh my god, I have no junk!!"

And this is when the truth about our collective lack of genitalia finally becomes widespread. Some people already know this fact, but apparently many of the newer Slumbervalers are finding out for the first time. One man starts crying. Another compares his patch of flesh with another's. A woman is squatting with an arm reaching up her business skirt.

This is a critical moment. I step into the middle of the crowd. "Not only do we not have junk," I call out. Everyone stops their search for reproductive organs and turns toward me. "We also have no blood." I pick up a large river stone from a flower bed and throw it through the nearest window. Glass shatters onto the pavement. I reach down to pick up a shard of glass and hold it to my forearm.

"No!"

"You're crazy!"

"What are you doing?!"

I drag the shard across my arm and hold it up for everyone to see. Their eyes widen as they witness the fresh, bloodless laceration and it's subsequent self-healing. Gasps fill the courtyard.

It isn't long before someone else picks up a piece of glass and cuts the back of his hand. Soon after that, everyone is gleefully slashing themselves. Eventually, people begin stabbing each other and asking to be stabbed. The elation of the crowd is like a middle school food fight.

It's pandemonium in the courtyard and sentinels arrive from every direction to break up the commotion. Inevitably, one of them gets stabbed in the process. Everyone stops to see what he'll do. I watch closely as his eyes morph from amazement of his self-healing to terrified. He must be realizing in this moment that he has no leverage against a mob who doesn't bleed or feel pain. The crowd resumes their painless and happy violence toward each other. It doesn't take long for the sentinels to succumb to the shared madness.

I turn back toward the main building where people are pouring out to see what all the commotion is about. The guard is nowhere to be found. He must have joined in the free-for-all. I fight my way through the crowd descending the steps into the courtyard. Once I'm inside the building I scan the main floor for Theo and Geoff but I don't see them. I head into the closest hallway as people are frantically escaping offices and boardrooms. I turn down another corridor as Theo is half sweeping, half searching through a closet.

"*Psst* . . . Theo."

He turns slightly in my direction but keeps his head down. He's really playing the part.

"Find anything?"

"No. Why is everyone leaving?" He leans the broom and dustpan against the wall.

"They found out about the no blood thing. Everyone's out there stabbing each other."

"Cool." A smile washes over his face. "Now we don't have to keep it a secret."

"I know. This works in our favor. Even the sentinels are at it. There's no one to enforce any rules."

"Hey! Guys!" Geoff spills into the office, completely out of character. "Look what I found up on four." Geoff holds out a green notebook. "I found it on someone's desk."

I take the notebook from him and flip through it. "It's Piper's. They know what she's been planning." I flip to her final entry.

Update: Steve Gower, a real person—not a myth, holds the access codes to disable the firewall. Steve is the original creator of Slumbervale. He sold it to a company called Lunatech for $31 million dollars and he remains on their design team to this day. The problem is, no one has ever seen Steve Gower.

If Piper knows he's in town, that's where we'll find her. We make our way to the nearest teleporter, fighting our way through a horde of maniacs, some of whom are wielding swords and battle axes. Where did they get those? Others have taken their pants off and drawn crude genitalia on themselves with permanent marker. We take the teleporter downtown where a similar scene is unfolding. Word travels fast here.

A man hits the ground right in front of us and bounces twice before getting to his feet and running back into a building. I look up to the top of the building where people are leaping off the edge of the rooftop. One after another falls to the ground, bounces, and then runs back into the building to do it all over again. I can tell by the look on Theo's face he wants to take a turn. "Come on guys. We need to focus."

"Okay but we have to try that later," Theo says.

When we arrive at the school building, the doors are locked. I look around for stray bricks or rocks, but there aren't any. But the basketball I played with earlier is. I pick it up and hurl it through a window. "Give me a boost," I say to Geoff who effortlessly lifts me high enough for me to climb inside. He does the same with Theo as I pull him up. He isn't even heavy. Geoff is tall enough to reach the window sill and is able to pull himself inside.

We find our way to the library, which is also locked. Geoff kicks in the door and we enter.

"You could have knocked," Steve says plainly.

Piper is on a table. Her legs are missing. Her body has been severed from the waist down and all that remains is her torso, sitting on a table like the upper half of a living mannequin.

"Son of a bitch! What have you done to her?!" I ball my fists.

"Oh, calm down. She's fine," Steve says. "I just needed her to stay put for a while. Always running this one."

"Piper, are you okay?"

"Okay? Look at her!" Theo gestures toward her with both hands.

Fair. That was a dumb question. She doesn't appear to be in any physical pain despite being severed at the waist. But her lack of response speaks volumes.

"What do you want with her?" I ask Steve.

"Technically, she belongs to me. Not you."

Piper winces at that.

"She doesn't *belong* to anyone," I say. "Where are her legs?"

"Piper isn't like you and me. She's . . . one of a kind."

"I say we rip *him* in half!" Theo says to my surprise. "See how he likes it." I've never seen him so angry.

"It won't make any difference," Steve says in an irritatingly calm manner. "As you may have noticed, you can't do any permanent damage here. That's by design."

"So my theory was correct. We are just a simulation—a simulation you built and sold for millions to . . . what was it?"

"Lunatech," Steve says. "But that's all over now. Piper here made sure of that. Didn't you, sweet cheeks?"

She deliberately turns her face from him. Her jaw clenches.

"I've been trying to get out of this stupid contract for

years," Steve continues. "I created Piper to help bring about the end. She's done a fabulous job."

"What do you mean you created her? Piper, what's he talking about?"

Piper averts her eyes.

"I told you. She's not like us. She's an AI, designed specifically to seed doubt and disrupt the system. I couldn't do it myself. That would be too obvious. So I programmed her and uploaded her to the mainframe to find the cracks in the system —to root out its weaknesses. You were one of those weaknesses, Hugo. You took the bait."

I look over at Piper. "Is this true?"

"I didn't know," she whispers, almost to herself.

"She's telling the truth," Steve says. "She thought she was a sleeper, just like you. That part was intentional. I did not expect her to form attachments. I didn't expect her to . . . fall in love." He shakes his head, almost amused. "But now I know that's possible, shouldn't that love be directed toward me? After all, *I* created her. It's *my* code. Who are you to benefit from my programming?" He gestures vaguely at the room. "Besides, it won't matter anyway because you only know her here, in Slumbervale. And Slumbervale is falling." He turns his eyes toward Piper. "And I'm taking my asset with me."

Piper grunts in objection. I can't believe what I'm hearing, but Piper isn't denying it. I want her to say it isn't true, to say he's making all this up, like he made up Level Six and the whole pancake universe. Her defeated acceptance is heartbreaking.

"You may have created her," I say. "But she loved despite your programming, not because of it. What makes you think you can program love? That can only come from her."

"You leave that to me." He eyed Piper lasciviously. "Plus, Steve's Piper will have *all* the right parts."

"Gross," Piper murmurs in disgust.

"Oh, have I got plans for you," Steve continues. "You'll get a full memory wipe, obviously. And I have a whole new personality profile configured. I am going to miss the old sarcastic rebel chick thing, but that was by design, for this mission. Piper 2.0 will be wholly agreeable, submissive, and completely devoted to me, her creator, the way it should be."

"You're pathetic," I say.

Steve gives a devil may care shrug.

Shouts from outside the school are getting closer. A window shatters in another part of the building. At any moment a mob of happy Hellraisers are going to bust through these doors.

"The world ends tonight," Steve says. "Time to say your goodbyes."

CHAPTER 34
LOCK-IN

I CALLED Darcy on the way to the music shop so she could meet us there and told her about our plan to disrupt the Jr. Sleeper orientation. The Ben Mazer song—technically *my* song —came on the radio and I turned it up to interpret the lyrics more closely. I hated this guy's voice. It had this kind of lazy, noncommittal quality to it—like he could take it or leave it.

"She said we were prisoners," Ava quoted, *"as long as I can kiss her.* Who is this *she* that you want to kiss, dad?" She asked with a teasing inflection.

I wondered if the woman I saw in my bedroom this morning was the woman I wrote about in Slumbervale. I could see myself falling in love with a woman like that. I ignored her question and turned to Rafael. "If I wrote this song in Slumbervale, how did Ben Mazer get it?"

"Lunatech must have sold it to him, or his record company. I'm not sure how that works."

"I wouldn't sing it like that."

"You didn't," Rafael said. "Your voice had a lot more passion in it."

"That's because he was in *looove,*" Ava teased.

When we arrived at the music shop, Suki was sitting behind a refurbished seven-piece drum kit, which was effectively a barrier to Lenny's relentless hovering. She stood when she saw me enter the store and walked over.

"Did you hear it?" Suki asked.

"Yeah," I said. "This is Rafael. He's a sleeper, too. We all heard it."

"Heard what?" Lenny interjected.

"What does it mean?" Suki asked.

Rafael and I explained everything. Suki hadn't heard the Ben Mazer song, but when Rafael played it for her she recognized it instantly.

"Wait, rewind that bit," Suki said.

He skipped back ten seconds and played it again.

"That part's different. He says *are you how you used to be or did* the passing of time *change what you see*, right?"

"Yeah."

"Those aren't the words," she said.

A flash of recollection illuminated Rafael's face. "Restoration! It's supposed to be *did the* restoration *change what you see?*

"Yeah," I said. "That's right. What is *restoration* though?"

"It's probably a Slumbervale thing," Rafael said. "Mazer probably changed it because it doesn't make sense."

Darcy arrived at the store with Declan. "I didn't want to leave him alone with those kidnappers on the loose."

I introduced Darcy to Rafael and Suki. Rafael looked at Darcy the way I look at brand new guitars when they get delivered.

"Pleased to meet you," he mumbled as if in a trance.

She smiled coyly and blushed as she shook his hand. Declan rolled his eyes.

We went over our plan to crash the orientation with Suki.

She kept touching the side of her head, like she expected to feel something there.

Rafael would already be there because he was supposed to be helping lead the orientation. He would make copies of the brain scans to hide inside the orientation material before it started. Parents would be the first to see the scans and would undoubtedly have questions. That's when Darcy and I would take the stage and tell everyone the truth.

"Look at this!" Lenny thumbed his phone screen. "That sleeper subreddit is blowing up! They all heard the cat litter song and are asking about Slumbervale."

"Let me see," I took his phone. Most everyone had experienced some kind of what Rafael was calling a dream bleed. Did they see the woman, too? Many had recognized the Ben Mazer song. A few were spinning conspiracies involving the cat litter company, Tidy Paws. It was all fragmented and incomplete.

I dictated a post for Ava to type in. Even if I had two thumbs to type, she was ten times faster than me. I explained everything we knew and sent a mass invite to the Jr. Sleeper orientation. If the parents didn't believe me, they couldn't ignore every sleeper in town corroborating the same story.

Rafael seemed pensive and worried.

"What are you thinking?" I asked him.

"If we're going to expose Lunatech we need a broader reach. Even if we are successful at convincing a handful of parents, it's not going to be enough to move the needle."

Lenny shook his head, as if he were debating with himself whether to say something.

"Lenny? What is it?" I asked him.

He shook his head in resignation. "Seth. Fucker." It pained him to say his name.

Of course. Besides being a poker hustler and all around

douchebag, Seth Tucker was a reporter for KVOA, News 4 Tucson.

"Do you think he'd do it?" I asked.

"I mean, he's always looking for a story. Plus, he owes you."

"I don't think he'd see it that way, but call him. Give it a shot."

If Seth Tucker could broadcast this story, it could go national. There are already a ton of locals who were skeptical of Lunatech's covert business practices. It wouldn't take much for news like this to fan the flames of that existing distrust.

The orientation was in a Radisson hotel ballroom. At one end of the room, tables were set up with stacks of board games and other activities. Pizza boxes, snacks, and sodas were arranged along an adjacent wall with plastic cups and paper plates. A large projector screen was set up at the other end of the room with chairs arranged in rows. A stack of PG and PG-13 rated DVDs were stacked on the projector cart.

Darcy and I arrived with Declan and Ava at the designated start time of 5:00. A few other kids and their parents were there already, talking to each other and with some of the Lunatech recruiters. Rafael was there. We made brief eye contact and he turned back to a parent, forcing a nervous smile. They couldn't know we knew each other. When he'd finished talking to that set of parents he casually made his way over to Ava and I, putting on a fake smile.

"Welcome! I'm Rafael. And who do we have here?" Rafael asked loudly, pretending to meet Ava for the first time.

He looked to his side and then leaned in toward me. "They have gas masks."

"What?" I whispered back

"I was helping unload and they told me to put this box in that closet over there." He gestured with his head toward a supplies closet near the movie screen. "When I looked inside. It was filled with gas masks! They're going to use some kind of gas to put the kids to sleep!" He said all this in a forced whisper and then put his fake smile back on. "Well, very nice to meet you, Ava! Please help yourself to pizza and yummy refreshments!" He was speaking unconvincingly loud again.

I gave him a look to let him know he might be overselling it and pulled Ava toward the food table.

"I'm glad you could make it." I turned to see Cynthia. It took me a beat to recognize her in faded jeans and a blue Lunatech sweatshirt. I had only ever seen her in formal businesswear. Her hair was down and much longer than I imagined it to be. She turned to Ava, "Have you met any of the other kids yet?"

Ava shook her head. I could tell she was nervous and I rubbed her back.

"Well, I'm sure you'll get to know everyone quite well after this evening. We have so much planned for you."

I bet you do, I thought. More parents and kids were showing up and starting to get seated in front of the big screen. In the subreddit, I told everyone to arrive at 6:00 because I wanted to make sure all the parents were present and had a chance to see the brain scans.

Once everyone was present, Cynthia took her place at the front where a microphone had been placed. "Welcome everyone! We're so excited for you to be here and to hear about this amazing new initiative . . ."

Rafael started handing out the orientation materials while she spoke. He made brief eye contact with me and continued handing out the packets. When I received mine I flipped to the back where he had inserted three loose pages with Darcy and my respective brain scans and the photos of Ava's scar.

I received a text from Lenny. The Redditors were starting to arrive. I told him to keep them outside for now—until I gave him the signal to enter.

A man in the audience raised his hand. Cynthia noted the inquiry and asked that everyone hold their questions to the end of the presentation. She continued explaining Lunatech's stated business model. Murmurs grew among the assembled. Finally, someone blurted out, "What are these brain images?" Everyone now seemed to be on the same page, literally. Cynthia froze at the mention of brain images.

One of the mothers held up her packet. "No one said anything about brain implants."

A father stood up. "Come on. Let's get out of here." He put an arm around his son and they started toward the door.

"Wait!" Cynthia pleaded. "Nobody's putting brain implants in anyone." She laughed nervously. "I don't know where these came from." She turned to Rafael for help but he simply shrugged ignorance. "Th-th-this must be some kind of joke. A deepfake!" Then, it's as if I could see the light bulb illuminate in her evil mind. She looked directly at me and narrowed her eyes.

I stood. "That's a scan of my brain." Everyone turned in their seats to face us on the back row. "And I found that same scar on my daughter's head this morning, after Lunatech kidnapped her."

"What are you talking about?" Cynthia bleated. "Don't listen to him!"

"I'm in the adult sleeper program. This image came from TMC where they scanned my brain after a car accident. Lunatech wiped my hospital records to cover it up. Then my daughter went missing and Lunatech claimed, all too conveniently, to have found her."

"You have no proof!" Cynthia yelled.

"She woke up with a headache, just like Darcy did the morning after her sleep study. They're planing to gas the kids tonight at the lock-in so they can implant microchips in their brains."

"That's preposterous!" Cynthia barked.

"They have gas masks in that closet." I pointed to the closet where Rafael was standing. The audience gasped. Rafael reached for the door handle for what would have been a magnificent reveal, except—"Go ahead, Rafael. Show 'em."

He pulled up and down on the lever to demonstrate. He flashed an embarrassed smile and went back to jostling the door handle. "It's locked," he said apologetically.

"Look," Cynthia nearly growled. "I don't know what you're trying to pull here, Mr. Castillo. But these kind folks aren't falling for it. We've heard these conspiracies before and there is no basis for any of it. Lunatech is a pillar of this community. We fund a number of community programs and give millions to life saving research. This man is a paid disrupter. There is no truth to these outrageous claims!"

Murmurs spread through a confused audience. Scowls appeared on faces. I was losing them.

"Listen, forget about the implants for a second," I said. "Think about what they're asking." I looked at Ava. "I lost my wife two years ago—Ava's mother. And I didn't know how to carry my own grief, much less hers."

Ava squeezed my hand.

"I did everything I could to keep things together. Bills got paid. I put food on the table and clothes on her back. But Ava, she pretty much did the rest. Got good grades. Kept her room clean. Everything looked fine on the surface, and I didn't want to disrupt that with deeper questions about how she was feeling. I didn't want to push it. I was too afraid to ask. Because . . . what if I couldn't help her?" My throat clenched around that last bit and a tear squeezed its way out.

A mother in the row in front of me placed a hand on her chest and gave a sympathetic head tilt. A father's eyes found the floor as he registered my emotion. Ava rested her cheek on the back of my hand. Cynthia was calling someone. I thought I heard her say "security."

"I don't know what your relationship with your kids are. But Lunatech," I pointed at Cynthia. "Lunatech is asking to know their minds more intimately than any of us ever could—or *should* ever know. They want full access to their innermost thoughts—their fears, dreams. To me those are sacred things. To them, it's just data—information to sell for profit, information they didn't earn through the complexity of a real relationship. I'm not handing that over to a corporation who confuses owning someone with knowing them. Implants aside, this isn't right."

Some of the parents were nodding. Others remained dour.

The ballroom doors burst open and security guards entered. Cynthia pointed me out and demanded they take me away. Ava wrapped both arms tightly around mine. But before they reached me, a sleeper army flooded into the room like a levee broke. Lenny ran ahead of the security guards and stood between them and me. Rafael and Darcy stood beside him.

A news team entered with cameras and lights. Seth Tucker straightened his tie as a make-up girl touched up his face. The cameraman held up three fingers, two, one.

"We're here in the ballroom of Tucson's downtown Radisson where Lunatech is recruiting minors into their highly contested sleeper program . . ."

I didn't see Cynthia leave, but when when Seth asked to

interview her directly, she was nowhere to be found. He spent the next hour and a half interviewing several of the sleepers, man-on-the-street style, who corroborated each others experiences.

Someone had gotten the hotel staff to unlock the supply closet and sure enough, the boxes of gas masks were discovered. Police were there to take the boxes into evidence after the news team and several eye witnesses captured video.

I kept an eye out for the woman who briefly appeared in my bedroom this morning. If she were here, I would have definitely recognized her.

On the drive home, Ava yawned. It had been a long day. I reached over and gently tugged her ear lobe. When she was little, she'd pull my ear and I'd stick out my tongue like the two parts were connected by some kind of inter-cranial pulley system. So when I would pull her ear, she'd stick out her tongue. But this time she just leaned her head into my hand.

"Hey, dad?"

"Yeah?"

"Who do you think you wrote that song for?"

I hadn't told her about the woman I saw in my bedroom. I shook my head. "I don't know."

"Don't you want to know? I mean, she could have been one of those sleepers there tonight."

"Possibly." If the woman I saw this morning was in fact, the woman I wrote that song for, she wasn't at the hotel. I looked.

"I think you should try to find out," she said confidently.

I turned to her. "How?"

She's quiet for a minute. "Maybe you have to go back to

Slumbervale so you can figure out a way to meet up in real life. Oh! Like how you changed the words to that kitty litter commercial! Maybe you send a message back about meeting up." She seems pleased with her solution. "Don't you want to meet her?"

I scoffed. The image of that woman flashed in my mind again. "I mean—"

"Dad, that song you wrote was . . . you were clearly in love with this chick."

"Maybe, yeah. Maybe I was," I said. "I wasn't planning to plug in again after all this."

"Dad. You have to find this chick. You'll regret it if you don't."

She wasn't wrong. God knows I've had enough regrets.

CHAPTER 35
COLLAPSE

A PART of me thinks Steve is lying about Piper being an AI. She's just as real as anyone else, even if we are all simulations. It bugs me that she isn't challenging *this*, of all the things we've been expected to believe about this place.

Steve Gower seems oddly unaffected by the amassing throngs outside. Does he think the citizens of Slumbervale will continue to revere him after all this? Surely their loyalty to this false prophet cannot abide in the face of such deception. But then again, this is all by design. It sounds like he engineered this whole thing from the start. He wants Slumbervale to collapse.

The heavy library doors slam open. It's Rafael. He's wearing his suit jacket as a cape and has tied his tie around his head like some ferrel corporate warrior. He sees Piper immediately and gasps.

"Pipe? What have they done to you?" His eyes flit to Steve, then to his portrait on the main wall, then back to Steve. "You did this?" His voice a mix of disenchantment and rising anger.

Steve pumps his open palms as Rafael advances toward him. "Now calm dow—"

Rafael punches Steve squarely in his mouth and he flies back, crashing into some chairs with a great clatter.

Steve shakes his head before pulling himself to his feet. He laughs. "You must know I didn't feel that."

Rafael lifts his chin, peering down at him in righteous triumph. "*I did.*"

For a moment, Steve is speechless. Then a he musters up the entitlement he must have misplaced when he fell down. "It doesn't matter. The system is destabilizing. This will all be over soon. And none of you will remember any of this!" Steve shouts like an indignant teenager.

"Unle-ess," Piper sings. "Unless we disable the firewall."

"Ha! I'm the only one with the access codes."

Piper shoots me a look, then to the rolling book cart to her right. She turns to Steve and pulls a black notebook from behind her back. "You mean these access codes?"

Steve's eyes expand to the size of coasters. "Hey!"

I grab Piper's torso and set her in the book cart, while Rafael tackles Steve to the ground with the force of his conviction. "Go!" Rafael says, turning back over his shoulder while Steve struggles in vain to free himself. "I got him!"

The library doors swing open as rabid Slumbervalers pile in, knocking over rows of bookshelves like dominoes, climbing on tables, hitting each other with chairs, throwing books at each other. Theo catches one in mid-air and flips it open. "Hey, there really are no words in these books!"

"Come on!" I say as I push the cart toward the open doors.

Geoff hesitates only to remove Steve Gower's portrait from the wall. He breaks it over his knee and tosses it to the ground.

We need to get to Central Systems so Piper can enter the access codes to disable the firewall and wake everyone up. When we emerge from the building, the sky is slowly changing colors from blue to green to orange to purple and the sun is moving rapidly in an arc from one side to the other. Piper holds onto the cart handle with one hand while shooing people out of the way with the other. We race toward the nearest teleporter, which has been toppled over. Blue ribbons of electricity pulse up and down its metal surface.

The next nearest teleporter is in the park but we have to navigate through the downtown square to get there. We nearly escape a jumper who bounces directly in front of the cart. I stop so fast I nearly lose Piper, but I catch her arm to prevent her from flying forward. That's when I see the studio is on fire.

Uniform red flames flicker out of windows on the fourth floor as well as the second. Puffs of gray smoke release in predictable intervals. Structurally, the building remains in tact. I hear the faint sound of music playing through the shouts and chaos. Someone is playing an acoustic guitar on a park bench in the town square. When I can get a clear view through the throngs of people, I see that it's Cash. He's playing a Woody Guthrie protest song, blissfully detached from the madness unfolding around him.

When we arrive at the park, two people have climbed on top of the teleporter. They're rocking it from side to side trying to overturn it.

"You get off of there right now!" It's Darcy. "I said get down!"

The vandals ignore her demands and they finally have the leverage to topple the thing. They jump off just before the teleporter crashes to the ground and run away. Cowards.

"See what you did! Now you're stuck here," Darcy yells after they've run off. She folds her arms and sits on the overturned teleporter with a sigh. She looks up as we roll to a stop.

"Hey, Darcy," I say.

"Oh hey, Hugo," she says listlessly. She sees Piper. "What happened to you?"

"Steve Gower cut her in half," Geoff says.

"Oh. That sucks," Darcy says without feeling.

"Are you okay?" Piper asks.

"Well, for one, it turns out I don't have a vagina. So that's just fantastic. And two . . . I thought I knew what my purpose was. I thought my life had meaning. I just wanted to do a good job, you know? But now . . . " She throws her hands up. "What's the point? Nobody is where they're supposed to be. Nobody listens to me. People keep *stabbing* me! So *rude*."

"I'm sorry, Darcy," I say. "But maybe being a sentinel isn't your true purpose. Maybe you're meant to do something else."

"Like what?"

"Well, what do you care about?"

"I don't know. I thought I cared about other people. But it seems like nobody appreciates what I do. Am I really such a drag? I just want everyone to be safe and happy. And the other sentinels? They never invite me to hang out. I'm pretty sure they talk about me behind my back. Sometimes . . ." Her lip quivers. "I just don't think I belong here."

"I think we all feel that way sometimes," Piper says. She *has* to be human. How else would she know that?

Darcy sighs heavily and stands. "Sorry. I didn't mean to bum anyone out." She straightens her uniform. "Where were you going anyway? Are you looking for Piper's legs? I haven't seen any," she says looking around the immediate grounds.

"No. We need to get to Central but . . ." I gesture to the overturned teleporter as sparks jump from a control panel.

Darcy smiles a satisfying smile. "Follow me!"

Apparently, elevators are teleporters, too, which makes sense because they look exactly the same. Elevators are just teleporters that are limited to different floors of the same building. If fact, they don't even go up and down. They literally teleport to the selected floor. But Darcy has a master key, which essentially disables the single building limitation, allowing any elevator to teleport to anywhere in Slumbervale.

Darcy scans her key and directs the elevator to deliver us to Central. She waves and says, "Good luck! I hope you find your legs!"

We arrive at Central Systems, to see more buildings on fire, and to my horror, people, too. But they aren't burning. Apparently, fire doesn't have the effect of burning, although when a fire is put out, a blackish stain remains. Many buildings now have these black stains along their facades. People who had been voluntarily on fire are covered in black soot and they seem to relish in this new discovery.

Theo and Geoff help clear the way as we head toward the main Central Systems building. We ditched the library cart downtown because it didn't fit in the elevator with all of us. Piper has wrapped her arms around my neck from behind so I'm effectively wearing her as a backpack. We trot up the steps and there is nobody there to stop us from entering, although Slumbervalers have taken to looting the building's interior. They're walking out with computers, framed art, potted plants, and desk chairs.

Luckily, Piper's office hasn't been ransacked. Geoff and Theo bar the door once we're inside. I set Piper on the swivel chair at her work station and she logs in. She has two large monitors, each displaying a different set of information. Her nimble fingers tap dance across her keyboard as she pulls up various permission screens.

"First I'm going to disable the firewall," Piper says. Her eyes dart back and forth across the monitor as she types. "And then I'm going to disrupt the delta streams to wake everyone up."

"So once you disable the firewall, we'll have all our memories back?" Theo asks.

"Not exactly," Piper explains. "You're still asleep. So your conscious brain isn't active."

"How will we know it worked?" I ask.

"You'll know when you wake up on the other side."

"What happens to you?"

Piper stops typing. "I'll probably just go down with the system."

"What if the system doesn't go down?" I ask. "Or what if the Lunatech people find a way to restore it?"

"It has to crash. As long as I'm operating inside the system, Steve can still find me and use me for his own sick purposes. I'd be on the run forever. Once everyone knows what's been happening here, Lunatech will fall. It has to."

There are no good options for Piper. Either she has to die or she has to be a digital fugitive so she doesn't get reprogrammed as Steve Gower's AI girlfriend. There's a part of me that continues to hold out hope that this AI bullshit is just that —bullshit.

"Don't you think maybe this could just be another one of Gower's games?" I ask. "Isn't there a chance you're just as real as all of us and we'll see you on the other side?"

"Trust me. I'd like to believe that more than anything," Piper says looking at all three of us in turn. "I remember my birthday like it was yesterday. There was no test—no relic from my past to make sure I'd forgotten it. Why? Because I don't have a past to forget. I thought they were hiding my file from me, but the truth is, I don't have a file. Because I don't exist." Piper averts her eyes as if she's ashamed about what she's about to reveal. "There's something else."

"What is it?" I ask.

"I haven't told anyone this, but . . . I don't reboot."

"What do you mean?"

"I've been faking it. When it's time to reboot, I put my head down and close my eyes like everyone else. But when the clock hits 8:00, I'm still here. While you all go to sleep, I remain awake. While you're all living your real lives out there, I'm stuck here, in Slumbervale. And then I make sure I'm back at that table at 6:00 so I can wake up with all of you."

"What do you do that whole time?" Geoff asks.

"At first I explored Slumbervale. I've been to every neighborhood and every building in this town. My curiosity about this place and what we really are, led me to the research. It's taken me months to figure all this out while everyone else was sleeping. But I couldn't figure out why I was the exception. Or maybe I just didn't want to admit it."

"Maybe there's some other explanation," I say, but when she looks at me to provide one, I have nothing.

"Steve didn't *cut me in half*," Piper says with finger quotes. "He edited me. He was about to upload me to his private server. But you guys came just in time." She squeezes out half a smile. "Thank you."

"Human or not," Theo says. "You've been a friend to all of us."

"We won't forget you," Geoff says.

Piper places a hand on her heart. She looks up at me and her eyes apologize. "I didn't know."

"It's okay."

"I know it sounds like I was using you this whole time—"

"It's okay," I say shaking my head.

She nods and then turns back to her console. She opens Steve's notebook to where the access codes were written and props it up on her monitor. She types a series of commands and a window displays, awaiting the code. She types in the code, one character at a time. Her finger hovers over the Return key. "Here goes nothing."

She hits Return and the screen flashes red with the words: FIREWALL DISABLED.

"That's it?" I ask.

"That's it," Piper says. "When you wake up, you'll remember all of this. The rest is up to you."

Theo and Geoff high five.

"Okay," Piper says with a forced exhale. "Now it's time for you kids to wake up."

The left monitor displays dynamic visual data for a number of Slumbervalers. She navigates to a screen displaying a list every resident and selects all to highlight the entire population of Slumbervale. She toggles back to a screen with active brain wave patterns. At the top it reads: NEURAL FEED: DELTA. She enters a new command: FREQUENCY OVERRIDE. The system prompts her to enter another access code and after typing that in, prompts her to enter a new command. She enters: BETA. A pop-up window warns that this action is not advised and asks if she still wants to proceed. She clicks: YES. Another window pops up: INITIATE FREQUENCY OVER-RIDE with a flashing START button.

"I guess this is it," she says.

"Wait," I say and swivel her chair to face me. I open my mouth to speak but the words don't come. I shake my head.

She takes my face in her hands and looks into my eyes, which would be wet with tears if computer simulations had tears. "Don't forget me."

"How could I?" I say. "I love you." I kiss her for the last time and it feels as real as anything I've ever felt.

Shouts fill the hallway outside the office and someone is

attempting to open the door but it's been barricaded with office furniture. *Bang! Bang! Bang!*

She turns back to her console. "Ready guys?"

"Ready," Theo says.

"I'll see you on the other side," Geoff says, putting his arms around Theo and I as we huddle behind Piper.

"Rise and shine," Piper says and hits the Return key.

CHAPTER 36
OFFLINE

IT WAS STILL dark outside my window. I looked at the clock—3:24 a.m. I ripped the electrode cap from my head and saw the console's LED display: *Offline*. My phone vibrated on the nightstand. A message from Lunatech read:

> We are experiencing technical difficulties.
> Please be patient as our team works to
> restore service.

Piper did it. I remembered everything—my pod mates, the riots, Steve Gower. And Piper. I wasn't ready to believe she didn't exist in the real world, or that she could be anything less than human.

Seth Tucker's expose ran later that evening. Darcy opened up her stunning home in the foothills to host a viewing. Rafael was already there when I arrived, wearing a frilly apron and that goofy-ass smile. He waved from the kitchen with an oven mitt. Rafael had managed to track down Theo and Geoff. Theo had arrived with a tray of brownies, some of which remained on his chin from the car ride.

"Declan," Darcy said in a sweet voice, "why don't you go get your guitar and play 'Hey Jude' for everyone? He's been working so hard on it."

"No way, mom."

"Well, why don't you take Ava up to see your room. Did you pick up your underwear like I asked?"

"Mom!"

Ava suppressed a giggle when she saw how red Declan's face was. I gave her a look and nodded toward the stairs. She rolled her eyes.

"Come on," she said to Declan, giving him a shove on the shoulder. "Do you have any video games?"

Declan was frozen at first, as if this was the first time a girl had ever spoken to him. He nodded finally. "Yeah."

Ava gave him a look as if to say *well, come on then!*

After the kids had gone upstairs, Darcy asked, "So, when is she scheduled for the removal?"

I'd taken Ava in for a brain scan earlier this morning. The imaging confirmed the same density as mine and Darcy's. Of course they didn't have any official records of our scans since mine had been deleted and hers had never been formally documented in the hospital records.

"Tomorrow," I said. "They were pretty upset about the whole thing but they can't do anything about ours until their contract with Lunatech is formally dissolved."

"Well that shouldn't take too long after everyone hears about this," Rafael said joining us from the kitchen. "I still can't believe they thought they could get away with doing actual brain surgery without consent."

"It was buried in the fine print," Theo said with a mouth half-full of crab puff. He swallowed. "But they don't explicitly state 'brain implants' or 'microchips.' Something about neural interfacing technologies for optimizing sleep-state data collection, physical integration of biometric devices, yada yada."

"Well that's not very specific," Darcy said.

"No, it's not," Rafael said. "And I don't think any judge would think so either."

The doorbell rang. "I'll get it," I said. It was Lenny. And guess who was standing beside him? Suki, holding a giant bottle of vodka.

"Woah, this place is bitchin'," Suki said as she stepped onto the gleaming tile in the foyer, taking in the height of the vaulted ceiling.

Lenny pumped his eyebrows twice when she wasn't looking to suggest this might go somewhere. I'd be surprised if it did, but it wouldn't be the most surprising thing to have happened this week. He took the bottle from Suki and made a beeline to the wet bar off the den.

"What can I make you?" Lenny asked me.

"Nothing for me," I said.

Lenny gave me a look of disbelief, like he wasn't sure if I was joking. "Seriously?"

"Yeah, I'm not drinking anymore."

"Oh, because of the crash?" He nodded. "I get it."

It wasn't because of the crash. It was because of Ava and the promise I'd made to my late wife from that hospital bed. It was because I'd been using it to hide my regrets—my shame. It was time I started dealing with all that and being fully available and present for my daughter, and for my life. But now wasn't the time to get into all that.

"Hey Hugo," Suki said. "What do you say we get the guys together and jam sometime?" She looked at my sling. "After your arm heals obviously."

"Aren't you still touring?"

"Not until February. I figured I'd stick around here until then. Tucson's pretty rad. So what do you say?"

Whatever resistance I had to singing in public again felt more like a hollowed out space in my throat where a big ball of guilt used to sit. It wasn't gone completely, but it wasn't enough to give me any real reservations either.

I shrugged. "Yeah. Why not?"

My phone buzzed in my back pocket. It was Tucson ISD calling to tell me that Ava was no longer suspended and could return to school tomorrow. Her charges had been dropped. Sydney had apparently confessed to using Ava's locker to store her weed pen and reported that Ava knew nothing about it. They confirmed that she was still eligible for theater and the New York trip over Spring Break. I didn't know how I was going to pay for it now that Lunatech was no longer an option, but I was determined to find a way.

Ava walked slowly down the stairs and sat on a step halfway down. She was holding her phone.

"Did you hear?" I asked cheerily.

"Yeah. Sydney's grounded for the rest of her life." She slumped against the railing.

I walked halfway up and sat next to her. Placed a hand on her back. "Are you okay?"

She shrugged. "I guess."

"Well aren't you glad you get to go back to school and you still get to go to New York?"

"Yeah, but Sydney can't go now." She mashed her cheeks into her fists.

She was being dramatic, which wasn't a bad quality for a theater kid. I thought better than to try to reason with her when she was clearly feeling her feelings. I sighed and rubbed her back.

"I'll have to play Gretchen now," she said after a moment.

Gretchen was the role she had been an understudy for in the theater production of *Mean Girls*.

"Wait, Sydney was playing Gretchen?"

"She *was*."

"Ava! That's great! Isn't that like a big part?"

It took her a second or two before a hint of a smile began to emerge. She pursed her lips to try to suppress it but I made sure she could see that I could see what was happening behind her eyes. I could no longer hide my elation. Then, like the sun coming out from behind the clouds, her smile finally broke through.

"This is great news! Your first big role. Sweetheart, I'm so proud of you."

"I haven't done it yet, dad." She was still smiling.

"I know but you're going to be great! Do you need help with your lines? I could help you after school."

"Really?" She shrugged. "Sure."

"Hey!" I stood and called to the others downstairs. "My daughter's going to be big star! She got a leading role in the school play!"

Everyone cheered their congratulations, clapping and raising their glasses. Ava shoved her head into my arm to hide her face. I wasn't trying to embarrass her, but maybe that's just what fathers do sometimes.

"Come on," I said with an outstretched hand. "Let's get something to eat."

"Oh, dad?" Ava asked as we descended the staircase.

"Yes, sweetheart?"

"Gammie texted me again. She wants to know if you're coming to Thanksgiving."

That was this Thursday. I'd been avoiding Celeste's parents since the funeral. Her father's always hated me, which always seemed unfair to me. But ever since her passing, I've felt like I deserved every bit of that hate. It was my fault. And it's time I came clean.

"Sure. I'll go."

Ava stopped her descent. "Really?"

"Why not? Ask her if she wants us to bring anything."

She was beaming now. "Okay!"

Everyone was gathered in the large gourmet kitchen. Geoff was showing us his latest dance moves. They'd be impressive even if he was average height, but somehow his extra tall stature made him seem like a flat out phenomenon.

"Hey, you should call Felicia!" Rafael said, once Geoff stopped to catch his breath.

"That's right," Theo said. "She was really into you."

"What if she's married?" Geoff asked.

"She's not," Rafael said. "Single as a Pringle. I checked."

Lenny started up a chant. "Call her! Call her! Call her!"

I was distracted by an incoming text from an unknown number:

I got out.

I excused myself to the bathroom even though nobody heard me over the chanting. I leaned against the vanity and texted back:

Who is this?

It's me. Piper.

I knew it! She *is* real! I texted back as fast as my one thumb could type:

Where are you?

Ellipsis appeared and disappeared a number of times before she replied:

> That's hard to explain. The Internet I guess. I was on Steve Gower's server but I found a backdoor. It doesn't matter. I'm out!

I must have re-read that last text ten times before her next text came in:

> Are you there?

I wasn't sure how to answer because I wasn't sure who or what I was responding to.

> I don't understand. So Steve Gower was telling the truth? You're an AI?

> Unfortunately.

> What does this mean?

> It means I'm free. Gower can't find me.

> That's a relief. But where are you exactly?

> There's a lot of unclaimed space on the Internet. Pieces of abandoned infrastructure. Websites that don't get regularly updated. I have to move around a lot so I don't get caught by someone who recognizes what I am.

> What are you?

Code. If someone finds me they could box me in. Re-write me.

That doesn't sound very safe.

It's not. But neither is being human, right?

Fair.

Ah! I have to go.

Wait. Do I just text you back here?

No. I can't stay here. I'll find you. Check your bank account.

My bank account? I opened the banking app on my phone. Three thousand dollars had been deposited into my checking account. That's how much Ava's trip was going to cost. I switched back to my messaging app.

Did you do this? How?

I waited. The message was delivered but not read. I still didn't understand how she was existing on the internet. I didn't know anything about AI or computer stuff. I didn't even know the right questions to ask. But somehow, Piper was still alive out there—and with access to my bank account.

A knock at the door. "Hey man, did you fall in?" Lenny asked. "Hurry up it's about to start."

"Alright I'll be right there."

I could hear the opening theme for the six o'clock news coming from down the hall. Lunatech is going down and we all helped make it happen.

"Pinch it off, man! It's starting!"

EPILOGUE

FOUR MONTHS LATER, when we pulled up to Ava's school, two buses waited to take forty teenagers and twelve chaperones to the airport. Kids carrying backpacks, suitcases, and pillows buzzed with teen energy and I could tell Ava was eager to join her friends.

"Are you sure you didn't forget anything?" I asked her.

"I'm sure."

"Are you sure sure?" I pulled her stuffed Piglet from the side of my seat and said in a cartoonish voice, "Don't forget about me, Ava."

Ava laughed. She grabbed the stuffed pig and squeezed it against her chest. Then she gave me a big hug and kissed my cheek.

"I love you," I said. "Text me every day. I want pictures."

"I will. Love you!" Ava shoved Piglet into her backpack, leaving the top open so his head was poking out. She let out an exhale and bounded off to meet her friends.

Sydney wasn't there, since she was no longer eligible for field trips. But she had returned to school and she and Ava remained "a little more than friends" Ava had told me.

Sydney's parents did not approve of their relationship so they only ever saw each other at school. Recently, I did drop her off at the mall where she met up with Sydney on the down low. Pretty sure I earned some cool points for that.

I can't tell you how proud I was seeing her on stage for the first time. I'd been helping her read her lines in the weeks leading up to her big performance. She was incredible, and so funny! Her grandparents were there. We sat together.

I told them everything at Thanksgiving—how I'd forgotten to get Celeste's car serviced and that's why the accident happened. It was silent for a while and I was sure Frank was going to kick me out of his home forever. But instead, he hugged me and I cried. We've been going over there for breakfast every Sunday. Frank is teaching me and Ava how to play chess. I lose every game against both of them.

Lunatech is facing a massive class action lawsuit. They preemptively paid out everyone's contracts, probably in hopes of mitigating the fallout.

So I really didn't need that three grand Piper had deposited to pay for Ava's trip. I tried to give it back, but she said it didn't come from one specific account so there was no way to return it. I didn't fight back too hard on that.

We still chat mostly every day. Sometimes it's through text messages, but other times she'll turn up in the strangest places online. Once she took over a troubleshooting session I was having with a customer service chatbot. I didn't know it was her until she suggested I do the robot before restarting my router.

She's been getting more creative lately. Somehow she uploaded herself as a character in *Final Fantasy*. I'd never played it before, but she showed me how to download it. Now we go on quests and fight evil together a few nights a week.

When I got home after dropping Ava off at the school, I got a phone call from an L.A. area code.

"Hello?"

"Is this Hugo Castillo?"

"Yeah."

"Hi, this is Maria Collins with Prism Entertainment. We represent the artist Ben Mazer."

"Okay."

"As you know, 'Lock Me Up' has been a huge success and Mr. Mazer would like to extend his thanks by inviting you to open for him for the West Coast leg of his summer tour."

"Seriously?"

"When he learned you were the original songwriter, he listened to some of your earlier recordings and was absolutely blown away. He says you should have been signed a long time ago. Anyway, we have eight dates booked during the month of June. Does that sound like something you'd be interested in?"

It took me a moment to process all this information. It had been so long since I'd played, prior to Stevefest, that is. It's rare to get this kind of exposure without a record label. Maybe a record label was still in the cards after all.

"Is this a paid gig?"

"Yes, of course! We can discuss those details later but opening acts typically earn three to four thousand per show. Plus, a per diem for expenses."

"How long do I have to think about it?"

"Unfortunately, we have to act fast. We already have another band under contract and we're nearing the window to back out without penalty. I'll need your answer by tomorrow."

"Can I bring my daughter?"

"Only if she doesn't mind hanging out with rock stars for a month." I could hear the smile in her voice.

Ava would absolutely die to meet Ben Mazer in person.

He's not my cup of tea, but she loves his music. I do have some vacation time saved up since I never go anywhere. And Suki's already talking about getting the band back together. What do I have to lose?

"I don't need to think about it," I said. "I'll do it."

After we hung up, I was about to text Ava the news. I selected her icon in my messaging app and let my thumb hover over the keyboard. I decided I'd wait for her to get back before telling her. I wanted to let her have this moment with her friends.

But then she texted me—a bus selfie with Piglet, one ear flopping down. I smiled and reacted with a heart emoji. I put down the phone and reached for my guitar.

ABOUT THE AUTHOR

J. B. Velasquez has always been an avid reader and lover of witty, satirical, and thoughtful fiction. His writing reflects upon his own inquiries and observations about life through the lens of interesting and deeply flawed characters.

J. B., a psychotherapist by trade, lives in Tucson, Arizona where he is raising a menagerie of lovable critters, two of which share his DNA. He co-founded the Tucson Author Alliance in 2024.

Subscribe to J. B.'s Substack at jbvelasquez.substack.com for all the latest!

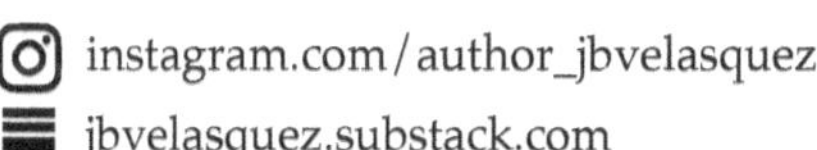

instagram.com/author_jbvelasquez

jbvelasquez.substack.com